NOT

QUITE

DEAD

DAWN HARRIS SHERLING

Not Quite Dead

Author photo by Sally Prissert

Edited by Parisa Zolfaghari

Cover and interior design by We Got You Covered Book Design
www.wegotyoucoveredbookdesign.com

ISBN: 978-0-578-40092-1

This book is dedicated to my father,
the bravest person I know.

PROLOGUE

Dr. Bill Withering slowly sipped his coffee, savoring the complex beans he had two-day shipped from Hawaii monthly, and wondered when, exactly, things had gone so horribly wrong. Ignoring the few bitter drops clinging to his thick mustache, he stared at the life-sized portraits on the wall of the faculty lounge. All venerable physician-researchers who had come before him. Decidedly, he would not be following in their footsteps.

The National Institutes of Health had cut research grants across the board just before the housing market had crashed. Withering had told his wife that a variable rate mortgage on the too-big house in Wellesley was a bad idea. But she just had to listen to her idiot brother, the real estate agent, who insisted that real estate prices never went down. Until they did. Since Withering's salary was supported by how much grant money he could generate, money became tight just as he needed it most. Luckily, the pharmaceutical companies had recently loosened the reigns a bit on their grant funding. Withering examined the grounds at the bottom of his mug and considered the disappearance of drug company-supplied pens to the clinical physicians and the appearance of more research grants to doctors like him. He let out a disappointed sigh. No matter how coarsely he ground the beans, there were still remnants left over at the end. And no matter how the regulators attempted to take drug company money out of medicine, the dollars always found their way through their filters. The millions spent on pens and other drug company trinkets were a visible sign of the companies' influence, one for which they and the doctors who partook of them, could be easily criticized and so were now relegated to the dustbin of medical artifacts. But the billions in research grants were less obvious, a mere footnote buried in a scientific article. And while the pharmaceutical companies couldn't have any direct influence on the research itself, they could certainly decide which research was worthy of their support.

Bill Withering wanted to be worthy, so he had shifted his research from the basic science of diabetes to the more profitable science of weight loss drugs. He could still help the mostly overweight and obese diabetics to whom he had devoted his career and, just as critically, he could also pay his delinquent mortgage.

But the money would only keep flowing if the results were good. Better than good. The drug company executives wanted dramatic results—ten to twenty percent of body weight gone in a few months. While the science had suggested humans would have this dramatic weight loss, the lab mice just weren't cooperating. Mice and humans were different, after all, Withering reasoned. His results with the mice had to be better or the grant to move the drug on to a clinical trial with humans would never be approved.

Withering and his house needed that next grant. So, after a slow start, his research began to show what it needed to—that after three months on the experimental drug, the mice were losing about fifteen percent of their body weight. Of equal importance, no significant side effects could be noted. So none were.

O N E

It was 2:00 a.m. when the nerve-jarring beeps of her pager summoned Autumn Johnson, breathless, to the fourteenth floor. Autumn's not-quite-curly hair was again attempting its nightly escape from the bun she kept having to readdress and the right leg of her pale blue scrubs bore a small ketchup stain, embarrassingly betraying her inability to keep it together on an overnight shift. Taking advantage of a rare moment of quiet, Autumn had decided to grab a day-old tuna sandwich and too-greasy fries from the twenty-four-hour hospital cafeteria instead of writing patient notes. A decision she was now regretting, both due to the angry rumbling of her stomach and to the pile of work she would never be able to get through before the end of her shift—and the sun—arrived. She ignored the protestations of her stomach and followed the raised voices to room 1428.

A skinny, wrinkled body lay supine on the tile floor.

His hospital gown bunched at his waist, bicycle-kicking limbs making it appear as if his sagging scrotum was the only thing anchoring him to the floor. The wild-eyed patient was screaming for all the saints in heaven to come to his assistance. As for the overnight shift nurses of the fourteenth floor, who actually *had* come to his assistance, he appeared ready to injure them in any way possible with limbs that flailed at any attempt to get him off the floor.

"Can't we give him something?" a red-faced nurse growled at Autumn, making her feel that, somehow, this delirious patient's fall out of bed was her fault.

Her pager went off again—a text message about someone on the seventh floor having chest pain. He would have to wait. She fumbled through the dozens of papers in her white coat pocket, each detailing the medical histories of the patients she had to take care of overnight. Because of a rule passed a few years ago, trainees couldn't spend more than twenty-four hours in the hospital at a time—down from the whopping thirty-six-hour shifts that were previously typical. So, Autumn, only a few months after graduating from medical school, found herself playing the role of the night-shift intern, taking over for eight of her daytime colleagues and covering up to 150 patients at a time. Her finger quickly traced over the three-line histories for the patients she was now responsible for. The night-float intern's chief task was to not let anyone die amidst nonstop action. And though she tried to sleep during the day, she just wasn't any good at it. Two weeks into her night-float rotation, she had a low-grade headache she just couldn't shake and her bones ached like those of a soldier in combat.

Finally, her now hyper-alert eyes landed on the typed-up summary of the distressed patient in front of her.

> Schafer. Eighty-two years old. Parkinson's disease,
> heart failure, chronic kidney disease.

The short patient history she had in her hands went on to explain that he had been admitted for congestive heart failure, improved with diuretics, and was probably going to be discharged the next day. His usual intern clearly hadn't dealt with his sun-downing—when the elderly become disoriented at night due to the unfamiliar surroundings of the hospital.

Three months into her job, Autumn distinctly remembered a medical school geriatrics lecture cautioning against using usual sedatives in the elderly. Ativan, a benzodiazepine, was a good choice in a young person, but in an older person, it could make their confusion worse. That Haldol, an antipsychotic, was a good choice in the older population floated up from somewhere in her brain. Autumn quickly shouted, "Give him a milligram of Haldol IV," and ran to the computer to type it in.

Her pager went off again. Someone else had a fever.

"A milligram isn't much," the red-faced nurse offered, pointing to the patient's clenched fists, feebly attempting to land a punch. "How about five?"

"Fine. Five," Autumn called back as she furiously clicked through the various order-entry screens and pop-ups on the hospital's electronic ordering system, turned, and ran off to the seventh floor patient with chest pain.

After taking care of the patient with chest pain—his EKG was normal and a little Maalox seemed to cure him—

but before she could get to the one with a fever, Autumn's pager went off again.

"Schafer is having a seizure," the text read.

No time for the sluggish elevators. Autumn ran up the stairs back to Schafer's room. Breathless, she took note that the previously flailing patient had stopped flailing. Thought the nurses had successfully gotten him back into bed, he now wasn't moving at all. He also wasn't having a seizure. His head was cocked severely to the right and his body lay miserably contracted.

Autumn's heart rate, which had started to come down from her jog up the stairs, began racing again. Schafer had dystonia. Autumn began to breathe heavily as she remembered something else. Haldol might be a good idea in most older people, but not in someone with Parkinson's disease.

"Oh God. Oh no!" she said out loud. She grabbed at the stack of papers in her pocket again and read:

Schafer. Eighty-two years old. Parkinson's disease.

She had given someone with Parkinson's disease Haldol. Five milligrams of it. *Please God, no!* She ran from the room and picked up one of the greasy black phones at the nurses' station.

"I need the neurology resident on call," she tried not to shout at the operator.

She glanced up at the clock. It was 2:33 a.m. and whoever it was was going to be pissed.

A few minutes later, the neurology resident, usually friendly, staggered down the hall looking just as disgusted as Autumn expected her to be. Residents' shifts could also be up to twenty-four hours.

"What happened?" the neurology resident asked flatly, none of the usual conviviality in her voice.

"He was sun-downing. He has Parkinson's disease. I ordered Haldol," Autumn reported, adding in a much quieter voice, "Five milligrams."

"You did what?" The neurology resident narrowed her eyes and looked at Autumn like she might just be the stupidest person in the world.

"I ordered Haldol," Autumn repeated even more quietly.

The bloodshot-eyed neurology resident laughed darkly. "Didn't the computer tell you not to do that?"

"No," Autumn barked back and felt the contents of her stomach rise. "I don't know. Maybe it did."

There were so many screens. So many warnings. If she stopped to read them all, she'd never get to the patient with chest pain or the one with the fever. Some days it seemed like a big game to see how quickly she could click through the screens to get to actually see her patients.

Just then, Autumn's pager went off. She still hadn't seen the patient with a fever. The neurology resident was making her way to Schafer's room.

"I'll be back," Autumn called out and ran for the elevator bay. Like hell was she going to run down seven flights of stairs now. Her legs already felt like jelly and her on-call night was barely half over.

On call. Before medical school, maybe even before internship, Autumn had thought that on-call meant you went to sleep in the hospital and they called you if something went wrong. But something was always going wrong. And it was her job to set it right. But it was hard to do that when all you did was run from one crisis to the next. And the people were so sick. Not sick like when you have the flu, but sick like dying. And modern medicine, even in this glorious place, couldn't really fix dying. Maybe just push it off for a little bit. Sometimes, though, death gave a big push back. Those seemed to be the nights Autumn was on-call.

A black cloud. That's what the more senior residents told her she was. She was a black cloud. Or followed by one. If something was going to go wrong, it was bound to go wrong when she was on duty.

Autumn would shrug when her colleagues called her that. Maybe it was bad luck. But maybe it wasn't all random bad luck. Maybe she was a terrible intern and would turn out to be a terrible resident, and, finally, a terrible attending physician.

Too bad there was no time for self-pity. She could get really good at that, but the elevator doors had opened onto the febrile patient's floor.

Two Tylenol, four sets of blood cultures, an enema, and twenty-three pages later, sunlight finally started to stream in through the partially shaded patient windows. Autumn made her way to the cafeteria to give the day interns back their sign-out sheets, her heart lightening each time her giant stack got smaller. At least no one had died.

"Sorry," Autumn mumbled as she gave Mark the run down on his now dystonic Parkinson's patient.

He shrugged as he took back his list and gave Autumn

a wan smile. "It's okay," he mumbled in response, clearly unhappy that his patient load would not be lightened. "I could have made the same mistake."

Autumn tried to smile back, but she doubted her friend Mark's words of encouragement. He had been an undergraduate chemistry whiz who broke the curve on every exam, while she was just lucky to be there. There was no way he would have made such a critical error. Mark, along with everyone else in the hospital, seemed so much smarter than she was. Autumn felt particularly stupid when she was sleep deprived at two o'clock in the morning.

Blissfully, though, her time as the night-float intern was coming to an end. Tomorrow, she would begin life anew as an ICU intern. That was bound to be better than this. After all, the ICU only had ten beds. There was no way taking care of ten patients, even if they were deathly ill ICU patients, could be as bad as 150.

T W O

Just get home. Just get home. Autumn mouthed this mantra to her steering wheel over and over again in order to keep herself awake. She concentrated on the long line of cars approaching as they drove into Boston, the beige towers of the hospital receding from view in her rear-view mirror. Those cars heading into the city for the day were surely driven by normal people who got to sleep in their beds at night and who showered in the morning. She supposed most of them got a lunch break and maybe even got to leave their offices once in a while to breathe fresh air and enjoy a mid-day meal that didn't come from large, aluminum chafing dishes.

As the approaching traffic thinned and she drove the last few blocks to her apartment, she recalled a meme that showed "what people think I do versus what I really do." When she told random salespeople and casual acquaintances that she was a resident physician, they assumed she already made big bucks and ran around the hospital saving lives all day, then went out for fancy dinners at night. Autumn snorted. She barely made enough to cover her student loan payments, pricey Boston rent, and food. And about the saving lives part? Mostly she did paperwork. Occasionally she got to talk to her patients who had led rich lives before becoming reduced to a collection of diagnoses. She let out an exhausted sigh as she parked in front of her apartment building. Lucky for her all those normal people with normal lunch breaks had left for their normal day jobs, gifting her with a prime parking spot. At least she had that. And Jay.

Jay Abrams. She had met him at a party five weeks ago. He was her age, twenty-seven, but still a medical student since he was also getting his Ph.D. Busied with his diabetes research, he hadn't done any of his hospital rotations yet. The realities of illness and death were still concepts in textbooks for him, not stains and smells on his scrubs.

Autumn wrinkled her nose as she walked into her apartment, still dark from the blackout curtains she'd gotten so she could make an attempt at sleep during the day. There was an unmistakable musty odor, which she quickly identified as a wet towel on the carpet. Jay must have left it there. He was normally much neater than that. She shrugged as she hung it on the towel rack, figuring he must have been in a rush to get to his lab, smiling slightly as she imagined his muscular, dripping, naked body. A slight heat in her belly, this time pleasant and unrelated to the greasy fries she had eaten the night before, spread through her as she recalled his smooth hands on her body and his wet, hungry mouth on her neck. Her fingers went instinctively to the last place he had touched, and so, she forgave him for the towel on the floor.

Autumn's body gave a slight shudder, which she decided to ignore, and pushed Jay out of her mind. It was the third time Jay had spent the night and she had no intention of getting into a serious relationship. Jay had never raised the topic of making things exclusive and she was too busy for that sort of thing anyway. He was a much-needed diversion. That was all.

Autumn pulled on the braided orange string holding up her stained scrub bottom, which then quickly fell to the floor. She walked out of them and her clogs in two slow, deliberate steps, climbed into bed, and pulled the comforter up to her chin. She settled her body even deeper into the heavy comforter in the hopes that sleep would follow. But despite the aching of her bones and the heaviness of her lids, her eyes refused to close for any length of time. Because when they did close, she didn't see the blackness she was hoping for. Instead she saw Schafer's unmoving, contracted body, his head cocked sharply to the side. Mark had said it was a mistake that anyone could have made. But anyone hadn't made it. She had.

THREE

JAY

For the first time in many weeks, Jay's mind had quieted. He had a plan. It wasn't a particularly great plan, but it would get him out. He carelessly ran a finger over the indentation on the cover of his well-worn lab notebook: Jay Abrams, no M.D., no Ph.D. Not yet, anyway. He slipped the data for his life's work into the side of the creaky metal desk. The drawer let out a tired groan as he closed it, a comfortingly familiar noise he welcomed. Science, he understood. Blackmail, however, was a new subject for him.

Jay leaned against the solid, well-worn desk and looked around at what had practically been his home for the past three years. He had spent more hours in Withering's lab than in his own apartment. Except for the occasional mouse scratching on the floor of its cage, all was silent. At this hour, he considered that the fluorescent glow emanating from the lab would be the only sign of life left on the fourth floor of the massive research building. He filled his lungs as if he hadn't stopped to take a good breath in all day and let it out slowly through his nose. It had been a long day. Oh hell, it had been a long year. His first two years in the lab had felt full of promise—a career in its infancy. Jay wasn't sure what had changed this past year, but the lab had become a miserable place.

Jay frowned, grabbed his bag, and looked around at his tired surroundings. One day it seemed like Withering was never going to let him get his Ph.D., and the next day, Withering acted like he couldn't wait to get rid of him. Well, Jay had had his fill of that self-important son-of-a-bitch, too. He was ready to get out of this hellhole of a lab, and if blackmail was the only way to do it, so be it. He deserved to graduate. He had done his time and had contributed his fair share to the advancement of science and medicine. More importantly, he had made his brother's life count for something.

He quickly scanned the black-tops. Everything had been cleaned and put in its place. He checked that the pair of computers had been powered down. And even though the mouse cages weren't his responsibility, he made sure they all had water and food and the doors to the cages were properly locked. They were. Withering's lab assistant, Luba, was a detail-oriented person who seemed to notice everything. Still, even though he didn't work with them anymore and was glad for that, Jay liked to look in on the mice and give them a little attention from time to time. Withering didn't like him messing with the mice, but Jay didn't much care what Withering did or didn't like anymore.

As Jay heard the soft pop of the fluorescent lights turning

off and locked the door to the lab, he wondered if anything interesting was happening around the campus. Now that his research days were coming to a close, he'd focus more on his social life. Time to take a break from being a lab rat. The girl he'd been seeing had been busy a lot. She was bright and fun, but dating a resident was a lot harder than dating someone who would have more time for him.

Jay thought he remembered something about an undergrad party one of the other medical students had mentioned. Was that today? He would find out when he got home. The female undergrads were competitive not only about their academics, but their looks, too. Since many of them had been wildly successful in high school, they needed to compete on a level beyond academics here. A great many of them were now trying to exercise themselves to perfection, and he could appreciate that. He spent whatever free time he could at the gym. Jay was sure he could find a pretty, fit, pre-med to chat up if he could figure out where this party was supposed to be.

Jay rode the service elevator down to the impressive marble lobby and waved to the abandoned security desk on his way out before realizing the guard was already gone. He crossed the perfectly manicured lawn onto the drab, cracked sidewalk that could have been any Boston street where the awe-inspiring structures intermingled with the mundane. Roman columns stood a few feet from chain pharmacies. Having lived in Boston for so many years, the bizarre juxtaposition no longer registered, and Jay hurried down the long tree-lined avenue, barely noticing the slight ache beginning in the pit of his stomach.

FOUR

CASSIE

Dr. Cassidy Ellison, senior ICU resident, watched patiently as her new intern, Autumn Johnson, carefully ran her gloved finger along Mr. Giannini's clavicle for what seemed like the hundredth time in the last fifteen minutes. Her face was visibly sweating underneath the light blue surgical mask, turning it a darker blue in small, coin-like patches.

"Shit," Autumn cursed out loud, as she slid the needle in again, pulled back on the syringe, and got virtually nothing in return except for a few drops of bright red blood that would inevitably clog the needle unless she flushed it immediately with saline. Cassie narrowed her gaze at Autumn as she turned to flush the syringe and considered admonishing Autumn for her cursing. What if Mr. Giannini could hear her? Cassie didn't think he could—the guy was practically dead. The cursing set a bad precedent though. Autumn might inadvertently curse while doing a procedure on a conscious patient in the future. Not good. Every year, the interns' lack of professionalism seemed to get worse. This was only her second year supervising interns, but Cassie felt that she was excellent at picking up on patterns. Instead of opening her mouth, she smiled encouragingly at Autumn from her slightly uncomfortable plastic seat. Autumn was new at this, and Cassie was sure there would be something more important to criticize at any moment. Like most medicines, escalating the dose of criticism all at once wouldn't provide as much benefit as well-timed, smaller doses.

Mr. Giannini had another subclavian line on his left side, so he could still get the two pressors that were keeping him alive, no matter how long the central line took her new intern. Cassie continued to observe quietly, the more experienced resident's hardest job, as Autumn plunged the needle in again, drew back slowly as she advanced, and for all her effort, got nothing back in the syringe. When Autumn's brow furrowed and the mask was turned nearly entirely dark from perspiration, Cassie finally got up and took a few careful steps toward her.

"Redirect inferiorly," she calmly instructed Autumn to point the needle downward. Though only two years ago she was in the same position as Autumn, it seemed like her internship had never really happened—a bad dream perhaps. Cassie was quite skilled at putting the negative things in life out of her mind, or at least pushing them away, and forging ahead.

"Okay, thanks, Cassie. But you know, I could do an IJ line much more easily," Autumn said, referring to an IV line into the internal jugular vein that ran next to the carotid artery in the neck. "I aced neck anatomy in med school—even found the *ansa cervicalis* on my cadaver!"

Cassie shook her head. "The subclavian line is cleaner." Cassie motioned toward the patient's mouth area, covered with mucous and tape, securing his breathing tube in place. "All that junk is bound to run down his neck into the IJ line. That's an infection waiting to happen."

End of discussion. The intern could do it. She would have to. There was no alternative. Cassie could and would stand there all night with her. But maybe they could break for dinner and come back if Autumn didn't figure it out in the next few minutes? Cassie motioned for Autumn to direct the needle a bit more downward, careful to stay out of the sterile field.

Nothing. She watched Autumn pull the needle out almost to the surface of the skin, and Cassie motioned for her to insert it again. Nothing. Cassie nodded and Autumn redirected again. Nothing. And again. Then finally blood! A rush of the dull, maroon stuff steadily filled the syringe.

"I'm in!" Autumn yelled through her mask, joy evident in her voice.

Cassie, smiling broadly now, jumped up and snapped on her own sterile gloves.

"Okay, don't move, I'll hand you what you need. Leave the needle in and take the syringe off," Cassie commanded.

She watched carefully as Autumn unscrewed the syringe. If, despite the reassuring maroon color of the blood, it was from an artery, the blood would shoot out like a geyser and the unfortunate Mr. Giannini would be even closer to death. But the dark blood only dribbled out, indicating the needle was in the vein. Cassie handed Autumn the long, coiled wire to insert through the needle. Guarded in plastic, the wire came out of the thin blue casing with a little bit of pressure from Autumn's thumb. Thankfully, the tip fit nicely into the end of the needle, and Autumn stopped the oozing out of the unconscious patient's vein with a quick motion. Slowly, she began to advance what seemed like a yard of wire into the needle.

"Grab the end," Cassie commanded. "Don't let go of the wire."

Autumn grabbed the end of the wire, as the emptied plastic container that had previously held it fell to the floor with a soft crack. Letting go of the guide wire, which was now sitting in the heart, or hopefully just above it, would result in the wire sliding its way into the heart completely, sending the patient immediately off to the operating room if he didn't die of a fatal heart arrhythmia first.

Cassie was ready to step in as Autumn pulled the needle out with her left hand, slid it along the inches of wire protruding from the skin's surface, and dropped it into the white plastic tray beside her. Blood had started oozing again, but it was only a tolerable trickle. Autumn now twisted the plastic dilator over the wire and then pushed it roughly through the skin and soft tissue beneath, boring yet another hole into poor Mr. Giannini.

The dark maroon trickle began to run faster as she yanked the dilator back through the skin. Quickly, Cassie handed Autumn the central line with its four hanging plastic tubes. Autumn pushed it over the guide-wire and into the subclavian vein, staunching the bleeding from Mr. Giannini's new wound. Success! Cassie had known Autumn could do it. They all learn eventually.

Examining the floor for any needles or pieces that might have fallen during the line insertion, Cassie instead spotted a pair of shoes belonging to Mr. Giannini's nurse, Joanne. Her eyes followed the old-style blue scrub dress up to Joanne's head—she had a sturdy frame but the skin hung loosely off her face, wrinkled in the tissue-papery pattern of a life-long smoker. "Done yet? Ya know I have things to do in here."

"Almost," Autumn nearly whispered as she made sure to secure the line in place.

"Interns," Cassie heard Joanne grumble on her way out of the room. Cassie was proud of her intern but couldn't help but agree with Joanne, who had decades of experience on both of them. The interns were a fair amount of work.

Cassie was almost done cleaning up the considerable mess Autumn had made. She had dropped the sharps into the specially-marked red bucket before she picked up the phone outside the room and called for a portable chest X-ray to make sure the central line had gone where it was intended and that no unintentional holes were poked into Mr. Giannini's lung. Then she grabbed the blue drape with its various gauze pads and spent syringes, bundled it all up, and dropped it in the huge waste bin that every room in the ten-bed ICU held.

Joanne would have to transfer the patient's pressors, antibiotics, and IV nutrition into his new central line before they could remove the likely-infected old one from the red, inflamed left side of his chest. That would take Joanne a good twenty to thirty minutes, prompting Cassie to finally decide that it was dinnertime. It was 8:30 p.m. Cassie had started her day at 8 a.m. and hadn't had time for much of a lunch. She decided that a greasy hamburger and fries, the cafeteria's specialty with just the right balance of protein, fat, carbs, and guilt about her choices, was just what she needed to keep her going for the rest of the night.

She turned to Autumn. "Time for dinner," she announced. As she and Autumn quickly made their way to the ICU's heavy double mechanical doors, Cassie called out cheerily to the nurses that they were leaving to eat. Though it was more a statement than a question, she paused in case anyone wanted to fill them in on an impending crisis before they were trapped in the painfully slow elevator for what could be valuable minutes as it transported them from the fifteenth floor to the first. As they walked resolutely past, the nurse-in-charge, Christine, who was normally agreeable, shook her head no.

"Not a good time. I just heard about a young fellow coming up from the ER. Sounds pretty bad. Better hang around for a while longer. I brought some cookies and put them in the back if you need something to hold you," she offered with her heavy Irish accent, adding a bit of warmth to the bad news. "We don't have a bed for the new guy though. We're going to have to clear someone out."

"Why do they never call me about new admissions?" Cassie asked no one in particular. Christine continued looking at her, smiling gently and waiting for Cassie to decide which patient to transfer to the regular medical floor—albeit in this hospital, the regular medical floor would qualify as an ICU in most others. Cassie closed her eyes as if deep in thought, though the answer to Christine's question was obvious.

"I think Mr. McAdams can go. He's the only one not on

a ventilator. They'll just have to deal with his pneumonia on the regular floor. He has great venous access, hasn't needed his pressors for the last eight hours or so, and they have antibiotics there, too," Cassie said, trying to convince herself that the patient would do just as well on a floor with less medical staff. There were only a limited number of ICU beds in the hospital and if a patient wasn't close to death, he would have to make room for someone who was.

Not missing a beat, Joanne held out the phone at the ICU desk and called out, "Hey, some ER resident is on the phone for the ICU senior resident. You want to take this?"

Christine called over to Mr. McAdams's nurse, "Sue, pack up your patient, he's got to ship out. We're getting one from the ER."

Sue scowled. "You know, he needed both Neo-Synephrine and Levophed to keep him alive until just this morning, right?"

"I'm taking alternative suggestions. What have you got?" Christine asked calmly.

"They either need to build another ICU or discharge the two ninety-somethings who have been here for close to a month waiting to meet their maker." Sue gestured to beds two and three, whose chronically debilitated occupants, everyone agreed, would not be making it out of the ICU alive. "But, for tonight, I guess not," Sue said and shrugged her shoulders, causing her large chest to retreat momentarily in defeat.

"Can I help?" Christine offered and went into Mr. McAdams's room with Sue.

Picking up the phone, Cassie motioned for Autumn join her at the main desk. Dozens of cubbies lined the walls, holding every form anyone might ever need or perhaps would never need. The residents spent at least an hour a day filling out these forms. Sometimes it was closer to two hours. The program director, who hailed from a time when there weren't three administrators for every practicing physician, would admonish them on their first day of orientation that "no patient had ever died from note-o-penia," signifying that they should prioritize patients over paperwork. However, it seemed he hadn't communicated that to the hospital administrators, who appeared to be creating new forms daily.

Cassie covered the mouthpiece with her hand. "Seems like this twenty-seven year-old guy is having some heart problems. How much do you want to bet he took something?"

"What do you mean heart problems?" Autumn asked, her mouth pulling down. Cassie knew what she was thinking. The medical ICU never got twenty-seven year olds. The average age of ICU patients was probably about eighty.

Cassie gave a curt, "Sure," to the ER resident, hung up, and shrugged in Autumn's direction. "I don't think the ER knows. The guy came in with nausea, vomiting, diarrhea, standard GI bug stuff. At first, the heart rate was in the forties, but well, he's young so no one made much of it. You know, it could just be an athletic heart. Then, out of nowhere he started going like 140, so they put him on a monitor. No one was sure what the heart rhythm was, but they figured it was just a fast sinus rhythm, and he was probably dry from all of the diarrhea and vomiting. They gave him a bunch of fluid boluses over a few hours hoping to discharge him right back home and all of a sudden, the guy goes into unstable VT at about two hundred beats a minute," Cassie said, explaining his path to ventricular tachycardia, a life-threatening heart rhythm, something fairly unusual in one so young.

Autumn let out a small gasp.

"Weird, huh?" Cassie continued rapid-fire. "So, they shock him, obviously, and he goes back into whatever slow rhythm he was in to start with, but this time they see lots of ventricular ectopy. They think he might go into VT again, so now they're sending him to us."

"Is he conscious? Can he tell them what happened?" Autumn asked.

Cassie smiled weakly, reminding herself that interns were still learning. The Boston Memorial ICU brand of patient didn't generally come in the conscious variety. "Well, he coded, so they intubated him. Not a bad idea since he was vomiting when he dragged himself into the ER and wasn't going to be protecting his airway. From what I can gather, they knocked him out pretty good. Succinylcholine, etomidate, Versed, fentanyl, and who knows what else. He won't be talking to us tonight anyway," Cassie said with a shrug. "Maybe if all goes well tonight we can extubate him tomorrow and have him help us figure out what he took."

"Didn't they send a tox screen?" Autumn asked.

It was a good question. The ER always sent a toxicology screen, and his symptoms pointed to some sort of overdose.

"Yup. Negative except for some THC," Cassie answered a little sharply. She needed Autumn to work right now, not ask a bunch of questions. She could deal with her questions after figuring out the logistics of making space for their new admission.

"Autumn, can you call the admitting team on the regular medical floor about Mr. McAdams while I start digging through the new admission's stuff so we can sort this out a little bit more?"

Having occupied her intern with the usual busy work, Cassie started to get ready for their admission. Cassie's own heart rate was picking up. She was pretty excited for this one—one they might actually save. Unlike the television shows, where people needed advanced cardiac life support, rolled into the ICU, and then skipped out by the end of the episode, almost no one made it out of a real ICU alive. How could they? Their bodies were old, cancer ridden, or with hearts that pumped blood out at a trickle. Tonight, though, they were going to admit someone young and vital. She just needed to figure out what he might have taken. Many new synthetic substances didn't show up on traditional toxicology screens. If she did her job right, he could walk out of here. That's why she had become a doctor—to fix people. Lately, it just wasn't working out like she had planned.

Cassie gave Sue a wave as she wheeled McAdams's stretcher out of the ICU, a bag of a pale yellow antibiotic hanging from the pole at the head of the bed, a monitor beeping steadily at the foot of it. Cassie huddled over one of the computer workstations, trying to find prior records for the patient they were about to meet. A shadow appeared behind her on the screen.

"Anything?" Autumn asked.

"Shockingly, no. I can't even find this guy registered with admitting at all. I didn't expect to find much in the first place on a twenty-seven year-old, unless he's a coke or heroin abuser, which maybe he is, but he's not even registered in the ER. Why isn't he in the system?" Cassie wondered aloud, the words flying out of her mouth faster than she intended for them to.

Cassie opened her mouth to offer a few suggestions, but the mechanical hissing sounds from the ICU doors opened, cutting her off. Cassie, with Autumn just behind her, jumped up and raced to meet the stretcher carrying their new admission. He was rolled in feet first. Chuck, the senior medical resident in the ER, was at the side of the stretcher. One of the ER nurses squeezed the ambu-bag supplying oxygen to the patient's mouth, obscuring his face with her large hands. Only a mop of his black hair was visible above all the equipment. Uncharacteristically, the patient had no hospital-issue gown on, the paddle burns exposed on his uncovered chest, his lower half covered only by a thin white sheet.

"Holy shit," Chuck boomed to no one in particular. "I had to shock him in the slow-ass elevator. He went into VT or VF in the elevator! Can you believe that?"

The slower beeps coming from the monitor let everyone know that the patient was not currently in ventricular tachycardia or worse, ventricular fibrillation, as Chuck had suggested he may have been only just before their arrival. Cassie tore off what seemed like a mile of two-inch-wide paper spit out by the monitor, quickly folded it, and put it into a pocket of her white coat to examine later. "Looks like it worked," Cassie said to Chuck dryly as they prepared to get the patient into the bed.

"No shit, it worked! I used to be pissed off they made

us come up in the elevators with ICU admits from the ER. What a pain in the ass! But this time, thank God I was there. I know your admission, if you can believe that, and he owes me a beer for that one! You guys need to get him to detox or something. I never figured him for a user." Chuck shrugged and his gaze drifted around the stretcher, stopping when he saw Autumn. His eyes bored into her, as if he expected something—Cassie had no idea what. But Autumn's eyes were focused on the beeping monitor, as though it might somehow give up the secret of what had happened to this young man. Cassie glared back at Chuck, willing herself not to ask him if he didn't need to hurry back to the ER. She was starving and Chuck's self-aggrandizement was only aggravating her.

"Let's get him in the bed," Christine commanded, frowning at Chuck and grabbing the ER run sheets from the foot of the bed. "And where's respiratory to get him hooked up to the vent?"

"Respiratory," called a soft voice emanating from the bright red lips of a slight woman racing a few seconds behind everyone else. The respiratory therapists, who inevitably spent their entire twelve-hour shifts running from one disaster to the next, were always the calmest people in the ICU.

"On three," Christine called out, as Chuck, Cassie, Joanne, the large-handed ER nurse, and Autumn gathered around the stretcher to pull the patient over to his ICU bed.

Cassie was at the patient's left side, still able to smell the burnt hairs on her new admission's chest. Autumn was at the patient's feet, while Chuck was at his head, though he ought to have been at a spot where his muscular build could have been put to more practical use, Cassie thought to herself.

"One," Christine called out.

So as to avoid the burnt flesh odor, Cassie turned her head slightly and looked over at Autumn, who was glassy eyed, staring at the patient's face and sweating more profusely than when she had been putting in Mr. Giannini's central line.

"Two," Christine commanded as everyone but Autumn reinforced their grip on the sheet beneath the patient.

Cassie could only watch in horror as she saw Autumn's fingers loosen their hold on the sheet. There was nothing she could do as Autumn crashed to the floor at the same instant Christine yelled, "Three."

Cassie turned her focus quickly to the bed and made sure that her new patient had been transferred with all of his tubes and lines still attached. When she turned back to Autumn, she found her awake on the floor, slumped over, staring straight ahead. "I've got this," Christine mouthed to Cassie, as she motioned for the respiratory tech to hook the patient up to the ventilator. Christine lifted Autumn to her feet, slowly guiding her to a chair outside of the room. Cassie watched through the glass as Christine grabbed a few four-ounce plastic containers of juice from the fridge at the nurses' station. She heard Christine ask Autumn if she had eaten yet that day and sighed. No. They hadn't.

Christine positioned Autumn semi-recumbent in the chair, raised her feet, and tore off the foil top from a cranberry juice as she handed it to Autumn.

Confident that Autumn would survive, Cassie began to enter orders for her newest patient whose name had miraculously finally appeared on the ICU list. She hoped Autumn would be coming back soon, but if not, she'd handle the admission herself. Ignoring the thumping in her chest, Cassie scrolled through the lab reports herself, writing down the pertinent abnormalities on a new four-by-six index card she kept for each of her patients. The card soon filled with her neat abbreviations and she reached for the stapler to have another card attached and ready as more data came in—she was certain that no detail could be overlooked—this was life and death. There could be no mistakes.

FIVE

Jay was jolted awake by a throat on fire. He tried to swallow but for some reason his tongue wouldn't cooperate. A cramp shot through his stomach. Should he get up to go to the bathroom? He felt so tired. He figured it must be early, but it was bright in his room. Brighter than it should have been for early in the morning. Very yellow. What time was it anyway? Jay turned his head to look over at the electronic alarm clock and realized he couldn't see. It was too bright. The world was awash in the brightest yellow, only occasionally disrupted by small black dots dancing across his vision. Oh God, what if he'd gone blind? His eye doctor had warned him about the possibility last year.

"You are extraordinarily nearsighted," Dr. Spencer had told him. "If ever you get a bunch of black spots in your eyes or experience a blinding light, get to the hospital immediately. It's called retinal detachment, and if I can get to it quickly enough, I can save your vision."

Jay's heart began to thump in his chest. But his chest was heavy—weighted down as if there were bricks stacked on it. He felt an immediate urge to expel the contents of his stomach. Bathroom, now! He tried to swing his legs off the side of the bed.

Nothing happened.

He tried again, but they wouldn't budge. Neither would his arms. They felt just as heavy as his chest. He tried to move his right index finger. That wouldn't move either.

"Calm down. You are dreaming. This is a dream," Jay told himself, realizing he wouldn't get retinal detachment in both eyes at the same time anyway. Fine, he was dreaming. He was dreaming he was blind. No more marijuana for him. That joint before the party he never made it to had been a stupid idea. Jay tried to listen as hard as he could to see if it could help jolt him awake. He could make out several voices in the room (in his dream?), but it was all distant mumbling. Beyond the voices, he could definitely hear beeping. After listening for a few seconds, it seemed that beeping was all he could hear, three different tones of it. A video game, maybe? Was it his younger brother playing a video game?

"Shut it off, Nathan," he tried to say. But he couldn't speak. Instead of the words being formed with an exhalation, he felt them violently pushed back inside his lungs. He tried again. "Nate, I said shut it off!" he thought and tried to say. But again, the pressure in his chest exploded as the words went the wrong way. The highest-pitched beeping got louder.

"Heesbuckink," Jay heard a woman's voice yell. Then

more mumbling.

He'd never experienced pain like this before in a dream. What the hell was going on? This couldn't be a dream. He couldn't move. He couldn't speak. He was paralyzed. Maybe he'd been drugged.

Every few seconds the pressure would build up in his chest, then he would let out a sigh. Jay felt a sudden urge to lie quietly and let whatever it was happen. He let his mind wander, trying to figure out whom he could have pissed off. The crazy animal activists? They wrote letters, but they didn't abduct researchers. He didn't even work with the mice anymore. No, they couldn't have kidnapped him. Anyway, why would they? He just worked in the lab, as Dr. Withering often reminded him whenever he had an observation that Withering didn't much care for. Withering? Would that son-of-a-bitch have kidnapped him to stop him from outing his lousy research to the higher-ups? Sure Jay had threatened him, but he just wanted Withering to give approval for his dissertation to go to committee so Jay could finally get his Ph.D. He was sure Withering knew he was bluffing—he was too vague about what he had on the researcher. Could Withering have found the notebook?

The beeping continued, but Jay could barely hear it now. There were the voices, too, but they had become even more indistinct. Jay tried to force his now incredibly heavy eyelids open. It took less strength to bench press two hundred and fifty pounds. Jay tried again and for a split second, his eyelids fluttered. Jay saw little green figures scurrying around him. Incredulous, Jay confronted the one thought that he'd been trying to push away for the last few minutes. It was the one explanation that could bring it all together. Occam's Razor: the simplest explanation was often the correct one.

He'd been abducted by aliens.

No, he hadn't. This was the pot talking.

He didn't even believe in alien abductions.

But aliens, as improbable as they were, could certainly exist. Jay remembered a statistical calculation he had made in a college astronomy course. The United States government sometimes supported an agency devoted to such things, SETI, the Search for Extraterrestrial Intelligence, he recalled. What were the chances? One in a million? Perhaps. But if there were intelligent life in the universe, why would they perform ridiculous experiments on humans? Jay used to chuckle at the supermarket tabloids with first-hand accounts of alien abductions. He had even read a couple of the stories standing in the interminable lines for their entertainment value. They seemed so absurd. But now it made perfect sense. The bright lights, being paralyzed, the weird noises. Wasn't this the stuff he had read about?

What were they doing to him, anyway? The tabloids were the only source he could refer to right now, so he tried to remember the articles he'd carelessly flipped through before. His thoughts were murky. He didn't think they would kill him. They didn't usually kill the people they kidnapped. Impregnate? It seemed there were a lot of stories about that sort of thing. But he was pretty sure he couldn't carry a pregnancy, alien or otherwise. Medical experimentation? He was a medical student. He could tell them what they wanted to know. There was no need for experimentation. He would willingly help them. He had to make them stop.

"Owwww." His mind shrieked in pain as he felt the right side of his neck sliced open, blood trickling down to his chest.

"Whareyoudoin," he heard the same woman's voice mumble. Maybe she was on his side. Maybe she would stop them from whatever it was they were trying to do.

"Owwww. Stop it. Stop it. Stop it." Jay's mind raced as he felt a hand roughly grip his penis and try to shove something hard and cold into it. Whatever it was passed into his urethra and the hand dropped his penis, leaving it with a dull ache.

That was it. He had to escape. He felt a tingling sensation in his toes and fingers, like they were coming awake. Maybe he could move his arms and legs if he tried. He needed to somehow get out of this. They seemed to speak English, sort of. He could tell them they were making a big mistake and that he'd help them voluntarily. He would tell them whatever they wanted to know. He couldn't speak, but he could gesticulate. He tried to throw his left arm up. It was heavy, but Jay thought it came off the bed.

"Heestrintatakeoutatube," Jay heard. "Fentanilahundr-andversidfore." It sounded vaguely like English. He tried to lift his arm again, but this time hands, almost human in appearance, grabbed it and forced it down. A cloth-like wrap quickly encircled his wrist, and he couldn't lift his arm anymore.

"Now," came a yell.

It was English!

He felt a rush of adrenaline at being able to communicate

with them. But why did the aliens speak English? The bright lights were slowly dimming. Why would the aliens speak English? It grew darker. Maybe they can speak all human languages. And darker. The voices were becoming distant, and his vision was now completely black.

Jay awoke to the sounds of even more beeping. He felt very drunk and very nauseated. Where was he? Oh yeah, spaceship. Aliens. He forced his eyes open, but everything was still blurry. The little green men were still there. His throat was burning, the side of his neck was burning, and his penis felt like it had been put into a vice grip.

"I wanna go home," Jay implored the aliens, but they couldn't hear him. He wasn't even sure the words had come out of his mouth. Suddenly, Jay felt a horrible searing pain on his chest. It was the worst pain yet. The overpowering smell of burnt flesh wafted up to his nose. What did these aliens eat, anyway? Him?

"To Serve Man." That was a *Twilight Zone* episode. No, it wasn't. That was right now. They were cooking him. He smelled the smoke rising from his chest. The aliens were going to eat him. But he was resigned to it now. He suddenly felt very calm about the fact that he was going to be eaten— until a very large alien started pressing on his chest.

"That hurts," Jay wanted to tell him. Were they tenderizing him? Couldn't they wait until he was dead? They seemed to tenderize him for a very long time, leaving him with a sharp pain every time he took a breath in. He tried holding his breath again, but the aliens were forcing his body to breathe. He was starting to feel much colder, and he was quite sure he was naked. But he was also very tired. More tired than he had been in his whole life—only he couldn't sleep. He would grow accustomed to one pain and start to drift off, but then another pain would jolt him awake. Every few minutes something would squeeze his arm tightly and then let go.

Sometimes Jay could see the blurry figures, but mostly he just saw colors moving and dancing around him. A lot of yellow. His head was in a very thick fog. He tried to count to himself but couldn't get past three.

The darkness was coming again and the smell of burning flesh was much stronger now. Maybe they were almost done cooking him. Maybe this would be over soon.

S I X

CASSIE

To the uninitiated, the ICU can be an intimidating place. When she was an intern, each time there was a beep, Cassie would jump. And there were a lot of beeps. Some were mono-tonal, not pleasant, but not bone-chilling. Then there were the beeps that got increasingly high pitched with each note. Those quickly conjured goose bumps on her skin and a thumping in her chest. The nurses' movements would quicken with the panicked intonations of the mechanical beeps. Their first glance was always toward the patient's monitor, electronic evidence of the patient's tenuous connection to this world. Sometimes, the nurse would push a few buttons and leave the room in a huff, clearly irritated by the machine's stupidity. Other times, hands started to move purposefully even as their expressions fell. Now that's when Cassie knew she needed to rush in, but that wasn't always the case. At first, she was paralyzed by fear; she needed to be told by the

42

senior resident to "start chest compressions" or "send off a chemistry panel."

Her first few days in The Unit, as medical staff called the ICU, were spent constantly on edge. Anything could happen and usually did. Patients started bleeding and didn't stop. They had seizures that seemed to never end. Their rapid and erratic heart rhythms couldn't be stopped, until they did, and then it was worse. If those things happened on the regular medical floors, the patient went to The Unit. If those things happened in one of the countless community hospitals throughout New England or as far away as Bermuda, they came to the massive teaching hospital's inadequately small Unit. As an intern, Cassie could always look up to her senior resident, watching over the patients, completely in control. Or so she thought then. Now she was the senior resident and she used bravado to mask her fear. That was the most important thing she had learned in internship. Fear and uncertainty had to be pushed down as far as they would go. She still got the goose bumps and the chest thumping but no one would know it from her steely expression. The attending physician, who made his or her appearance on rounds and then left to write the papers that would get him or her into the prestigious medical journals, always said "call me if you need me," but it was a sign of weakness to call—that much was understood. If she wanted to be respected at all, she would handle whatever came her way. She was the last line of defense against death and she had to act like it.

No one wanted to die. And no doctor was prepared to let them. Codes, the resuscitation effort the nurses and residents wield to fight the forces of death, could go on for a very long time. Some believed a code that had gone on for more than twenty minutes should be stopped or "called." But it wasn't always that simple. When the blood pressure comes back for a few minutes, should that be subtracted from the count? Should the timer be restarted from that point? What if a little more time would be the few minutes that would make a difference? And so, in the very large teaching hospital with the very smart doctors who should know better, codes went on for thirty or forty-five minutes or sometimes for more than an hour. The younger and healthier the patient, the harder it was to give up—to accept defeat and welcome the enemy, Death. That would make Death the victor, and all of the medical school studying and long days and nights of internship and residency would have been preparation for nothing.

Cassie felt the adrenaline course through her veins as her heart bounded from her chest. She couldn't stop. It had all been for this, hadn't it? The moment when the doctor swooped in dramatically to save the patient. In the movies or on television, after all of the heroics, the patient either lives (and walks out of the hospital after the commercial break) or dies. But Hollywood tended not to give enough credit to either medicine or nature. Medicine could help a person hang on to what little threads of life he or she still possessed, seemingly indefinitely. And when he or she seemed to possess none, medicine had the ability to create the illusion they were still there. Very few patients died dramatically. Far fewer patients got up and walked out of the hospital after they were coded. The vast majority went on to live somewhere between life and death, in a nether-region Hollywood has not yet discovered. It's a place where few who have worked outside of an ICU have heard of, and there were only hospital legends of patients who have gone on to tell of this purgatory—the land of the not quite dead.

At 10:12 p.m., forty minutes after their new admission had begun coding, it was over. He was not quite dead. Unfortunately, he wasn't really alive anymore either. Cassie replayed the timeline in her mind.

At 9:20 p.m., they had barely gotten Jay Abrams into his bed when Autumn nearly passed out on the floor of his room. In addition to the multitude of drugs they had given him in the ER, they had already put in an internal jugular central line into the right side of his neck. Chuck drove her crazy, but Cassie had to admit that he did his work and did it well. They needed that central line.

Christine had barely gotten Autumn settled in a chair when Abrams went into VT again. At 9:32 p.m., Cassie started the code clock ticking.

"We've got a code! Get the code cart," Cassie commanded. Instantly three nurses appeared in the room. The respiratory tech reappeared. "I need a blood pressure, please, now," Cassie barked to the room, using the forced "please" that she used after every request during a code. It was important to keep one's manners in a code—not because of any social convention, but because to not do so would be the first sign that she had lost control.

Joanne raced to the cuff already strapped around Jay's left arm, adeptly expanded it, then deflated it and listened closely for the pulsations to return to his arm. "Seventy over palp," Joanne called out.

The lanky, male nurse changed the IV flow so it would

rush in as quickly as gravity. He sprinted awkwardly across the room for another bag, kicking the ventilator on his way to the back of the room and cursing no one in particular.

"Get me the paddles, please," Cassie demanded as Christine was in the process of handing them to her. "Two hundred joules. Everyone clear, please."

Cassie planted the rectangular metal paddles onto the soft pink burns on his chest, one below his left pectoral muscle and the other on his sternum. She pressed the button below her thumb and arched her body into a C-shape to make sure she was clear of his bed. His body gave a soft jerk as the joules of energy traveled to his heart. "Can someone turn the monitor toward me, please?" Cassie ordered. "What's my rhythm?"

"VT," Autumn offered from behind Cassie.

"Charge to three hundred," Cassie ordered, turning back to Autumn, who seemed quite pale, but at least she was upright. "You okay?" she asked Autumn.

"Yeah. Fine. I know him," she said quickly, stepping behind Cassie.

"Clear," Cassie barked and pushed the red button. The body jumped again, but the rhythm stayed the same. "360, clear," Cassie said firmly and pressed the button again. "What's the pressure?"

"I can't get one. Hang on, I'll try to Doppler," Joanne said, reaching for the tiny ultrasound machine that helped find pulses when they were otherwise not audible.

"Start compressions please and one of epi and two of mag," Cassie called. Christine came forward with a syringe she had drawn up in anticipation of the shocks not working.

"Clear," Cassie ordered when Christine had finished

pushing the medication into the IV. Cassie shocked Jay three times, and each time his body gave little jerks of acknowledgement.

Joanne went back to kneeling by the patient's arm with her ultrasound headphones on, listening carefully for any signs of life. "I can't Doppler anything," Joanne reported.

"We've got pulseless electrical activity," Cassie called out. Pulseless electrical activity—a PEA arrest. She tried to remember if she'd ever seen someone survive this heart rhythm without blood pressure. She couldn't.

She turned to Autumn. "I need to know what his new chemistries and tox screen showed now, please." Autumn raced to a computer without saying a word. Cassie then turned to the only man in the room. "Dan," she said to the lanky male nurse, "can you help Sue with compressions?"

"Where did she think I was going?" he mumbled to Joanne as he made his way to the head of the bed, having just retrieved another bag of IV fluids.

It was 9:39 p.m. when Dan started using the palm of his hands to transfer his body weight onto Abrams's chest in the hopes of temporarily, if only weakly, circulating his blood for him. The sound of two ribs cracking couldn't be heard by anyone in the flurry of activity in the room. The diminutive respiratory technician stood at the head of the bed, adjusting the ventilator to try to keep the air flowing to Abrams's lungs and provide oxygen to the rest of his body, attempting in vain to silence the beeping alarms. Dan stood a few paces down and to the right of the body, vigilantly compressing the chest, working hard enough that he had broken into a visible sweat. Joanne stood to the left of the body, waiting for "hold compressions" to be called out so she could try to listen again for a pulse with her Doppler machine. Christine was readying the medications that Cassie called for, diligently writing each one down, recording the time of each intervention on her flow sheet. Cassie stood away from the body, her eyes trained on the patient's monitor, glancing occasionally over to the patient, though she could see very little of him through all the bodies working on him.

PEA. If she couldn't find the underlying cause of it and reverse it, it was all over. No one survived these codes. It was either something this guy had taken or some very strange metabolic derangement. He was too young to be having a heart attack, had no reason she could think of to have fluid around his heart, and couldn't have thrown a huge clot to his lungs—could he? She took a couple of quick steps to his legs and pressed down hard on his shins. No swelling. Probably no clot.

Autumn raced back, her activity returning the color back to her face. "Tox screen still only shows THC. His chem 7 just looks like he's been having diarrhea, but his liver enzymes are up: AST is 213 and ALT is 150. He also looks like he's got some pancreatitis with a lipase of three hundred," Autumn reported flatly.

"Hold compressions, please," Cassie commanded. "Any pulse yet?" she asked Joanne.

Joanne focused intently on Abrams's groin, moving her Doppler probe to the left and then the right with very slight motions. She lifted her head after about ten seconds, her face heavy with disappointment. "Nothing."

"Resume compressions, please." Cassie turned to Christine. "What have we given so far?"

Christine looked up, her face revealing her waning hope. It was 9:55 p.m. and there was probably already some brain damage. Christine began to read off her list in a monotone voice.

"One of epinephrine at 9:35. Two of magnesium at 9:36. Amio given at 9:38. Compressions started at 9:33," she said, looking up at Cassie as if to suggest that it was time to stop. But Cassie chose to ignore it.

"Can you get a blood gas?" Cassie said to Autumn. "And can someone call the cardiology fellow? I think we need a stat echocardiogram to rule out tamponade. He can maybe see if there is heart strain from a pulmonary embolus, too."

"Sure," Autumn replied stiffly, as Christine handed her a blood gas syringe. Sue, who was outside of the room now, quickly dialed her phone to summon the cardiology fellow.

Autumn knelt beside Jay's right wrist. Joanne looked down at her with a frown. "Sorry, honey," she said softly, "you're not gonna get anything out of his wrist. You better go for the bigger vessels in the groin."

Autumn's face reddened with embarrassment. Joanne handed her the Doppler, and as Dan pounded away on the patient's cracking chest, he generated enough of an artificial pulse for Autumn to be able to plunge the needle into the femoral artery deep in Abrams's groin, bright red blood flowing as Autumn pulled back on the syringe. She left the room quickly to send the blood gas, and Cassie noticed that Autumn's face was as white as the wall she flew past. That intern needed to keep it together. She had said she knew the patient. So had Chuck. Who the heck was he, Cassie wondered. Is he, she corrected herself.

It was 9:59 p.m. While waiting for the results of the blood

gas, Cassie requested several other medications, treating her own need to feel useful more than her patient. At 10:02 p.m., a haggard-looking cardiology fellow appeared, probably having spent the better part of the last couple of days in the hospital, wheeling the large heart imaging machine in front of him. He quickly said hello, was brought up to date on what had happened over the last half hour, and got his machine ready. By 10:05 p.m., he let everyone know that there was no fluid around the heart and, while he had no way of knowing for sure if a big clot was sitting in the lungs, he didn't think there was. He asked Cassie if he could help with anything else and when she replied, "No. It's been over thirty minutes," the cardiology fellow responded with a simple shrug and wheeled the echo machine out of the ICU while the resuscitation continued.

During the echocardiogram, Autumn had reappeared with the results of the blood gas and declared that the patient's pH was a little high and his level of blood carbon dioxide was slightly low, but the information was incidental, providing no real assistance. Cassie had already asked for more epinephrine, which was given without any effect that anyone could notice. It was a couple of minutes after the Levophed started dripping into Abrams's arm, when Cassie decided to "call it"; end the code and pronounce the patient dead.

"Hold compressions, please," she asked, much more softly than her usual orders were issued. "Do we have a pulse?"

Joanne went back to listen again, her head hanging down before she even began to listen. But this time her head quickly bounced up. "There's a pulse," she yelled out. "Let's get a cuff pressure."

Dan was already inflating the blood pressure cuff around Jay's left arm. Everyone stood very still, with only the occasional beep from the other machines in The Unit interrupting the silence. Dan placed his stethoscope on Abrams's arm and slowly deflated the blood pressure cuff.

"I'm getting eighty," he said.

"Let's start some dopamine at five, please," Cassie asked, her spirits lifting slightly. The monitor showed a fast sinus rhythm. She had done it—ripped a victory from Death's hands tonight. She breathed a heavy sigh of relief, snapping off her gloves, not fully appreciating what exactly she had done.

Two hours later, Cassie slipped into her on-call room adjacent to the ICU and absentmindedly flipped on the switch to the blinding fluorescent light. In stark contrast with the dimmed lights of the corridor, the harshness of it gave her a start. No matter. She didn't want to be soothed into a few hours of sleep tonight. Maybe the brightness would help to focus her thoughts. The nurses would page her if there were any emergencies.

She looked over at her on-call bag and considered the ten Xanax tablets in a Ziploc buried at the bottom of it. Six months ago, a patient had quietly pressed her Xanax into Cassie's hand each morning and afternoon, swearing her to secrecy. The nurses had wanted to calm the nervous patient down and were surprised when she didn't much improve after the drugs. The patient had told Cassie that she liked her anxiety. It kept her sharp. Cassie found, however, that she didn't much care for her own anxiety, and the Xanax was a welcome escape from it. At first it was just one pill every couple of weeks to help her get to sleep after a particularly stressful day. Lately, however, she found herself taking one almost every day. The only problem Cassie saw with this was that she would soon run out. Not tonight, she admonished herself. She needed a clear head, and she was running low anyway. In her mind, she replayed her post-code conversation with Autumn, who wasn't particularly worse than any other intern she had worked with, but who seemed to be unnecessarily complicating this already worrisome admission.

"We've been hanging out. I've slept with him," Autumn had blurted out to her as soon as they sat themselves down in the hard, plastic chairs of the charting room in the back of the ICU. Cassie opened her mouth and then promptly closed it, realizing she didn't quite have a response for her intern reporting that she had previously slept with a patient who just nearly died. Instead, she gently rested a hand on Autumn's shoulder, breathed in deeply through her nose, and responded with the only statement she could bring to mind. It was one of her stock go-to comfort phrases: "That must have been very difficult for you to see."

Cassie had used that sentence a lot recently with the families of her patients. Why not stick with what works? It was one of those phrases that provided comfort, sidestepped guilt, and avoided the question of responsibility. It also served to break the awkward silences that came up so regularly in the hospital.

"I think I'm still in shock. You know, we weren't super close, but I just saw him and he was fine . . ." Autumn drifted off.

Cassie nodded sympathetically. But, in fact, she did not know. She had only ever had sex with her college sweetheart, and they had split up six months ago. He was a good guy, a high-school teacher, but their paths had diverged too sharply. She rarely had an acceptable response to what began to feel like his daily interrogation. "So how did your day go?" He would tell her about his shining star student trying to get into college. But she had no appropriate stories with which to reciprocate. How exactly was she supposed to respond? *Little old Myrtle tried to die today and defecated all over herself, then bled all over me.* Residency was all-consuming, and it had consumed her relationship. Cassie looked down at her well-worn, sensible, water-proof watch given to her as a medical school graduation present by her ex: 12:15 a.m. Then she focused her gaze on her visibly dazed intern.

There was a slightly too long pause before Cassie remembered it was her turn to speak. "We'll call him your friend," she offered Autumn diplomatically. "Why don't you give me your pager and try to get some sleep? The Chief Resident should be in at around six. You can go to his office then and see if you can get some time off to deal with this."

Cassie tried to smile encouragingly, but she was dreading the next few hours. It wasn't that she couldn't handle the ICU without an intern. It was the pre-rounding and presenting the patients in the morning that she didn't want to deal with. It was one of the least glorious jobs in the hierarchy of doctors and thus relegated to the intern for its "learning potential."

"I think I'll go sit with him," Autumn said, gesturing back

to the room, most of the color still absent from her face.

"Absolutely. Don't worry about the other patients," Cassie said more firmly now, holding out her hand to take Autumn's pager.

"Thanks so much," Autumn said, smiling weakly as she handed over the beeping menace for the night. She lumbered off, leaving Cassie with a lot of unanswered questions. Chuck said he had known Abrams. Autumn intimated that she had knowledge of him in the biblical sense. But Cassie had never seen him before. Was he a resident in another program? Autumn didn't seem the type to travel in the same social circle as Chuck. Chuck was a clean-cut jock, played football in college, and most definitely would have been in a frat. Autumn still bore the remnants of her goth-girl days, her facial piercings just barely still visible. But, she considered, you never knew what people did in their spare time.

As Cassie stared at the dingy white walls and ceiling of the call room, she could only pose her questions to the yellow water stain on the ceiling over her head. Did this guy use? Did he take something knowingly? And what the heck would have thrown his heart so out of whack? His EKG showed depressions of his ST segments. That usually meant strain on the heart. Cocaine? But his tox screen didn't show coke. Maybe it was wrong. No test was perfect. The tox screen, however, was fairly accurate, at least for substances that had been recently used. And for a drug to have sent Abrams's heart into these wild rhythms, it would have had to have been taken in the last day.

Okay, so not cocaine.

PCP? Could PCP do this? Cassie climbed off the bed

and sat at the small desk, turning on the computer that connected her to the rest of the hospital and most of all the relevant medical literature in the world.

She clicked on the icon linking her to the globe's medical journals and quickly typed in "PCP and arrhythmias." Within seconds, the screen produced a list of dozens of articles, all unfortunately related to Pneumocystis carinii pneumonia, which had been renamed to something else she was quite sure and was of no use to her. That wasn't what she had meant. Cassie carefully typed in "phencyclidine and arrythmias" instead. Dozens of articles appeared detailing the cardiac problems patients had experienced with PCP. But PCP was not on the routine toxicology screen the hospital used. She was sure she could call the lab to add it on to the blood or urine they already had.

Cassie reached for the phone but quickly stopped herself, remembering the new hospital policy of a written lab slip needing to accompany all additional testing requests. No telephone-only orders would be accepted. Cassie was sure this was a new Medicare compliance law. After all, one seemed to come out every week and make her life just a little more complicated. The rules didn't help the patients, but if you forgot one, Medicare, or the private insurers that were sure to adopt similar rules, could deny the claim and save itself some money. She stopped her drowsy mind from drifting too far into the realm of complaining, since she had already mentioned to the Chief Resident that this year it seemed the interns hardly got to see their patients at all, busied instead with paperwork and computer work.

She decided to refocus and think about all the tests she might want to add on so that she could get it all done at the same time. After the code, they surely had enough of his blood sitting in vials in the lab. She reached into her white coat pocket and picked out the smooth paper strip she had pulled from Jay Abrams's telemetry monitor when he had first been brought into the ICU. Reading it from left to right, she focused more intently as the slow beats quickly plunged into a wide and fast rhythm. Convinced this could not be a natural phenomenon and there had to be something in his system causing it, Cassie typed "drug-induced bradycardic and tachycardic arrhythmias" into the search engine. Her eyes quickly scanned down the page, stopping suddenly near the middle. She looked at the EKG strips again. Were the ST segments smiling at her?

"Oh no, oh no," Cassie said to no one in particular, placing her right hand on her forehead and pressing on her temples. She had seen something like this rhythm before, though not as dramatic, at the Veteran's Hospital as a medical student—the slow rhythm, fast rhythm, and upsloping ST segments, curved ever-so-slightly into a mocking grin as if to tease her: "You remember me, don't you?" Cassie shot out of her chair and bounded into the ICU.

"Good morning," chirped Carolina, one of the night-shift nurses. Picking up on the distress on Cassie's face, she then asked, "What's wrong?"

"I don't know, but I'm hoping to find out in the next couple of hours," Cassie called back as she raced toward the central desk where forms were housed. She pulled a chemistry slip from its stack and hastily wrote in Abrams's patient identifier number, his name, her name, and her hospital ID number. Then she carefully spelled out "DIGOXIN LEVEL" in the white space provided for the test request and hastily signed it. Her hand had started to shake visibly.

"Hey, Carolina, when's the next lab run?"

"At four, and calm down, you're making me nervous."

Cassie looked up at the clock on the wall, 3:45 a.m. She put the slip in the bag and picked up the phone to call the lab. The phone rang and rang as she waited for the lone overnight chemistry tech to pick it up (or so Cassie pictured it, never actually having been in the lab after hours). She let her eyelids, heavy with fatigue and the burden of not getting it right, droop. Behind her closed lids she could see one line, over and over again, the title of the seventh article on the first page of her search:

Review: digoxin overdose as the cause of both brady- and tachy-arrhythmias

Of course she wouldn't have thought of it when Abrams first rolled through the door. Why should she have? The drug wasn't actively prescribed anymore—only the oldest patients, who had been taking it for their atrial fibrillation or heart failure for decades, were still on it. There were newer drugs, better drugs now. And as far as she knew, people didn't get high off of digoxin. Did Abrams have a heart condition? Chuck and Autumn would have said something if he had underlying medical problems, wouldn't they? There was just no way she could have suspected dig any earlier. Cassie felt a chill travel up her spine, trembled for a moment, and then shook it off, gripping the phone tighter.

When the lab tech picked up after what felt like the twentieth or thirtieth ring, with a curt, "Chemistry," it almost didn't register. "Hello?" he asked.

"Oh, sorry. I need to add on a lab please. Patient number 1578229574. Digoxin level to your earliest sample. I'm provider CE189. Thanks," Cassie blurted out in one breath.

The lab tech, not picking up on the urgency in Cassie's voice, or perhaps just ignoring it, responded dryly, "You know the rules. I need a written request, too. And don't forget to sign it. In black ink."

SEVEN

AUTUMN

Autumn's eyes locked on the rise and fall of Jay's chest, now properly covered by the thin, blue patient gown. It was as if his chest no longer belonged to him. The chest was a lifeless metronome, rising and falling steady and regular, with each of his breaths generated in precise time by the ventilator behind him. Inhale. Pause. Exhale. Pause. Inhale. Pause. Exhale. After a few minutes, a loud beeping from an IV machine clogged in the neighboring room broke the hypnosis. Autumn's eyes wandered down to Jay's hands, locked in clenched fists, with a hint of bruises forming on the tops, the sites of multiple failed attempts at intravenous access. Her gaze continued downward, unable to bring her eyes to meet his face. The beeping next door had been silenced and Autumn was again lulled into a meditative state.

With her eyes focused on the pale green tile floor, Autumn's introduction to Jay's mother was a pair of shiny black heels, which stopped advancing beside her rolling chair. These were immediately joined by another pair of equally expensive-looking shiny black loafers. Autumn's head sprang back reflexively to see the rest of the well-dressed couple. Feeling like an intruder, she jumped to her feet.

"Oh my God," the woman exclaimed as she ran to grab Jay's tightly closed hand, forcing Autumn to take a quick step backwards. "Jay, Jay!" She was screaming. The man, in a Lacoste polo shirt with a soft yellow sweater draped over his shoulders and serving no useful purpose, wrapped a nearly hairless arm around the shaken woman's waist as if he was a stand supporting a doll and turned to Autumn.

"What's going on here?" he demanded forcefully, but not unkindly.

Autumn shifted her weight from her right foot to her left foot and inhaled deeply. "You are Jay's parents?" she asked dully, falling back into medical-professional mode.

"I'm his stepfather, Pierce Morris. This is his mother, Marsha," he offered, squeezing the now crying woman's shoulder and not extending a hand.

"I'm a friend of Jay's, Autumn Johnson," Autumn said slowly, testing the words, forgetting to offer her hand as well.

The man raised his eyebrows at her hospital attire. The woman didn't look up. "And you're a nurse here?" he asked.

"No," Autumn shook her head, now fully out of her trance. This wasn't the first time she had been mistaken for a nurse. That had been going on throughout her four years of medical school. She had a ready response. "I'm a doctor, in training. Right now, I'm an intern—a first year resident—

here in the ICU, and I'm helping to take care of Jay."

The woman turned to Autumn, wiping away tears mixed with mascara with her palms, and almost too quickly to follow, began asking questions. "What happened to my son? Is he going to be okay? And what is going on in this hospital? He's not even listed under his own name. We had to argue with security downstairs for the last fifteen minutes, and I've just about had it."

The husband's arm went back around his wife's waist as she began to cry again. Autumn pushed the rolling chair nearer to her, partly out of kindness, but more out of a fear that she might collapse.

Apparently, Jay's parents had to face the same problem Cassie had encountered when she'd tried to find their new admission in the computer system last night. They couldn't, Autumn realized, because in accordance with hospital policy regarding staff privacy, there was no Jay Abrams in the hospital right now, which was probably what security had conveyed to Jay's parents. During the day, the reception staff probably would have known better, but in the middle of the night, security might have forgotten that there were some patients listed differently from others. Anyone who was affiliated with the hospital or medical school, or any famous people coming in, simply got a Y or a Z in front of their name when admitted. That way, the hospital staff wouldn't inadvertently (or purposefully) see their colleagues' rooms and diagnoses. And if a celebrity or politician were in the hospital and the press called, the person on the other end of the phone could reply truthfully that they couldn't find that name in their system. Family members were supposed to be told about the precaution, but this didn't always happen.

"He's had a rough night," Autumn began as Jay's mother crumpled into the chair. In medical school, she had been a bit taken aback by the peculiarities of a physician's speech, but now, she was adopting the language just as an immigrant quickly learns the slang of his adopted country. "He's actually pretty sick," she added, nearly wincing at her choice of words.

In order to qualify as "sick" to a doctor, you have to be near death. Colds, fevers, or anything else easily cured never got the designation "sick." When a doctor says to another doctor, "Mr. or Mrs. So-and-so is sick," it's immediately understood that the situation is grim. When a doctor says the same thing to a family member, perhaps using the phrase, "very sick," to make his point clear, the family member cannot possibly ascertain the doctor's true meaning. Very sick means dying.

"What happened to him?" Marsha pressed.

"We are trying to find that out and maybe you can help us with that." Autumn was in full doctor mode now. "His heart stopped a few times, and we had to shock him back to life. We have to help him breathe right now and that's why that tube is in. I'm very sorry." Autumn reflexively bit her lip. She sounded so detached. She didn't want to sound that way—like just any intern taking care of any patient.

"I don't know what I can do to help," Marsha looked up at Autumn, withdrawing her hand from its position around Jay's involuntarily clenched fist. "He's healthy," Marsha stated firmly, in direct conflict with Jay's decidedly unhealthy appearance. "No medical problems that we know of."

"His brother had diabetes, right?" Autumn prodded. "Anything else run in the family?"

Marsha closed her eyes and wrapped her arms around herself in reply. Pierce answered.

"No, no other problems in the family. Actually, if you were Jay's friend, I'd like to hear your thoughts about his state of mind recently. I got the impression from talking to him that he was pretty upset, depressed even. Could he have taken something? Done this to himself?"

Marsha brought her hand to her mouth and looked as though she might be sick. Autumn caught her give a sideways glance to her husband as she softly asked, "Depressed?"

Pierce nodded once. "I didn't say anything. I thought it would pass. But his experiment wasn't going well, and he was pretty upset about it."

Autumn's face scrunched briefly, but she smoothed her expression before they noticed. Jay had made it seem like his lab work was going great, like he was on the verge of a breakthrough. He certainly hadn't seemed depressed to her, but she decided to keep her thoughts to herself for now.

"I guess he talked to you about those things," Marsha replied to her husband. "You understood his work so much better than I ever could."

Pierce nodded his head once more and gripped Marsha's shoulders tightly. She began to cry softly into his stomach.

Autumn took this as her cue to leave the room, excusing herself by saying, "I'll leave you guys to be with Jay. The team will be in soon. It was nice meeting you," she finished awkwardly.

Cassie had told her she should ask the Chief Resident to

transfer her out of the ICU that morning. Autumn initially hadn't felt right abandoning her responsibilities, but she had just convinced herself that that would probably be a good idea. Jay and his family were more than she knew how to handle right now. As she pushed his room's curtain aside, she glanced up at the clock behind the still-empty ICU secretary's desk : 5:45 a.m. What should have been the start of her hospital day. Autumn pressed the pad to open the hydraulic ICU doors, walking out quickly, lost in thought about how she would bring up her situation with the prickly Chief Resident. She barely registered the scruffy-looking, balding man in dirty jeans moving purposefully past her.

E I G H T

C A S S I E

At 5:45 a.m. Jay Abram's digoxin level was still listed as "pending" on her screen. Staring blankly at the computer, she had already scanned dozens of articles, pausing about every fifteen minutes to check if his labs had been updated yet. Despite two hours of combing the medical literature, digoxin was still the thing that made the most sense, though why this supposedly healthy, at least according to Autumn, medical student would take it didn't.

What else could she remember about digoxin? She remembered Dr. Goldberg, their ICU attending, joking that in his day all they had was digoxin and lidocaine to treat heart conditions and both of them were just as likely to kill a patient as cure them. But they were both still used under special circumstances today. Cassie had just reviewed the pharmacology of digoxin and the medicine could do it all really, sometimes to the patient's great detriment. The heart cell has many ion channels and by blocking the sodium for potassium exchanger, digoxin made the cells in the heart build up their internal supply of sodium. This then caused another path, the sodium for calcium exchanger, to get revved up and force sodium out of the cell and consequently calcium into it. Since calcium made muscle cells contract, digoxin could help increase the strength of the heart muscle in heart failure patients. It could also decrease conduction through the heart and slow it down. But if too much calcium was forced in, as in an overdose, this could make the cells start going wacky and send all kinds of signals for the heart to contract when it shouldn't. So, it could make the heart go both slow and fast depending on the dose in someone's system at any given time.

"The dose makes the poison," Cassie whispered softly to herself. Digoxin was a medication that required careful monitoring and a medical student like Jay should have known that. And it wouldn't cause a high. No one took digoxin if they didn't need it.

And yet Jay's symptoms could surely be consistent with digoxin poisoning, especially the nausea and abdominal pain that had initially brought him in to the ER. Chuck had told her that Jay had taken a cab to the Emergency Room and complained of nausea and abdominal pain to the triage nurse before passing out in the waiting room and being rushed back. Still, couldn't nausea and abdominal pain happen with almost any intoxication? Cassie supposed that it could. His body was trying to reject something. She hoped the digoxin level would be back in time for rounds. At least then she would have something useful to present to the rest of the ICU team.

As she was considering ordering up some Digibind, the

antidote to digoxin, from the pharmacy, just to have in case she was right, she heard screaming coming from down the hall. Her pager went off. She silenced it without looking down at the message. Somehow she knew she had to run to Abrams's room. What she didn't expect to find there were three shouting middle-aged people, one of whom was on the ground, while every nurse in the ICU stood between them, keeping them apart from one another. Cassie's heart bounced around in her chest, uncertain as to what she should do as she stood outside of the chaotic room.

As she was contemplating whether or not to go in and try to help sort things out, the ICU doors hissed open and two uniformed security men bounded in. A broad shouldered, bearded security guard grabbed the preppy-looking man who was sitting dazed on the ground, while the smaller, stocky security guard with a close-cropped Marine-regulation haircut grabbed the disheveled man who was gripping his right hand like it hurt. When he let it go, Cassie noticed his knuckles were red. With the men attended to, the nurses then surrounded the well-dressed woman who was crying and shaking. The three were promptly escorted out of the ICU and would probably be kicked out of the hospital, Cassie thought.

"Family drama," Joanne said to no one in particular as she watched them depart the ICU.

"What happened?" Cassie asked.

"Don't ask me," Joanne shrugged. "I just work here. But, thankfully, not after seven this morning."

Cassie looked up at the clock. It was 6 a.m. Apparently her intern had taken her advice and was nowhere to be found. Pre-rounds, gathering the overnight data on the

ICU patients to present to the rest of the team, would be her job this morning. The rest of the ICU team would be arriving in an hour. She left her questions on the early morning drama unanswered and got to work. She'd see the overnight nurses again soon enough and get the story from one of them.

After she finished compiling the overnight vital signs and urine output from her ten ICU patients, Cassie logged onto the computer again. Jay's digoxin level was back! But what should have been nothing if she was wrong—and very high if she was right—had returned in the so-called therapeutic or non-toxic range at 1.2. He had taken the medication, but not enough that it would have caused any problems. So, if the digoxin wasn't trying to kill him, what was?

NINE

Autumn began to consider how she might explain why she needed to be excused from her ICU rotation as she rode down the elevator to find the Chief Resident, Randall, but call-me-Randy Chin. He lived and breathed the hospital. He had willingly signed up for an extra year of residency— she had little doubt he would be in his office this early in the morning. But what would she say to him? Maybe "hooking up" was acceptable in college or even medical school, but she had a professional reputation to protect now. Despite the proliferation of women in medicine, it was still a man's world and men could do what women couldn't. She didn't need rumors about her character to follow her throughout her residency and possibly beyond. Also, she had the sense that Randy wouldn't provide the most sympathetic ear. Rumor had it that when an intern's grandfather had died suddenly in a car accident and the intern had asked for a day off, he was met with a curt,

"Well, do what you think is right, but it's not like *you* got hit by the bus."

Autumn considered that she hadn't been hit by a bus either, but she certainly couldn't care for Jay appropriately in the ICU. She had pretty much proved that by nearly passing out—definitely the low point of her career so far, and that was saying something. She knocked timidly on the Chief Resident's door.

"Come in," came the booming voice.

"Hey, sorry to interrupt," Autumn tested, "you look busy."

And he did, with a large stack of documents to the right of his mouse pad, creating a slightly disordered look on his usually painstakingly ordered desk.

"Not at all," Randy replied, the smile on his face not reaching his eyes. "I was just working on a grant proposal, and I needed a break anyway. Have a seat."

If he needed a break already, Autumn wondered how long he had been working this morning as she softly sat in the chair beside his desk.

"I have a fairly odd request." Autumn paused, trying to read Randy's face. His lips were tightly drawn into a straight line—neither a smile nor a frown. It was a blank anticipatory look, and Autumn couldn't read him at all.

"Well, I'm in the ICU right now," she began.

"Okay," Randy replied less than favorably.

"So, this guy I've been seeing, my boyfriend," Autumn said, trying to make it sound more official. "He was brought into the ICU last night and coded and we, well not so much me, resuscitated him and uh, I think we don't know which way it's gonna go right now."

Like Cassie had a few hours before, Randy's jaw dropped open for a split second before he quickly closed it. This clearly wasn't the conversation he might have anticipated.

"I'm so sorry," he replied in what she recognized as his practiced sympathetic-doctor voice, the one she had begun working on.

"Thanks." Autumn shrugged. "The reason I'm here is that I'd like to be moved to another service while Jay is in the ICU, please. I can send out an e-mail to the intern class and see if someone will switch with me so no one has to be pulled off an elective or anything to cover," Autumn offered quickly, sensing that Randy didn't actually want to have a long chat about her ill boyfriend.

"Of course. Whatever you need," Randy replied absently, looking back at his stack of papers. Autumn surmised that he hadn't wanted to take a break from that stack after all. "You're post-call, right?"

Autumn nodded and slowly exhaled the breath she had been holding, all she could do in her surprise to his amiable response. Perhaps the tales of his toughness had been exaggerated. Maybe Randy Chin wasn't all that bad.

"Fine. Take the day off today." He waved his hand dismissively. "They can get along without you for tomorrow, too. It's your swing day anyway—not on call and not post-call, so you don't have many responsibilities. You can switch with someone after that, okay? Make sure someone is there to be on-call for you in two days."

Autumn's eyebrows went up in surprise as she nodded in agreement again. She hadn't expected it to be this easy. Then again, she was basically just dumping on her fellow interns. And Cassie. No one else would be affected, so why should Randy give her a hard time? Maybe it was Cassie's wrath she should be worried about. She had noted plenty of exasperated sideways glances from her senior resident last night. She hoped that Cassie wasn't the type to start spreading the word that she wasn't up to par.

Autumn exhaled a "thank you" and excused herself. She wasn't sure how, but she would make it up to Cassie, who was probably going to be stuck with her workload on top of her own. Maybe she could save a little money and treat her to lunch? Not like they got to leave the hospital for lunch very often. Or ever. Except for today. She was getting to leave, never having pre-rounded *and* skipping the hours-long ICU team rounds. And though it seemed cruel and unfeeling that she should be experiencing any joy given the events of the past twelve hours, she allowed her spirits to lift just a little as she bounded out of the glass doors of the hospital.

T E N

C A S S I E

Two and a half hours later, when the ICU team had finished examining all of the patients and had gathered in the back room to finish up their rounds, Cassie placed Jay Abrams's EKGs on the table in sequence, putting the initial ER EKG at the top followed by the four remaining EKGs. All the chairs were taken, so she propped herself up with her palms on the white, plastic desk behind the display she had just set up. She hadn't gotten any sleep the night before and her legs were starting to quiver with exhaustion.

"Do we have an old one for comparison?" Nicolas, one of the interns, asked. It was a routine question and a way he could contribute to the conversation. Always compare a new EKG with its predecessors.

"He's twenty-seven without any past medical history. We don't have a baseline EKG," Cassie snapped back. She didn't have a lot of patience for the usual rounding rituals this morning.

"Nicolas, perhaps you would like to read the first EKG for us," Dr. Goldberg commanded, foiling Nicolas's obvious plan of an early contribution exempting him from further participation.

"Well, it's a sinus bradycardia at about forty-eight beats per minute. Umm, normal axis and normal intervals. No ST or T wave abnormalities."

"The intervals aren't quite normal," the other intern, Mei, offered softly. "I think the QT is short."

"How short?" Dr. Goldberg pressed. Cassie noted it didn't take the doctor long to fall into PIMP mode. PIMP-ing, or Putting Me In My Place, was a long-held tradition, used to ensure young doctors never got too full of themselves.

Mei reached over Cassie for the EKG and held it close to her nose, her lips moving as she counted the very fine one-millimeter lines on the page.

"240 milliseconds."

Dr. Goldberg held out his hand for the EKG and pulled a pair of fine-tipped metal calipers from his white coat pocket.

"You're right." He smiled encouragingly over at Mei. "Do you think that's okay?"

"Given what happened last night, I would say no."

"Right. So if the QT interval is the time it takes from the first electrical signal to hit the ventricles to when the blood is pumped out of the heart, and the ventricle resets itself for the next electrical signal, a short QT means this is happening too fast. Why?" Dr. Goldberg asked.

"Something is wrong with his electrolytes. His potassium was a little low." Mei shrugged.

"Not low enough to cause any real problems. What else?" Dr. Goldberg pressed.

But Mei had been PIMP-ed too far. She just shook her head. She didn't know.

"It's digoxin," Cassie offered as she pulled a thin, white rhythm strip from her white coat pocket. "Just look at these ST depressions. The digoxin is pushing the calcium into the cells of the heart, so even though his blood calcium level is normal, to his heart cells it might as well be much, much higher."

"Good, Dr. Ellison. Now the question you need to ask the cardiologists is whether or not the level of digoxin we found in his blood stream could have this dramatic an effect and what we should do about it. Call the cardiology fellow ASAP. I will see all of you later this afternoon. I'll be in my lab if you need me before then."

Anurag Singh, the same cardiology fellow who had been in the ICU the previous night to perform the echocardiogram, came to do the formal consultation. Though he couldn't have gotten much sleep, he had cleaned up and was now wearing the more formal cardiologist's uniform of a simple print tie and white coat instead of the hospital-issue green scrubs. Anu seemed surprised Abrams was alive at all. He and Cassie walked through the EKGs together, and he agreed that the first was consistent with digoxin use, though not necessarily overdose. The rest, however, implied a much higher digoxin level than the lab found in the patient's blood. "Good pick up, Cass. Even if the first EKG is acceptable, when you put them in sequence, like a story, it tells one of digoxin overdose. I don't know how you got him out of all this without Digibind. I'm sorry I didn't stop to look at these last night when I was here."

"That's okay. It was probably too late for him anyway." Cassie shrugged. Anu had looked a mess last night. He had been her resident when she was an intern and she knew he was very dedicated and a treasure trove of esoteric medical knowledge—he had placed almost every year in the state medical association's medical jeopardy competition for residents. He also had two small children at home and was probably just worn out. "Do you have any ideas why his digoxin level is normal now?" she pressed.

"This may sound crazy, Cass, but he wasn't supposed to be on digoxin, right? The parents said nothing was wrong with his heart before he came into the ER. So maybe you're measuring the wrong thing. Maybe this isn't digoxin, but *digitoxin*. The assay for digitoxin cross reacts with the test for digoxin. The digoxin level may look low, normal, or even non-existent when in reality the digitoxin level is through the roof."

"Digitoxin? Isn't that just an older version of digoxin? Do they even still make that stuff?" Cassie asked skeptically.

Anu smiled broadly. "I don't know if it's been commercially available for a hundred years. But it grows in a lot of gardens up here. Maybe he ingested some by mistake."

Cassie's head tilted to the side as her brows furrowed. She had no idea what Anu was talking about, but it didn't surprise her that he was a horticultural expert as well.

"Foxglove is a beautiful purple flower, Cass. It's how they extracted the initial version of digitoxin—the precursor to digoxin. The problem then, as is the problem now with herbal medications, is that you often don't know how much you are getting. It was unpredictable. Now we have digoxin and a whole lot of other more predictable medications thanks to synthetic chemistry."

"But why would he have ingested any plant if he didn't know what it was?"

Anu shrugged. "Smart people do dumb things all the time. I dunno. I've seen some weird ingestions over the years."

Cassie nodded in agreement. She had seen people put all manner of interesting things in their bodies. Often they couldn't give her a good, or even a bad, reason for it.

"Can we still test for digitoxin?"

"Sure, but you may not get the results back for a couple days. I think it may be too late, but why not give him some Digibind anyway? It won't hurt. I'll come up with some estimation of the dose and get back to you ASAP."

Cassie looked down at her watch: 12:30 p.m. She'd been awake and in the hospital for close to thirty hours. It was well past her time to leave. Since all of the patients were stable, the team was going to grab lunch in the conference room downstairs. Nicolas mentioned that the drug company reps were bringing Chinese food today. Cassie wasn't particularly interested. She needed to get out of there.

But first she called the lab and asked to add a digitoxin level to Abrams's initial blood sample. While there wasn't enough in the original tubes from the emergency room, there was still a good deal from the samples that had been sent down during the code in the ICU. That would have to be good enough, and sometimes good enough, despite their best efforts, was the best anyone could do. Only she didn't really believe that. People were depending on her to be better than good enough. Good enough was for repairmen who could come back and fix their mistakes. Or perhaps salespeople who could get the next sale instead of the one they missed. Or even for her ex, a teacher. He held himself to a very high standard. He loved the kids he taught. But he could have an off day, a lecture that didn't go very well. He could fix it the next time. His students loved him right back and would forgive him a boring lecture. Cassie knew she only got one try to get it right. No, good enough just wouldn't cut it.

She sighed heavily as she trudged to her on-call room and quickly threw her toothbrush into her bag. She needed to be better. Sleep and food could wait. She needed to know exactly what Anu was talking about. What else did digitalis do and why might Abrams have taken it? She slumped into the hard plastic chair in front of the call room computer, gave the mouse a quick shake to wake up the screen, typed in "digitalis," clicked on the first link and started to read.

Digitalis – Wikipedia[*]

"Digitalis is a genus of about 20 species of herbaceous perennials, shrubs, and biennials commonly called foxgloves.

The name is recorded in Old English as *foxes glofe/glofa* 'foxs' glove, though there it does not refer to Digitalis.

[*]Digitalis. In *Wikipedia*. Retrieved March 3, 2016, from https://en.wikipedia.org/wiki/Digitalis.

Digitalis species thrive in acidic soils, in partial sunlight to deep shade, in a range of habitats, including open woods, woodland clearings, moorland and heath margins, sea-cliffs, rocky mountain slopes and hedge banks. It is commonly found on sites where the ground has been disturbed, such as recently cleared woodland, or where the vegetation has been burnt."

Useless. Cassie scrolled down further and kept reading.

"A group of medicines extracted from foxglove plants are called digitalis. The use of *D. purpurea* extract containing cardiac glycosides for the treatment of heart conditions was first described in 1785. It is used to increase cardiac contractility and as an antiarrhythmic agent to control the heart rate, particularly in the irregular (and often fast) atrial fibrillation. Digitalis is hence often prescribed for patients in atrial fibrillation, especially if they have been diagnosed with congestive heart failure. Digoxin was approved for heart failure in 1998 under current regulations by the Food and Drug Administration on the basis of prospective, randomized study and clinical trials. It was also approved for the control of ventricular response rate for patients with atrial fibrillation. Despite its relatively recent approval by the Food and Drug Administration and the guideline recommendations, the therapeutic use of digoxin is declining in patients with heart failure—likely the result of several factors. Safety concerns regarding a proposed link between digoxin therapy and increased mortality may be contributing to the decline in therapeutic use of digoxin.

Digitalis toxicity (*Digitalis intoxication*) results from an overdose of digitalis and causes nausea, vomiting and diarrhea, as well as sometimes resulting in xanthopsia (jaundiced or yellow vision) and the appearance of blurred outlines (halos), drooling, abnormal heart rate, cardiac arrhythmias, weakness, collapse, dilated pupils, tremors, seizures, and even death. Bradycardia also occurs."

That sure sounded like Abrams, Cassie thought, and scrolled down further.

"The entire plant is toxic (including the roots and seeds). Most plant exposures occur in children younger than six years and are usually unintentional. More serious toxicity occurs with intentional ingestions by adolescents and adults. Early symptoms of ingestion include nausea, vomiting, diarrhea, abdominal pain, wild hallucinations, delirium, and severe headache. Depending on the severity of the toxicosis, the victim may later suffer irregular and slow pulse, tremors, various cerebral disturbances, especially of a visual nature with objects appearing yellowish to green, and blue halos around lights, convulsions, and deadly disturbances of the heart. Vincent van Gogh's "Yellow Period" may have been influenced by digitalis therapy which, at the time, was thought to control seizures."

Cassie shrugged at this bit of art history and skipped ahead again.

"In some instances, people have confused digitalis with the relatively harmless comfrey plant, which is often brewed into a tea, with fatal consequences. Other fatal accidents involve children drinking the water in a vase containing digitalis plants. Drying does not reduce the toxicity of the plant. The plant is toxic to animals, including all classes of livestock and poultry, as well as felines and canines."

Could Abrams have mistakenly ingested the foxglove plant? Cassie sighed heavily as her eyelids begged to close. She hadn't learned anything that could help her patient. She decided to just skip to the end.

"Digitalis poisoning can cause heart block and either bradycardia (decreased heart rate) or tachycardia (increased heart rate), depending on the dose and the condition of one's heart. Notably, the electric cardioversion (to "shock" the heart) is generally not indicated in ventricular fibrillation in digitalis toxicity, as it can increase the dysrhythmia. Also, the classic drug of choice for ventricular fibrillation in emergency setting,

amiodarone, can worsen the dysrhythmia caused
by digitalis."

Cassie could feel the acid rising from her stomach as she
rubbed her temples, stopped reading, and powered down
the computer. So, if this was a case of digitalis poisoning,
she had done just about everything wrong. Her shoulders
slumped, and a tightness enveloped her chest. It was
suddenly much harder to breathe. If this was digitalis
poisoning, she hadn't just missed it, she was responsible
for the near death of her patient.

E L E V E N

When Autumn had started her internship, she'd realized that the key to sleeping in the middle of the day was to block out all light from her apartment. She had invested in too-long, heavy navy curtains that bunched on the floor and, out of laziness, kept them drawn most of the time. Instead, she filled her waking hours with incessant fluorescent lighting. Though she hadn't realized it yet, a day and a night filled with artificial lighting slowly drained the spirit. The momentary joy she had in leaving the hospital had evaporated upon entering the dark apartment.

And so her tears, which had been held at bay by a cocktail of adrenaline and fatigue, now came fast and hot. Ostensibly she was crying for Jay, but she was also crying for the people under her care who had died too young or too painfully. And she was crying for herself. No one pictures themselves in internship when they dream of becoming a doctor. The sickness and death were expected, though maybe not to the extent that was found at the large teaching hospital. The abuse from all sides, however, was thoroughly unanticipated. Thankfully, the pace of internship was so fast that if you didn't stop to think about what was happening and just kept going, you could survive on sheer momentum alone. So, Autumn wiped her eyes and nose on her sleeves, stopped thinking, closed her bloodshot eyes, and collapsed in a heap onto her bed.

"Autumn. Hey! Autumn."

Autumn rolled over in bed and opened her eyes. Jay was lying next to her.

"What are you doing here?" she asked. "Aren't you in the ICU?"

"Yes, but I need you to help me. I'm hungry. I need a burger."

"You're a vegetarian," Autumn reminded him.

"Oh. Yeah. Then can you get me out of here instead?"

"How? Why are you in the ICU anyway? Your stepdad thinks you might have taken something to try to hurt yourself."

"What do you think?" he asked, smiling and showing off his adorable dimple.

"I don't think you would have done this to yourself. You seemed pretty okay to me."

"I am okay. Or was okay. Who would have wanted to hurt me? All I did was spend eighteen hours a day in that lab. Working. Remember? I told you I was about to get my Ph.D. I would have been home free."

The ringing of the phone jolted Autumn out of her

deep sleep and her all-too-real dream. Disoriented, she thought it was her pager going off, but then recognized her darkened room and reached for the phone.

"Autumn? Hi, it's Cassie."

Autumn glanced over at her alarm clock; it was 8 p.m. She sat up and turned on her lamp, trying to wake up for the conversation.

"Cassie?"

"Word on the street is that you've gotten a couple of days off. That's great. You need it."

Autumn very seriously doubted the sincerity of her words. After all, she hadn't found her replacement intern yet. Cassie would be stuck with her work until she did. She wasn't awake enough to respond, so she kept listening instead.

"I was wondering if I could get your help with something? I mean since you have a few days off."

A day and a half, Autumn thought, not "a few days," and managed to find her voice. "Sure. What is it?"

"I think Jay may have ingested a poisonous plant called foxglove. Have you heard of it?"

It sounded familiar. Did it have some medicinal properties? She couldn't quite remember, though she had tried to pay attention to the medicinal plants lecture in medical school. Her mother, who favored long floral dresses and fancied herself a modern hippie, liked to try the latest and greatest herbal supplement being touted. Autumn, at least, needed to know the ones that could kill her.

"Yup," Autumn answered.

"Do you know what it looks like?"

"No, I definitely don't know that."

"Well, it's like a bell-shaped purple flower. Do you think you could go to Jay's apartment or work or something and look for it?"

She didn't recall him having any plants in his apartment. And hadn't he told her that it was lucky for him that he wasn't responsible for any other living thing since he had a tendency to neglect his things, focusing all his energy on his lab work?

"I don't think he had any house plants," Autumn offered.

"Did he work in a lab? Could you check there?"

His lab? She was sure his research was around diabetes treatment and stem cells. Why would there be plants in the lab? She'd never seen a non-plant lab with plants in it. Still drowsy and hoping to get off the phone, she said, "Sure. The building will be locked up now, but I can do it in the morning."

"Thanks, Autumn. And just so you know, I think you were very helpful yesterday."

Autumn thanked Cassie and hung up. Cassie's words had sounded pinched and Autumn realized that they both knew she'd been no help at all. She could do Cassie this small favor. So much for her day off. So much for not thinking about Jay. She had nearly passed out when Jay was brought in to the ICU. That was barely tolerated in green medical students—it was certainly not okay for an intern. Now Cassie was asking for her help. For Jay, whom she was not at all able to help the day before. Well, she could certainly make an attempt at doing a better job now. A vague remnant of her dream lingered. Cassie was asking for her help, but so was Jay.

She decided to get to the lab as early as possible in the

morning since she would have to be back in the hospital the day after as she had promised Randy. The next day! Oh shit! She had yet to find a replacement for herself in the ICU. As she typed the all residents' listserv address, she thought about how to word her e-mail. She didn't want anyone to help her out of a sense of obligation, and she didn't want to be so cryptic as to start off a flurry of rumors. She decided against using the word "boyfriend." She couldn't deal with people coming up to her all day and asking if she was okay. Plus, she still wasn't sure Jay *was* her boyfriend.

She finally decided on the simple and not untrue, "A friend of mine is in the ICU, and I would be able to do a better job somewhere else in the hospital for the time being. Please consider switching with me for the next few weeks," for the body of her e-mail. It wasn't too desperate and she hoped that someone out there would take her up on the offer. If no one did, she'd have t go back to the ICU. Face Jay and his parents. Try not to embarrass herself again. *It's not like you were the one hit by a bus.* She wondered if Randy had actually said that to someone. Not that it mattered. Even if it was just hospital legend, the spirit of the statement was true. If you could stand, you could and should do your job. The patients and your fellow residents were counting on you.

Autumn sighed deeply and finally noticed the rumblings of her stomach. When had she last eaten? She sent off the e-mail and shut down her computer. She still had a few heat-and-eat burritos in the freezer, but the thought of them made her stomach turn. She decided on a package of macaroni and cheese from the pantry cabinet. The milk had expired a couple of days ago, but it still smelled okay.

When the macaroni was ready, she poured most of the three servings the package claimed to contain into a large bowl and planted herself down on her sofa. With a spoon in one hand and the remote control in the other, Autumn was ready for her usual post-call ritual of vegetating. After an overnight in the hospital, her mind was usually incapable of processing anything more complicated than *The Simpsons* reruns, but tonight even that required too much thought. She stopped flipping through the channels and finally settled on The Weather Channel, which she wound up watching for two hours, falling back asleep to the sounds of smooth jazz saxophone.

The following day, after having slept for a total of fourteen hours, freshly showered and newly optimistic, Autumn parked in the hospital lot. When she'd woken up, she'd briefly considered the possibility that the improbable events of the past two days had been a dream. But after turning on her computer and loading her e-mail, that possibility faded away. The first email was from Chiwete Awolowo. He would be happy to cover for her in the ICU. Apparently, he loved the ICU. And since no one else seemed to want to take her up on the offer, she hastily drafted a "thank you" email to Chiwete and got herself ready to go. She grabbed the large, now mostly empty beige tote she crammed with her overnight stuff, tossed out the carefully zipped toiletries bag, and slipped on the only fall coat she owned. It was one of two coats hanging in the free-standing wardrobe. As a born and bred Floridian, Autumn had figured you only needed one coat—a big puffy down one to keep yourself warm when the air turned cold—and had found herself without words when Mark presented her with a long tan trench-coat as a welcome-to-Boston present. It was a sweet gesture, but Autumn still wasn't quite sure what good it did besides make a nice fashion statement. The wind seemed to cut right through it and she would have been just as happy in her puffy down coat. But she would have been the only woman in Boston wearing one this time of year and lately she was just trying to blend in.

After parking, Autumn bounded quickly out of the hospital lot, hoping she wouldn't see anyone she knew. She cinched the long coat tightly around herself and strode past the hospital to the collection of laboratory buildings near the medical school, a few blocks north. The early morning air was brisk and she breathed it in deeply, letting the outside world fill her lungs. It felt good.

Autumn knew that Jay worked in Dr. Bill Withering's lab across the street from the impressive marble medical school building. Jay had complained to her about his principal investigator a few times. In Jay's opinion, Withering was an academic climber who got where he was on the backs of the hard-working M.D.-Ph.D.s with whom he populated his lab. Jay blamed him for the delay in getting his Ph.D., but on their last date, he had told Autumn that he finally had enough data to convince Withering to support him in finishing up his dissertation. He was pretty matter-of-fact in his tone. She thought he ought to have been happier about his new data and being done and told him so. He had simply shrugged.

She continued down the long avenue. The medical

offices, medical shops, and research buildings seemed to stretch for miles down the perpetually congested road. Withering's lab wasn't in the marble, Roman-pillared medical school building that Autumn had yet to set foot in since starting her residency—her place was in the hospital— but in a smaller brick one across the grassy quad. She pulled on its heavy glass door, took a few steps inside the nondescript lobby, and came face to face with a large, uniformed guard.

"ID, please."

The guard was middle-aged, balding, with a gut that hung over the shiny black belt holding up his pants far below his waistline. He was intimidating nonetheless at what Autumn figured was at least 6'5". He looked up skeptically at her as she handed him her hospital ID badge. It was a good thing she needed it to get into the parking lot or she may not have brought it at all.

"Where are you headed?" he boomed again.

"Dr. Withering's lab. I have a meeting," she lied, not sure why.

"Please sign in," he commanded, taking two steps toward the podium that housed an old-fashioned logbook.

Autumn printed her name and then signed it as seemed the custom in previous entries in the book.

"I'll write down the date and time for you," the large guard said without much enthusiasm, turning the logbook back toward himself. "You can go ahead, the elevators are to your right."

"Uh, can you remind me where Dr. Withering's lab is again?" Autumn smiled up at the guard as innocently as she could, as though he was a bouncer at a much more popular venue.

He raised his eyebrows, stared at her for a second, then looked down at another sheet of paper on his desk.

"Labs 410 and 412."

"Thanks," Autumn said brightly and made her way to the elevators.

Though the lobby had been updated, the elevators were circa 1970, and no light appeared when Autumn repeatedly pushed the "4." Mercifully, though, the machine moved and a minute later the elevator doors opened onto the fourth floor hallway. The fourth floor looked like any other lab hallway anywhere in America. While equipment worth millions sat within its rooms, money wasn't wasted on aesthetics. The plain gray-green walls supported emergency showers and eyewashes every twenty feet, and brightly colored paper diamonds with their large black numbers on the outer doors warned of the hazardous materials contained just beyond. Large red bins and silver cylinders of various sizes, also labeled with the diamond-shaped hazardous materials stickers, narrowed the hallway. Autumn walked confidently down the hall, quickly scanning the room numbers. Just as every hospital was essentially the same on the inside, so was every lab hallway.

About halfway down the hall, Autumn arrived at lab 410. Its warning diamond had a 2, a 3, and a 4 on it. Autumn had forgotten what the numbers stood for but decided it was always safest to keep one's hands to oneself in an unfamiliar lab. The door was closed, so she knocked gently. When no one answered, she knocked more firmly. Still no answer. She walked a few more steps to lab 412 and knocked on that closed door with no more luck.

Autumn wandered farther down the hall to see if she could find anyone who worked in 410 and 412 chatting with colleagues nearby. Many of the doors were closed as Autumn made her way past the 420s. Not as social a hallway as the one she remembered from medical school, where the doors were often left open, once leading to quite an incident when a lab assistant had left a mouse cage unlocked and people were finding mice in their labs for days.

Autumn found a door two doors down only a crack ajar. As she slowly approached it, she was nearly toppled over by a short woman with strawberry blond hair making her way out, balancing a tray of small plastic wells, containing a clear liquid.

"Soddy," came the accented apology.

"Oh no, pardon me," Autumn also apologized. "I'm looking for Dr. Withering's lab?"

"I am Luba," the woman said. "I work for Widdering."

Autumn's heart rate picked up at her good luck. "I'm Autumn," she said a bit too enthusiastically, sticking out her hand, then withdrawing it when she realized that Luba needed both hands to carry the wells. "I'm a friend of Jay's."

"Jay? He is sick, I hear. He will be okay, right?"

"I don't know," Autumn answered honestly, wondering how Luba knew he was unwell. "I wanted to look around the lab to see if I could find anything to help figure out why this happened."

"Come with me," Luba commanded and strode quickly but carefully back to lab 410. "Jay is a good boy," Luba said, softening her tone with a real fondness.

Balancing her tray carefully on one arm, Luba unlocked the door to 410 and led Autumn in, putting down the wells on the large black-top table. Autumn's eyes wandered around the lab. Most of it was filled with standard mice, except for the ones that were very, very fat, waddling around their cramped cages. Autumn followed Luba to the back of the lab where there was a large executive-style chair and desk, piled high with books and journals. The wall behind it was filled with framed awards honoring Dr. William H. Withering, M.D., Ph. D. Reaching for her enormous key ring, Luba made her way to the door to the left of the desk.

"Jay's lab," she said as she unlocked and opened the door. She turned on a light. It must have been the adjoining lab, 412. It was much smaller than the room next to it. It seemed fairly tidy and empty for a lab. Autumn knew that Jay was more of a neat freak than his carelessly tossed towel had suggested. She looked at the black-top table and found only a few empty petri dishes. On the far wall there was a standard metal filing cabinet, which Autumn made her way toward, with Luba trailing behind her. As she got closer, she saw that the key lock had been broken off the far right corner.

"Lost the key, I guess?" Autumn joked, running her finger along the pock-marked metal.

Luba didn't smile. Autumn wouldn't try to lighten the mood any further and moved her hand away.

Instead, she opened the four drawers of the cabinet and found a few hanging folders in each. The pages inside were anything but neat though, sitting at angles to one another. *Too messy to be Jay's*, Autumn thought. She walked around the center black-top table, making her way around the room with Luba just behind her. There wasn't much of anything really. And there were certainly no plants. Autumn checked the small laboratory refrigerator near the door. It was empty but for a small brown stain on the white, plastic floor of the fridge.

When she turned to speak to Luba, the quiet woman had produced a black-and-white-marbled lab notebook and a photo. Autumn had no idea where they had come from. She hadn't seen Luba touching anything.

"This belonged to Jay," Luba said simply, handing the book and photo of what must have been an eleven or twelve-year-old boy to Autumn. "I take it from his drawer and save it. Please keep it safe for him."

Autumn screwed up her face, not quite understanding. Why was Luba keeping Jay's things safe? She was acting like Jay was being let go instead of in the hospital. Suddenly, Luba grabbed the large leather tote Autumn was carrying and quickly dropped the book and photograph into it. Autumn opened her mouth to question Luba's behavior but noticed Luba looking past her. Autumn turned to see a tall, lanky shadow standing in the doorway.

"Dr. Widdering," Luba said sternly to the shadow. "This is Autumn, a friend of Jay's."

"Autumn, so nice to meet you. I'm Dr. Withering. Can't say that I've met many of Jay's friends."

Autumn looked up at the tall, broad-shouldered man. With his expensive suit and perfectly coifed hair, he struck her as possibly a bit more pompous than the average tenured professor, and she resisted the urge to introduce herself as Dr. Johnson.

"Autumn Johnson," she said stiffly, shaking his outstretched hand. "I'm an intern at the hospital."

"Autumn," he repeated pointedly. She knew he was trying to emphasize their respective positions in the medical hierarchy, and she willed herself not to roll her eyes. "How is Jay? I heard he was in the hospital."

He'd only been in the hospital a day, and Autumn wondered how Luba *and* Withering already knew Jay was there. "Fine," she lied again. Why stop now? "His mother just wanted me to get something of his and bring it over for him."

"Really?" Withering looked up at Luba. "Jay didn't keep many personal effects here, did he?"

Luba shrugged and turned to walk back to the larger, adjacent lab. Autumn wanted to know the answer to Withering's questions, too. She also wanted to ask Luba more questions of her own, but it was clear that Luba wouldn't say anything more around her boss. Autumn stared at Luba's back for a moment, thinking it odd that she had shut down as soon as the doctor arrived. She turned back to Withering.

"Got a photo right here," Autumn said tapping on her tote. She thought it better not to mention the notebook, though she couldn't quite figure out why she felt that way.

"Well, alright then. Anything else I can do for you?" Withering asked, his eyebrows arched, distinctly communicating that he wished to do nothing else for her.

Autumn decided to press her luck anyway. "How is Jay's research going, if I might ask?"

"Fine, I suppose. He isn't the most productive student I've ever had in my lab, but he was finishing up what he could."

"He was doing some sort of stem cell research, right?"

Withering's eyebrows had come down. Jay's research was also his research since Withering was the principle investigator. Withering was clearly the kind of man who liked to talk about himself, and he didn't hesitate to launch into an explanation.

"Right. His research involves type 1 diabetes and stem cell therapy. He had compared fresh human fetal pancreatic tissue to purified human adult islet cells and found that the fetal cells worked much better."

"So that's what he was going to get his Ph.D. for?" Autumn pressed.

Withering stretched his mouth into a wan smile. "Not quite. The scientific community is not going to be impressed by someone showing that embryonic or fetal stem cells work better. We knew that already. I think almost everyone knows that now. If they didn't work better, there wouldn't be all this controversy around stem cell research, now would there? Jay was trying to actually grow the fetal cells in culture."

"Did he?" Autumn asked.

"Not very well. The cells that proliferated well did not produce insulin efficiently and those that did produce insulin did not proliferate well."

"But he was finishing up, you said." Autumn's hands went reflexively to her hips; she couldn't hide the frustration in her voice. What did Withering want from Jay? An actual cure for diabetes? As a student?

"It had been several years. I had to let the boy try for his Ph.D. at some point," Withering said with a bit of disdain in his voice, his brow furrowing again.

Autumn's eyes darted once more around the lab. No plants. Why would there have been? Living things in labs were possible sources of contamination for the experiments. So why did Cassie think there would be foxglove here? She had been sent on a fool's errand, but maybe she could still get some useful information from Withering.

"Do you know of anyone who didn't much care for Jay?" Autumn tried, reprising the innocent tone that had worked on the guard earlier. This time, however, Withering's eyes widened in apparent anger. Despite her efforts, she had made it sound like Withering might have been involved in Jay's hospitalization. Softening her tone further, she corrected, "I mean stem cell research is pretty controversial like you just said. Do you think some extremist could have wanted to hurt Jay?" She didn't need him angry at her. That wouldn't do her any good. What she needed was information, and he was the only one giving her any. She took a few measured breaths.

Withering sighed deeply. "My dear, there are a great many people doing stem cell research and as far as I can tell, there are but a few lunatics out there, thankfully. If you've gotten what you came for, then I think it's time for you to go. We're very busy here." As an afterthought, he added, "Give Jay my best wishes when you see him."

Autumn bit her tongue and nodded. Withering was a pompous ass, and she didn't quite believe that Jay's research wasn't good enough, although she had to admit that she didn't know much about the science behind what he did. She did know that the world of research was a competitive one, and she assumed Withering didn't climb the mountain of academic medicine by being a nice guy.

He likely used Jay to get whatever it was that he needed to get ahead. Autumn just didn't know what that was. She wondered what else she didn't know.

Withering nodded back to indicate their conversation was over but didn't offer his hand. He turned and Autumn quickly walked out to the hall. She tried to catch Luba's eye on her way out but couldn't see her in the adjoining lab. Perhaps she had gone back to processing her wells. She was sure Luba would know what Withering had needed from Jay. But Luba wasn't talking to her. Not today anyway.

Making her way into the waiting elevator, she dug into her purse for her cell phone. *Damn tote, nothing ever stayed organized*, Autumn thought as she stuck her nose into the bag. A harsh ding alerted her that the elevator had reached the lobby, and she walked out while still looking into her purse. Her elbow knocked against something in motion.

"Oh, excuse me," Autumn said, startled, instantly looking up to find the familiar face of a drug company rep who often brought the residents lunch. The attractive man was in a tailored suit carrying a paper shopping bag that smelled distinctly of Chinese food. He smiled warmly at her, showing off a prominent dimple on his right cheek. Autumn felt her face warm. She did have a thing for guys with dimples. Especially those who brought her food. She never realized drug reps brought food for anyone but the doctors. Although the doctors were prescribing the drugs, the researchers were the ones doing the work to get them approved in the first place. It made sense that the drug reps would happily feed them, too. Schmoozing with docs and researchers. *Nice work if you can get it*, she thought.

"No problem," he sang out, pressing for a floor with his

free hand. The guard glared at her as she smiled back at the drug rep, her glance lingering for just a moment too long.

TWELVE

LUBA

Lyubov Myshkina hurried back to her work. She was in the U.S. on a J-1 visa, which meant that if she lost her job, she would have to leave the country. Luba shuddered at the thought of going back to Russia—she had nothing to go back to. Her parents had both died too young. Her husband drank too much and her marriage had ended in a conflagration of broken liquor bottles, accusations of infidelity, and slaps flying in both directions. Her research job in Moscow had been dependent on whether or not the lab director was able to come up with the requisite bribes for the right officials. She had dreamed of coming to America since she was a girl—the land of the free, the home of the brave—and most importantly, she thought America was the place where, if you worked hard, you could be successful no matter who you knew or didn't know, no matter how much money you had or didn't have. Science was the great equalizer anywhere, but especially in America. Though now that she was finally here, Luba had to admit, she hadn't gotten it quite right.

American bosses seemed to be more honest than the ones she knew back home, but not all of them. Dr. Withering hid some of his results, that she knew. It wasn't especially surprising to her. That had happened a fair amount in her previous Russian lab. The right results were needed for continued funding everywhere. Withering knew how to hide things properly and if Luba hadn't come of age knowing the slight of hand involved in concealing errors and covering everything with a brilliant sheen, she might not have noticed. Though discretion was more of a Russian skill than an American one, Withering was quite Russian in this regard. Americans, Luba had noticed, tended to be brash and brazen, quite taken with their assumed freedoms. Jay was an American through and through.

She collapsed in her seat at the black-top table. She hadn't liked Jay at first. But in her two years in the lab, he had endeared himself to her. She figured that he would be very successful as an M.D.-Ph.D., and she had initially assumed that he had traveled an easy path in life and would continue to do so. He'd have a nice house in the suburbs and drive a Mercedes or Lexus. Why should she bother to help him? He didn't need it. She minded her own business. But, for six months, Jay had persisted with his wide grin each morning, his cheerful, "Hi, Luba" each time they passed one another, and his offers of assistance when he wasn't busy with his own work. So, one day, Luba took Jay up on an offer to help catalog a new shipment of mice. He had stayed well past the time he could have left. She came to the conclusion that he was what the Americans called "a good guy."

And now he was hurt. Luba hadn't asked what had happened. She wasn't sure she wanted to know. She had assumed he had been in an accident when Jay's father or some male relation had called the lab early that morning to report that Jay was very ill in the ICU and would not be in to work that week. She could only answer that she was sorry and would inform the boss. The sun had barely begun to stream through the lab's windows, and Luba had only had a few sips of her tea. Still, after that phone call, there was a gnawing in the pit of her stomach that had nothing to do with missing breakfast. Jay had confronted Withering about falsified records several times in the past month. She had heard him quite clearly. The boy had no discretion. Such an American! She had seen Jay scribbling data into his lab notebook after his own work was done. She wondered if Withering would take Jay's notes in his absence. She wondered what was in the notebook besides Jay's own work. She couldn't say anything about what was going on in the lab. Her job, and therefore her visa and her ability to remain in the U.S., was dependent upon her silence. She closed her eyes and reviewed what she had done that morning. She was almost certain that nothing could be traced back to her.

It had been 7 a.m. when she had arrived, realizing that Withering wouldn't be in for another hour. She had begun opening drawers and turning over papers as neatly as she could. She knew Jay's notebook was in the desk's locked drawer and she needed the key. She searched 412 for several minutes and had turned up nothing. It quickly became 7:15 a.m. and still no key. Never mind. Her husband had locked his liquor away. She knew how to get around locks. Especially flimsy metal drawer locks. But after five minutes of trying with a straightened paperclip and sweat starting to bead on her brow, the stubborn drawer had refused her entreaties to open. Luba figured that she should just give up but remembered that a screwdriver and hammer would work, although this would certainly not be discreet. If Withering noticed the broken lock, which she doubted he would, she would tell him that Jay had lost the key and had broken it weeks earlier. So, at 7:20 a.m., Luba had gone to the storage cabinet in the back of the lab and had taken out the toolkit used for minor repairs, removing the barely used screwdriver and hammer. If he spotted the broken lock, Withering would curse Jay as Luba had seen him do before. Why would he think anything else? After a quick insertion of the screwdriver and a blow from the hammer—loud, but if no one was there to hear it, she figured, it hadn't happened—the drawer slid open with a small groan. She had grabbed the bound notebook, startled by the picture of Jay's brother just behind it. The dead one. Jay had told her he had died when they were children. It turned out his life was not as easy as she had originally imagined it to be. She grabbed the picture, too.

The other labs had started to come alive, and footsteps had startled her into quickly stashing the hammer and screwdriver back in the storage cabinet and then absently placing the notebook and picture underneath a stack of papers on her desk. She hadn't yet thought about what she was going to do with Jay's items and busied herself with her work down the hall when the young doctor had shown up. She wanted to know about Jay's work. What could she tell her that wasn't already in the notebook? So, she decided to give her the notebook. As Luba sat huddled over in her chair, she wondered what, if anything, the girl would do with it.

A kiss on her cheek brought her out of her trance. She knew who it was, but the suddenness of it caused her to startle and spin around in her chair.

"Chris!" she exclaimed. "Not in the lab!"

Chris smiled his Hollywood-actor smile. He was from the heart of coal country, beautiful land raped by American oligarchs, like her hometown had been by the Russian oligarchs. Chris had a Russian soul—deep and troubled beneath the well-polished veneer. Luba could see this clearly, although he tried not to let on. He was so much like her that she had decided to let him take her out to dinner after he wouldn't stop sending her flowers and showing up at her lab. He had even started bringing Withering and Jay their lunches in his pursuit of her. They had had a fancy Italian dinner the night before and he had taken her home afterwards. It was only their second formal date and she said "goodnight" with a long kiss. She needed to be careful with her heart but was willing to open it slowly. Fate had placed him in her path, she was sure of it. What other explanation could there have been for her meeting him in the parking lot on her way to work two months earlier? He was lost and needed to get to a meeting, and she had always prided herself on her excellent sense of direction. The meeting was between hospital officials and Zeno-Graphium Pharmaceuticals. It turned out that he worked for the same company that funded one of Dr. Withering's studies. Their meeting couldn't have been just a coincidence. They had too much in common. She smiled back up at Chris. He resembled Clark Kent, the Superman character from the first comic book she had ever seen as a teenager.

She had a good job now and a handsome boyfriend. She just needed to keep quiet about what she knew. She had done her part today and she had done enough.

THIRTEEN

CASSIE

A bone-chilling cry jolted Cassie out of her trance. It had been eerily quiet in the ICU up until that moment, and the rest of the team had gone to lunch and the noon conference. Cassie had stayed back to catch up on the mountain of paperwork she was doing in Autumn's absence. Making no progress, her pen held in midair, she kept replaying the night Jay Abrams had been brought in, mentally correcting her missteps. Rather than stuffing the EKG strips into her pocket, when she replayed the night, she looked at them more thoroughly and had instantly recognized digoxin toxicity as she kept admonishing herself she should have. She had called for the Digibind before Abrams entered into his dysrhythmias and the antidote had arrived well before he would have sustained any brain damage, which he now most certainly had. Cassie was picturing Abrams's distinctive EKG strip when the cry coming from a patient room pulled her back into the real world. The wail was a familiar one across all cultures and religions, forgotten by many in America, though readily recognizable in all hospitals. It was the sound of one soul saying goodbye to another—a death wail.

Mr. Giannini had been in the ICU for a week and his course had trended steadily downwards. Cassie knew that it would and had anticipated this moment. Like most in the ICU, he was a cancer patient, but unlike most in the ICU, he was also on dialysis. How much could a body take, she wondered. Mr. Giannini had to endure years of being strapped into a machine and having his blood slowly drained and replaced three times a week. Then he got cancer and had to be poisoned with chemotherapy in an effort to kill the cancer cells before they killed him. He essentially had no kidneys, was down half a lung, and had virtually no immune system left. His family was composed of an incredibly sweet and devoted wife along with a son and grandchildren who visited daily. They thought he could get better, pull out of this. "He's a fighter," they liked to say.

"Well, who isn't?" Cassie often wanted to reply. All of the oncologists claimed that their patients were fighters, and who were they in the ICU to argue otherwise? She had just met the Gianninis a few days ago, and it's hard to change a family's mode from "fight" to "do-not-resuscitate" overnight. So, Mr. Giannini was still a "full code," though shocking his heart would do nothing if it went into a fatal arrhythmia from all the stress it had had to endure. He had a bad cardiomyopathy, the pump just didn't work anymore, and they would just be shocking the heart back to useless.

Cassie wished she could have explained that better to the family. Cassie told the family as sternly as she could, "a miracle would have to happen" for him to pull out of this, only to learn that this family was hoping for just that.

Cassie careened into Giannini's room, shaking off her daydreams of having saved Abrams. She steeled herself with a cold, antiseptic filled breath. The nurses were in the room already, ushering the family outside. The defibrillator had been brought to the bedside. Cassie placed the paddles on Mr. Giannini's bony carcass, resembling a taut canvas-covered stick tent more than a human chest, and watched the machine's small screen showing his heart rate of twenty-five. He had no pulse that she or the nurses could find.

Cassie looked up at Christine. "One of atropine," she said as Christine was already pushing the medication into the central line. No response. "One of epi," Cassie said blandly. Christine, who had the epinephrine ready, pushed the medicine into the small blue port. A fatal ventricular fibrillation appeared on the monitor.

One of the nurses frowned as she charged the machine to two hundred joules. "Ridiculous," she muttered under her breath. Cassie heard, though, and felt a chill run through her own body. Her insides churned as she prepared to shock his battered body in its final moments. Her training commanded her to go on. She couldn't just stand aside and watch his death. She would have to be an active participant in it.

"Clear," Cassie said, though everyone already had. She pushed the discharge buttons on the paddles and Mr. Giannini's body, somehow both swollen and stick-like in all the wrong places, gave a small jerk. She had stopped the ventricular fibrillation of his heart, but that hadn't really helped. Cassie kept the paddles on and watched as his heart rate fell to twenty.

"Three hundred," Cassie commanded, sweat starting to bead on her forehead. She shocked the wrinkled, ghost-white man again, watching intently as his chest jumped inches from the bed. The heart rate was fourteen, then nothing. She took the paddles off his chest and put them back onto the defibrillation cart. His heart had stopped. It was over.

She took her stethoscope from around her neck and listened for heart or breath sounds. There were none. She ground her knuckles into the sternum of the frail chest and shook him, looking for a response. Nothing. Then, as she was obligated to do, Cassie forced open Mr. Giannini's swollen eyelids with the thumb and forefinger of her right hand and shined a pen-light into his blank eyes. No pupillary response. Cassie looked up at the clock and then over at Christine and the nurse who had muttered that their ministrations were ridiculous. She couldn't spare Mr. Giannini the pain of a resuscitation at the end of his life, but at least she had kept it short. A chill ran through her again.

"Calling it at 12:20 p.m.," Cassie said simply, steeling herself as she walked out to tell the family that their beloved husband, father, and grandfather was gone. While she did that, the nurses would disconnect the multitude of lines and tubes, trying to make Mr. Giannini look as human as possible in death, with the hope that the family would be able to remember him as a loving, doting grandfather instead of the blown-up pin-cushion he had become in the ICU.

As the tearful family collected in Mr. Giannini's room to say goodbye, Cassie made her way back to the charting room to quickly dictate the events that had transpired in his short code and send the death certificate to admitting. The body couldn't be released until she had completed this task. She would check off the box that said the family had refused the autopsy. She didn't feel like asking them, even though she knew hospital policy said she had to ask every family of a deceased patient for an autopsy so the pathology residents could learn. But Cassie reasoned that Mr. Giannini had been enough of a learning tool for the residents in his life. She would let him finally rest in peace.

After dictating a death note and signing the death certificate, Cassie looked over at the mountain of paperwork she still hadn't completed and frowned. Whatever. She was done for the day. She had already clocked in too many hours for the week, she told herself, nearing the end of the eighty-hour limit. But she also had to acknowledge that she felt like a raisin that had fallen to the bottom of her overnight bag—exposed and dried up. As soon as the rest of the team got back from lunch, she was leaving. She strolled back out from the charting room. A cleaning crew had already been summoned and all traces of Giannini and his family had been scrubbed from the ICU as if he had never been there at all. She went back to thinking about Jay Abrams. He was very much still there and entirely her responsibility. You break it, you own it. She peeked her head inside Abrams's room. His mother was there, her hair perfectly blown out, in stark contrast to her cheeks, which were streaked with mascara. She looked up at Cassie from her hard plastic perch next to

Abrams's hospital bed. Cassie figured he was most likely brain dead from his prolonged code. Had anyone spoken to the family about this yet? No, probably not. It would be her job. She blinked her eyes hard.

"Hi," Marsha Morris said, forcing a smile. "How's my boy doing today?"

Cassie opened her eyes, took a deep breath in, and said as softly as she could, "He is still in a coma." Her gaze drifted to Jay's lifeless body, shrouded in the starched white hospital sheets.

"I know."

"The neurologist will be by tomorrow to assess his chances of recovery, so we'll know then how things are going. She'll do an EEG, brain wave testing. That will give us a better idea." Cassie ground her molars together hard and was jolted by a shot of pain that ran through her jaw. Good. She deserved that. She was fueling false hope. She knew the prognosis was grim.

"I lost another son," Marsha said out of nowhere, focusing on a black mark on the floor. "Jay is all I have left. Do you have any idea how smart he is?" Anger started to creep into her voice as her speech came faster. Cassie tried to relax her face and listen. Her jaw throbbed.

"Jay is gifted. He's doing research that would have helped his brother. He is going to be a doctor, too. How many people can do that? Not many. Did you know he is an MSTP scholar? There are less than a thousand of those in the whole country. He is going to make a huge difference in the world. You have to help him."

Cassie's jaw throbbed with each of her pulsations, a drum beat traveling to her brain. *What? Did? You? Do?*

Marsha looked at Cassie directly now, her stare boring through all of Cassie's defenses. As mascara-stained tears collected anew in her lap, Cassie rested her hand on Mrs. Morris's shoulder. Cassie blinked back her own tears as the silence was quickly broken by the gregarious voices of the team coming back from the noon talk—bellies and minds full. Cassie had never felt emptier.

F O U R T E E N

A U T U M N

Walking out into the daylight, Autumn had to squint at the display on her phone, which she had finally located in the bottomless pit of her bag. It was 12:30 p.m., and her stomach was growling. She thought briefly about heading to the hospital for noon conference and the free lunch to be had there but decided that she didn't feel like talking to anyone at the moment. She wanted to have a look at the notebook Luba had basically shoved into her bag. The smell of French fries or fried something was beckoning her from the collection of restaurants nearby. She decided to get some greasy brain food to help her try to decipher Jay's notes.

Autumn settled on fast-food Indian from the nondescript building housing the food court, which, without any signage, somehow managed to support thriving businesses in between the hospitals and research buildings. *Must be that you can smell the glorious non-hospital food from a block away,* she thought. She settled on the least sticky-looking table she could find to place her tray and dug into her tote, first pulling out the photograph she had gotten from Luba. The boy was small and cute and not yet into his awkward teenage years. He had the same piercing green eyes as Jay, but it clearly wasn't Jay. His hair was light, almost blond. Autumn wondered if the picture could be of Jay's brother, who had died while Jay was still in high school. In the short time she had known Jay, he had mentioned his brother several times. Autumn laid the photo next to her tray.

She then pulled out the smooth marbled lab notebook and placed it on her lap. The front cover was labeled simply as "Jay Abrams 4/30-." The lab notebook seemed almost entirely used. Autumn scanned the pages, huddling over her chicken tikka masala, carefully transferring small plastic forkfuls into her mouth.

For the first twenty pages or so, only the front sides of the pale blue lined pages were used. After that, Jay had taken to using both sides of the page, but not consistently. When there was writing on both sides of the page, the indentations made by the ballpoint pen he was using made the writing on the other side of the page more difficult to read.

Not very neat of him, Autumn thought, holding her fork in the air for a second too long and letting a drop of bright orange tikka masala sauce drip onto the page.

"Shit!"

So much for criticizing someone else's ability to keep tidy. She grabbed a thin paper napkin from her tray and wiped hard at the greasy orange sauce, leaving behind an inevitable stain. She futilely wiped at the now yellow-orange mark on the paper, sighed, tucked the photo gently into the front cover, and put the book away. She should have been more careful. What did she know about stem cell research, anyway? She would look at the notebook later, away from food. She was due back at the hospital tomorrow morning and still had a lot to do to get ready.

She had to send a more thorough e-mail to Chiwete, who would be taking over for her in the ICU, and let him know about her ICU patients' histories. She would have to review the reciprocal e-mail he was sending about her new patient load on the regular medical floor. Autumn thought about stopping by the hospital to visit Jay but decided instead to see him first thing in the morning. She was weighed down with heavy cream sauce and the anticipation of all she had to learn and do before the next day. And maybe something else was keeping her away. She shook off that possibility as she tossed out the remains of her meal and began the walk back to her car, casting a sideways glance at the hospital, its imposing beige towers making her stomach turn over. Heavy grey cloud cover had begun to obscure the bright sun.

Tomorrow, she would be back on the dreaded medical floors, with their seemingly infinite number of patients and things that could go wrong. But, this time, she vowed, she would do better. She figured she couldn't do any worse.

FIFTEEN

CASSIE

A sliver of sunlight poked out of the heavy gray sky as Cassie made her way to the parking lot. She hadn't seen the sun in what felt like weeks. It barely registered. As her car filled with the midday warmth, she stared ahead and breathed in deeply of the non-hospital air. The smell was distinctly of stale car, but anything was better than the over-cooled, antiseptic hospital miasma that had been filling her lungs. She quickly pulled her Honda Accord into the open parking space behind her apartment building, eager to be alone in her own space—no patients, no interns, no nurses, just her. Silence. No screaming, no alarms, no tears.

As she slipped the key into the lock, she felt her phone vibrating from the back pocket of her scrubs. Sighing, she thought for a second about not picking it up but didn't recognize the number and decided that it might be important.

"Hello," she answered, unable to keep the annoyance

from her tone.

"Hey, Cassie. It's Autumn."

Not sure what Autumn wanted, Cassie didn't respond. She had completely forgotten that she had sent Autumn on the quest for foxglove.

"I'm going to be back tomorrow on the General Medical Service. Chiwete will be taking over for me in the ICU. I hope that's okay, and I'm sorry for the extra work I stuck you with."

"Oh, no problem. Really. I needed to practice my presentation skills anyway," Cassie lied, thinking of the mediocre job she had done substituting for an intern on pre-rounds. She considered that Chiwete could work on the mountain of paperwork she had left behind.

"How'd Jay do today? I didn't get a chance to stop by. I hope his mom is okay with that. I think she was expecting me."

Cassie gritted her teeth and felt the jolt of electricity shoot to the back of her head. *No more hospital talk*, she silently screamed, but said, "I wouldn't worry. I'm sure it's fine. He's no better, unfortunately. He'll have his EEG tomorrow, but I think he may have some pretty bad anoxic brain injury."

A longer than expected pause followed her words. She shouldn't have been so direct. Her free hand went to her jaw which was now throbbing. "Autumn?"

"Sorry. That's so insane. He's our age, you know? He can still improve. He's a fighter."

Cassie cringed. That's what Mr. Giannini's family had said about him.

When she didn't respond, Autumn said, "Well, like I

told you, we weren't exactly together, but I don't think he would have done this to himself. He was too smart to ingest something." Autumn paused again. Cassie still didn't have anything to say.

"Oh, and I looked for the foxglove, like you asked me to. I didn't find any."

Cassie finally responded with a snort. She had stopped caring about the foxglove. The ingestion. The precipitating cause. What did it really matter? The neurologist would likely end this all tomorrow. Pronounce Abrams brain dead.

"Doesn't matter. He took the stuff. Probably an accidental ingestion. His mom says he's all she has left." Cassie swallowed hard; her head was starting to spin unpleasantly. "She lost another son, and Jay was doing his research to make whatever happened to his brother better." Cassie's words drifted away.

"That's right." Autumn's tone brightened just as Cassie hoped her tone was signaling she was done. Her oblivious intern kept going. "That's also why he was a vegetarian. His brother wanted to be but couldn't since that would have limited his diabetic diet too much. Jay became a vegetarian after his brother died. I think he felt like he needed to honor his brother in some way. Then with the research, it was as though he could redeem himself for not being able to save his brother."

"He sounds like a complicated guy," Cassie replied blandly. "Trying to save people you can't save is a tough way to live. Maybe it's no way to live," Cassie wondered out loud, her head now beating a drumbeat for her to get off the phone.

"Uh no." The brightness drifted out of Autumn's voice.

"He had made some big breakthrough and was going to get his Ph.D. for it. He told me at dinner a few days before he came in to the hospital. I think his PI wants to play it down and is acting like Jay could barely tie his own shoelaces. Did he come by the ICU? His name is Withering. I got the strangest feeling from him. Like maybe he's involved in this in some way."

Cassie straightened, her eyebrows shooting up. "No," she said. If someone else had had a hand in what happened, then Jay Abrams's unconscious state couldn't all be her fault. Cassie sighed. No good trying to get out of this one Ellison, she admonished herself. "Autumn, let's face it. Odds are, Jay did this to himself."

Cassie could almost hear Autumn shaking her head over the phone. "No. None of this makes any sense. Look, Cassie, there weren't any plants in the lab, but I have Jay's lab notebook. I'm not really sure why I have it, but Withering's lab assistant gave it to me. I've just started to go through it, but something is weird. Why don't I take some time to sort out what was going on with his research and we can talk about it at lunch tomorrow if you can break away from the ICU."

"You sure you're okay?" Cassie asked, realizing that no one usually asked her that question.

"Yeah, I'm fine. I just wonder what the heck Jay had gotten himself into. Maybe there was more going on with his research than he let on. I'll let you know tomorrow, okay?"

Cassie relented, "Sure. I'll see you at lunch."

Cassie hung up the phone and sat on the cool concrete steps collecting her thoughts. Withering. His PI. What was Autumn implying? That Withering had poisoned Abrams? It didn't make any sense. That didn't actually happen. And even if he had, she was the one responsible for Abrams the minute he was wheeled into the ICU. She had tried her best for Abrams and completely failed. She'd tried with Giannini, too, but that was different. Of course, an elderly cancer patient in that kind of shape wasn't going to be shocked out of a code. But like Autumn had just said, Jay Abrams was their age. She could have saved him if she had been just figured things out just a little sooner. Conversely, no amount of guts or brains could have saved Giannini but still, she had to try anyway. Why? What had she been trying to do? Satisfy her own insecurities and please a family instead of doing what was best for the patient? Abrams. Giannini. She had screwed up on both. The wrong treatment for both of them. She had gotten it so right for so long. Why couldn't she get it right anymore?

Cassie tore into her overnight bag, yanking out the small bag of dwindling pills, ignoring the desiccated raisins that hit the carpet. She emptied two Xanax into her palm and swallowed them without water. Within minutes she felt the reassuring and familiar wave of calm wash over her. She was okay. Everything she did today was okay. She breathed a sigh of relief, stumbled into the apartment, and collapsed onto her sofa, staring blankly at the ceiling.

S I X T E E N

A U T U M N

It was still dark when Autumn began her walk from the parking lot to the hospital. Only the interns showed up this early, and the nurses wouldn't start arriving for change of shift for at least another thirty minutes. It was a three block walk to the hospital entrance from the parking lot and Autumn was used to only hearing the sound of her own footfalls along the way. This morning, the sensation of ants under her skin made her turn around. Her ears hadn't heard something as much as her body felt a presence behind her. But when she looked, there was no one there. And yet, she knew something was wrong. She pulled her white coat tightly around her chest. Cassie thought Jay had taken the Digitalis by accident. But what if it had been no accident? Luba had given her Jay's notebook, and the notes in it didn't make sense to her. Withering. What was Withering up to? Jay didn't like Withering, and it was clear Withering didn't like Jay. It was also clear that Withering hadn't wanted her in his lab. Autumn quickened her pace with only one block remaining in her walk. She could make out the human figures in front of the hospital, two security guards and a few patients milling around the entrance to the Emergency Department. She let out the breath she had been holding and crossed the street to the hospital. She was safe. But from what?

Autumn pushed all of that away as she strode into the brightly lit atrium. She didn't have time to lose it right now. Besides having to pre-round on ten patients she had not yet met on her new General Medical Service, she wanted to visit Jay. But not really. She didn't really want to visit him as much as she had to visit him. She felt guilty for not having stopped by when she told Marsha that she was going to be back, but she felt her skin peeling away from her body at the thought of going back to the ICU. Not her real skin—the newly acquired layer she wore as protection. Seeing Jay unconscious with the tubes and lines creeping out of his body spooked her as nothing else ever had. People thought they weren't supposed to get sick or die young, but Autumn was quickly learning that that was a lie. She had seen plenty of young people admitted to the hospital for cancer, infection, autoimmune disease. And though it was increasingly more likely the older one got, death could come at any time, she knew she wasn't safe—hence the protective layer she had mentally fashioned for herself. But seeing Jay lying motionless in the ICU stripped her bare.

Despite her misgivings about seeing Jay and Marsha again, walking into the ICU was surprisingly comforting, with its rhythmic beeps and eerie fluorescent lighting. The nurses were gathered around, looking at pictures of Sue's new granddaughter, and Autumn passed them silently, striding quickly into Jay's room. She released the breath she had been holding.

Upon hearing the sliding glass door open, Marsha Morris stirred in the reclining chair but didn't wake up.

Autumn approached Jay's bed. He was neatly positioned underneath carefully lain and smoothed sheets. His hair was flat against his head and his pillow was creased only where his head lay. He was in exactly the same position as when she had last seen him two days ago. A flexible plastic tube emerged from his left nostril and snaked down to mid chest, where a beige liquid was being pumped in from a small clicking machine, providing him with nutrition. The corners of his mouth bore the tell-tale ulcers of someone who has been recently intubated, but the actual endotracheal tube and ventilator were gone. He was breathing on his own.

Was he recovering? Instinctively, Autumn grabbed his left hand and pushed down with the side of her thumb as hard as she could onto his index finger's nail bed, looking for a pain response from the patient. But Jay did not withdraw his hand. He didn't even flinch.

"Autumn?"

Autumn dropped Jay's hand, which fell like the inanimate weight it was, and spun around to find a bleary-eyed Marsha Morris staring at her.

"Hey, Marsha," she said softly. "How are you?"

"Okay, I suppose, under the circumstances. I was hoping to see you yesterday." A frown pulled at Marsha's mouth for the briefest moment, and Autumn could almost feel her disappointment. "I suppose you were too busy," she tried to add brightly.

Autumn hesitated, unsure how to respond. Jay's mother didn't need to hear about her visit to Jay's lab or her suspicions about Withering. She had enough to worry about. But maybe she knew more than Autumn did about his work. Maybe Jay had confided in her. "Marsha, did Jay discuss with you anything that may have been going on in his lab? Maybe things he was worried about?"

Marsha's eyes welled up with tears, but they didn't fall. "He didn't tell me much. He stopped confiding in me after his brother's death. I think he blamed me for not being able to prevent it. Maybe there was a lot about my son I didn't know." She squeezed Autumn's hand. "Maybe you can help fill in some of the blanks."

She couldn't help Jay anymore—the dead weight of his hand portending the death of so much more—but maybe she could help Marsha figure out how Jay had gotten here. Plus, she needed to know, too.

Yes, Marsha had a lot to deal with right now, but if Autumn was going to sort anything out, she needed a team. There were no one-man or one-woman shows in the hospital. At least not for an intern. And she figured that she was even less of a detective than she was a doctor. She was going to need help anywhere she could get it.

She took a gulp of air and decided to let all the information flow out of her like a breath. "I went to Jay's lab to look for a plant. One that he might have ingested that caused all of this." Marsha nodded knowingly. Someone must have told her about the digitalis. Autumn went on. "I didn't find any foxglove, but I did get a notebook of Jay's that may be useful if I can sort it out. It's been a while since I did any basic science work."

Marsha looked quizzically at her. "Do you think he wrote down the reason he got hurt? In a notebook? Like a journal?"

"No. I don't know what it is. It doesn't make a whole lot of sense to me, but I feel like it might give us some insight into Jay's work and maybe why all of this happened," she said, motioning to Jay.

Marsha stared at her shoes. "Maybe you could ask my husband for some help. He was a bioengineering major in college and before he got his M.B.A., he did some work in that field. He and Jay would talk about it sometimes, but it was too technical for me."

Autumn shrugged. She'd ask Mark for his help first. To Marsha, she said, "Maybe."

Mark might be able to make some sense of things. He always was pretty good at figuring out the unknown substances in organic chemistry, and this was the biggest unknown she had ever seen. She cursed herself for agonizing over the notebook last night when she could have just called Mark for help. She glanced down at her watch: 6:30 a.m.

"Marsha, sorry, but I have to get going and see my patients. I'll stop by later." As an afterthought, she added, "if I can," not wanting to get the woman's hopes up again if she was going to let her down.

"Sure. Today's his EEG, so we'll know more this afternoon if you can make it."

Autumn smiled weakly. "I'll try," she said and walked to the door slowly, giving a quick, awkward wave goodbye on her way out.

Picking up her pace, she strode to the elevator. She figured she had a good twelve hours of work ahead of her before she could sit down with Mark and go over the back pages in the notebook again. Chiwete had a lot of sick, hospital sick, patients on his service that was now, as of this morning, her service. On second thought, she didn't think she'd make it back to the ICU that evening but promised herself she'd go again first thing in the morning.

Autumn decided to check on McAdams first. At least she had met him before. Autumn's body gave a quick shudder as she recalled that he was the one they had sent out of the ICU to make room for Jay. She slid a printed copy of Chiwete's e-mail out of her right white coat pocket to review the pertinent patient information.

> McAdams, forty-seven-year-old man with ALS (Lou Gehrig's Disease). Recent pneumonia, sepsis, now improving on IV antibiotics. Unable to ambulate. If stable overnight, consider pulling central line and setting up dispo.

Autumn walked over to the nurses' station to review McAdams's vital signs from overnight. His temperature had been normal and his blood pressure was stable, too. She went into the supply closet to find a suture removal kit and get rid of the central line she had put in herself three days ago when he was in the ICU. An internal jugular line, her favorite. Autumn was fascinated by neck anatomy in medical school and had meticulously dissected her cadaver's neck. Unlike dissecting the abdomen, the neck required precision and delicateness and appealed to her need for order. She also loved the way *ansa cervicalis* sounded and made her dissection partners spend an entire morning identifying the tiny, looped nerve bundle and teasing it out from the surrounding fat and muscle. Autumn pictured the triangle made by the sternocleidomastoid muscle, pictured holding her hand over the carotid pulse, and then striking! She could slide the line right into the huge vein sitting just outside of her fingertips. She had put the central line in during the day, and Brooke had supervised. Unlike the overly fastidious Cassie, Brooke was a fan of the easier IJ line, too.

"Crap," Autumn said to herself. Although there were about a thousand IV bags and other supplies the nurses needed, no one ever thought to stock the supplies the interns needed. There were no suture removal kits. After searching for another few minutes, Autumn located a pointy scalpel, its pale green handle protruding from the small white cardboard box labeled #11. The last one. It would have to do. She slipped it into her overfilled white coat pocket and walked into McAdams's room. To her surprise, he was already awake.

"Mr. McAdams, good morning. I don't know if you remember me, but I'm Doctor Johnson. I helped take care of you in the ICU a few days ago. I'm going to be your new doctor here on the regular floor."

"Hey, Doc," he said with a thick Boston accent and a broad smile. "Of course, I remembah you. You put this thing in my neck."

"And now I'm here to take it out," she said, producing

a small piece of gauze and the scalpel from her pocket. "How are you doing?"

"I can't complain. You know plenty of folks in here ah much worse off than me."

Autumn smiled back at him but thought that wasn't quite true. He was only forty-seven and quite nearly completely paralyzed from the ALS he had been diagnosed with just eighteen months prior. He had likely gotten his pneumonia from food going down the wrong way because his muscles for swallowing were failing. But Autumn remembered that when he had come in he had mentioned that he had been with the Boston Police Department for more than twenty years. She had had a few patients who were BPD and knew they were generally from some pretty tough stock.

With two quick slices, Autumn removed the stitches tethering the central line to the skin of his neck.

"Okay, now take a deep breath in and hum it out." Autumn demonstrated, pursing her lips and humming rather badly. If he did that, an air bubble wouldn't invade his heart as she pulled the wide catheter from his neck. She quickly applied a sterile piece of gauze she had in her free hand and held pressure for a few minutes, listening with her stethoscope to his heart and lungs from the front as she did so, maximizing her efficiency.

She applied a small piece of tape to hold the gauze in place and collected the spent IJ catheter and scalpel, depositing the catheter into the hazardous waste bin and looking for the red "sharps" container on the wall to deposit the scalpel into.

She found it full to the point of overflowing, grabbed the small plastic sheath that had previously covered the blade, covered the dangerous end of the scalpel, and slid it back into the pocket of her white coat. She needed her hands free to finish examining her patient and rather than try to cram another item into the box in this room, she'd drop it off in the box next door when she was done. The scalpel was clean—it hadn't nicked the patient. They had taught her not to cram things into the sharps boxes the first day, and she knew an intern who didn't heed that warning and wound up sticking himself with a needle protruding out from one of the boxes. HIV, Hepatitis C, and who knows what else lurked in the needles and on the blades threatening her from that sharps container. She wouldn't be so foolish.

She turned her attention back to her patient, quickly pressed on his abdomen and his lower legs, and finished with, "I'll come by and see how you're doing later today. You may be able to leave soon," she said with a smile.

"Now, Doc, that's what I wanted to heah," he said enthusiastically. "Thanks fah taking this thing out of my neck."

"No problem," Autumn replied over her shoulder, making her way out of the room to examine her other nine patients. She raced down the hall with only forty-five minutes left to do it in before she had to meet the rest of her team.

Another patient, another set of vital signs, another physical exam, another note to write. Rinse and repeat. And somehow, she got it done in forty-five minutes, though, in the process, the slightly used scalpel had drifted down to the bottom of her white coat pocket, the much needed "sharps" container having been forgotten.

SEVENTEEN

LUBA

Luba's head was spinning. At the same time, it seemed that her heart wanted to leap out of her chest. She had already called in sick that day and assumed she would start to feel better by the afternoon. She prided herself on her strong constitution. When the weather was nice, she used her sick days for working in the garden her landlady let her share. She correctly assumed that Withering didn't suspect anything, although she always got sick during the nicest months of the year instead of in the brutal winter months when everyone else did.

Luba enjoyed her trips to the Russian markets in Brookline and would unfailingly replenish her stock of old-world remedies, remembering the names of the pills and herbs her mother had made her better with as a child. It was just such a remedy that would be needed now. Luba dug into her purse, only to find the bottle of vitamins she took two or three times a day. She would need something a bit stronger for this odd illness that had suddenly descended upon her.

As she walked into the tiny efficiency's kitchenette to select the appropriate cocktail of carefully stocked remedies from the end cabinet, her right leg locked and Luba was forced to the cold, tile floor.

"Ahm! Boleet," she called out softly, grimacing and grabbing her right leg, which had begun to shake uncontrollably. *"B'lyad,"* she yelled to no one as her right arm started to do the same. Soon her entire body had tensed up, shaking. Her jaw clenched, and she bit down painfully onto her tongue, not having the ability to release it. She could no longer cry for help, but forgot that she wanted to as the convulsive energy wrapped itself around her cerebral cortex. The only sounds Lyubov "Luba" Myshkina could make were a few soft, involuntary wails as the jerks forced every last bit of air from her lungs.

EIGHTEEN

CASSIE

"Coding" is one of the most detested words in all of medicine, though it is colloquially used to mean two very different things. To a resident, it meant that a patient is making a very active attempt at dying. When a patient coded, either their heart stopped pumping or they stopped breathing or both.

But to a practicing attending physician in the United States, coding is also the process by which he or she gets paid. Every diagnosis, from "arthritis, osteo, knee, left side" to "heart failure, primary diastolic, decompensated" had its own special alpha-numeric code. Coding is the process where the doctor fills out a form to send to the insurance company to be paid for services rendered.

Cassie wondered if it was only a coincidence or if it was someone's intentional wicked irony that the word was shared in this way. Though she wouldn't be a resident much longer and wouldn't have to deal with the respiratory and cardiac codes of dying patients on a regular basis, the word code would still be in her vocabulary and a part of her daily duties. It would never go away. The only thing definite in the uncertainty-filled world of medicine was that she'd be "coding" something for the rest of her life. And the reason she was learning to hate that word was that she was slowly discovering that a positive outcome from either type of coding was often elusive.

Cassie had brought Jay Abrams back from the brink of death by coding him for as long as she had. But now he couldn't eat or speak or likely even think. When they loudly called out his name, there was no reaction. And when they rubbed hard on his chest or pressed down on his fingernail bed to evoke a pain response, so basic and pre-historic, there was nothing still. His body wouldn't even tense up in the flexed or extended postures assumed by other brain-damaged patients.

Cassie sat back in her chair and recalled that she had gone to her CCD classes every week as a kid. She had learned her catechism, done her first communion, and had been confirmed. She still had her rosary beads near her bed, though she hadn't picked them up in a while. She enjoyed the rituals and the rules of the Catholic Church—it helped make sense of the world. And she thought her religious education had prepared her for life's tough decisions. Even in medical school she could argue from a point of certainty when they discussed abortion and end-of-life in what seemed like the pointless humanism classes they had to take. It was so easy to discuss life's big issues when you weren't in the middle of them. Bring the philosophers and priests to the ICU. Force them to stay for 30 or more hours every other day. None of this flitting in and out for an hour here and an hour there. Bearing witness to suffering is transient and clean. Covering yourself in it with no chance to wash it off, letting it seep into your pores, is how a soul is truly tested.

Did God want the brilliant M.D.-Ph.D. student to live out his days lying inanimate in a nursing home somewhere? Or did God want them to disconnect the life-giving feeding tube and allow him to pass away peacefully?

Cassie didn't know. Religion was supposed to provide solace and answers. And she hadn't had either for as long as she could remember.

Cassie unfolded her body out of the chair, the lack of fat that wasn't cushioning her tailbone causing it to ache. *Not my job to figure this out*, Cassie thought. Jay's parents were charged with that responsibility. From what she had seen of this family, agreement would be probably not come easily.

By sheer force of her will, she had made the team round at breakneck speed this morning so that she would have time to talk to Pierce, Marsha, and the violence-prone Larry, Jay's dad, who she'd met the same day he'd started a brawl in Jay's hospital room and who somehow had gotten permission to return to the ICU. She wanted to prepare them for the EEG results, suspecting they would not be good. She was sure she could reason with Pierce. And he would reason with Marsha. He seemed to have a calming effect on her when she was most fragile. Larry was another story. She suspected he didn't have much in the way of a formal education and maybe had a harder time understanding what she was saying to him. She imagined Larry getting frustrated. Then she imagined Marsha getting frustrated in response. She assumed Pierce would get frustrated somewhere along the way as well. She hoped that she could steer things in a more positive direction.

The EEG tech had just started to disconnect the small, carefully placed color-coded wires from Jay's head when Cassie knocked on the door frame. As she expected, Marsha and Pierce Morris sat on one side of the bed, holding each other's hands, and Larry Abrams sat, holding his son's hand, on the other side. The small, still patient might as well have been a great wall through which neither side could see each other. Marsha and Pierce smiled at Cassie as she walked into the room. Larry did not.

Larry Abrams appeared slightly more disheveled than he had on the first day they had met, now dressed in a stained T-shirt to go along with the battered jeans. The leather of his sneakers, in stark contrast to the well-polished shoes worn by his ex-wife and her husband, was starting to peel off in several areas. He hadn't shaved since the day Cassie had met him, and he was not one to offer conversational pleasantries.

"When are you going to have the results from all of this?" he demanded of Cassie as she walked in.

Cassie wondered if he was drunk. "Hi, Mr. Abrams. After lunch today sometime, I hope."

"What kind of an answer is that? In my line of work, when someone asks me when something is going to be ready, I say, one o'clock, two o'clock, first thing in the morning. But I guess that's the way you people work around here. I should know that by now."

Marsha and Pierce shook their heads in disapproval.

"I'm sorry, Mr. Abrams. We have to wait for the

neurologist to read it. I know that you are putting a lot of stock in the EEG, but I need you to understand that it may not add much more to what we already know. Your son is not responding to the outside world."

"No, my son is not responding to you. He is responding to me. I can see his eyes fluttering when I talk to him."

Cassie blinked her eyes hard and swallowed. This was going to be harder than she thought. "That may be involuntary movement. A primitive instinct from his brainstem, like his breathing, but not real consciousness. The EEG could potentially help us sort that out and maybe help you decide what you ultimately want to do."

"What do you mean what I want to do?" Larry snapped.

"What we all want to do, Larry," Pierce said, looking at Cassie. "Do what would be best for Jay."

"What the hell is he talking about, Marsha?" Larry glared with laser-focused eyes at his ex-wife, in an attempt to pierce through the imaginary wall they had erected.

"We may need to let him go, Larry," Marsha replied flatly, looking only at Pierce, keeping the wall with her ex-husband intact. To the untrained observer she appeared more put together than when Cassie had first met her at four in the morning a few days before. Gone were the mascara streaks and hand wringing. But she now seemed to be looking increasingly toward her husband for the answers. Cassie had seen this before. She was shutting down.

"Like hell I will! We've lost one son already, and I don't intend to lose another one. How could you give up on him like this?" Larry clenched his jaw and his fists as if he could, by physical force, drag the other two to the conclusion that their son must live.

Marsha bowed her head.

"Why don't we just wait for the EEG?" Cassie offered, backing down on her plan to discuss anything else with the family. Again. They needed more time. And like so many times before, she took the hope from the family around her and internalized it. After all, she wanted Jay to live, too. Maybe there'd be more brain function than the neurologist who had seen him yesterday thought. Maybe he'd be able to regain some function. Perhaps she hadn't failed after all. A shudder ran from her scalp to her sore tailbone. Maybe he could still recover. She'd wait for the EEG as well, deciding to put off consulting the care coordination staff about finding the former M.D.-Ph.D. student a nursing home until the results had come in.

"Let's talk again later today, after we have the results," Cassie said diplomatically as she turned to go, startling to Larry Abrams's grunt as she walked out. Mr. Giannini's family had wanted a miracle for him, and she knew that was hopeless. But now she was praying for a miracle for Jay Abrams. Sure, if someone had tried to hurt Abrams, as Autumn suggested might have happened, then this mess wasn't entirely her fault. But if he could recover, even just partially, then she hadn't failed either. She strode out of his room with her shoulders back, looking straight ahead, all the while thinking, against all odds, maybe he could recover. This hope was absolutely irrational, she reminded herself. But this hope was human.

NINETEEN

AUTUMN

Autumn hadn't spoken with Mark since the morning she had given him sign-out on his Parkinson's patient whom she had frozen in dystonia with a dose of haloperidol. She hadn't wanted to face him. The day interns entrusted the night interns with the care of their patients, and she had failed not only a fellow intern, but a friend. Now that she was out of the ICU and on the regular medical floors, running into Mark was unavoidable. She had known him for a long time and she knew that the way to his heart was most definitely through his stomach.

"Are you compensated?" she asked from behind him as he stuffed his patients' records back into his white coat pocket, having just checked off the bottom of his to-do list.

Mark spun around, his open grin greeting her without any hesitation. "Yup," he exhaled.

He didn't seem to be upset with her so she carefully returned his smile.

"It's lunchtime," she intoned, pointing at her watch.

"So, what are we doing here?"

"How's your Parkinson's patient?" Autumn asked and gritted her teeth, not sure she really wanted to know.

Mark shrugged. "Better," he said, staring straight ahead.

Autumn supposed the only other alternative was worse, so she nodded. At least it wasn't that.

"I'm sorry," she started. Mark put up his hand.

"A mistake," he said. "And not one that killed anyone. I'm sure we'll all make those one day, too. Want some words of wisdom from Chuck?"

"Chuck, the senior resident?" Autumn asked with raised eyebrows.

Mark grinned again. "Yeah. Him. Can't stand the guy, but he's smarter than he lets on. Chuck says if you meet someone who says they haven't had a complication, they are either lying or haven't done whatever it is for long enough."

Autumn snorted. "A fancy way of saying we all make mistakes?"

"Yup."

"So, what was Jay Abrams's mistake?" Autumn raised her eyebrows at Mark. Mark had inferred that Jay was the "friend" Autumn had referred to in her email asking for ICU coverage and had confirmed it with a short reply email. Autumn knew it was a privacy violation, but she couldn't keep Jay's admission secret from everyone, and she emailed back to Mark that he had guessed correctly. In her heart, she would always be the rule-breaker her mother had taught her to be. If there was a good reason for breaking it.

Mark shrugged. "Who knows? These things happen, Autumn. People get sick. Let the ICU take care of Jay. You kinda just met him."

Autumn prickled at that. Mark had been at the party the night she had met Jay. Mark had driven her there, but Jay had driven her home.

They rode the elevator down to the first floor in silence. Instead of risking accidentally mentioning private patient information, nurses and doctors generally rode the elevators staring straight ahead, not even bothering to exchange pleasantries, save a pursed-lip smile. It was common knowledge that there were those who laid in wait for indiscretions around patient privacy to occur—hospital staff called them the "HIPAA police" after the law that made it very expensive for hospitals not to guard against the leaking of patient information. Rather than be falsely accused by the HIPAA police, all conversations had quieted in public areas of the hospital.

"Kinda just met him," Mark had said, implying that she shouldn't care too much about him? Instead of talking, Autumn replayed the night she had met Jay five weeks earlier.

After Mark had coasted his beaten up Toyota into a parking space right outside of the imposing glass building, a beat they could feel deep in their chests quickly directed them to apartment 19G. Mark caught the door as a group made their way out.

The lighting was dim and the furnishings bare. But for the absence of tobacco or any other kind of smoke, it seemed like any party Autumn would have gone to in college. She surveyed her freshly cleaned up colleagues, somewhat unrecognizable out of their scrubs, and laid a finger on her vanishing nasal piercing. It was unmistakably a room full of grown ups and she, too, had grown ten years older in as many weeks.

"Hey, Johnson!" Chuck called out using his usual surname-only style, waving as soon as Autumn stepped into the dimly lit hallway. "Tell these guys what an idiot Tomlinson is." Mark squeezed Autumn's shoulder and pointed his chin to the other end of the room where he was heading to join their fellow interns. Autumn knew Mark didn't care much for Chuck or his bombastic buddies, but she hadn't wanted to be rude to her supervising resident.

Autumn attempted a smile as she headed over to Chuck and the three other third-year residents gathered around him. With his squared off jaw and broad shoulders, he reminded Autumn of a few football players she knew in college. She had briefly thought about asking him if he played when he was her resident a week ago on the oncology service, but she never had found the right time. Dr. Tomlinson had been their attending physician for all the patients with solid tumors and those patients kept them too busy for much idle chatter.

Tomlinson frightened some of the residents, and Autumn thought that he might also frighten some of his patients, though they were probably much more terrified of their cancers to notice his appearance. He was tall and gangly and often held his head to one side. His eyes bulged out of their sockets in the way a person's with Grave's disease of the thyroid might. Making matters worse, he was farsighted and wore glasses that made his eyes seem even bigger and more buggy.

Autumn brushed aside the image of Tomlinson and sighed heavily, her shoulders slumping down with the weight of having to recall the horrible events of her oncology rotation. She opened her mouth to begin.

"Wait. You need a drink for this. Anyone else need a refill? Rob?" Chuck offered as he turned toward the kitchen. "Go ahead and start, I'll be right back. Corona?" he asked.

"Sure. Thanks," Autumn said, unsure of where to begin the story now that her thoughts had been interrupted. After a pause, not so much for dramatic effect as to muster up the emotional courage, Autumn began. "Well, Mr. G is this seventy-two-year-old guy with non-small cell lung cancer, metastatic to brain," using the standard first initial to protect confidentiality, though by now she would automatically refer to patients in this way without even thinking about why she did it. "The patient and his wife are this really nice Italian couple. When he was well enough, she would bring in a thermos of coffee every afternoon to drink in these tiny ceramic cups. She would bring in pastries, too, but I don't think Mr. G ate very much of it. Mrs. G would just wind up leaving them for the nurses."

Someone snorted. "Yeah, like they need it."

"Anyway, he was in for pneumonia. I don't think it was post-obstructive, but maybe it was. He wasn't getting better on Vanc and Levo, with more of an oxygen requirement every day. He was also really forgetful and couldn't remember, or maybe didn't want to remember, that he had a brain metastasis. He had been on dialysis for many years, too—I forget why—and the nephrologist wanted a family meeting to discuss goals of care and making him a 'do not resuscitate.' She asked me to set it up," Autumn explained.

"Hah! Lemme guess," Rob, a half-head taller than the rest of them, interjected, "Tomlinson said no way DNR. I bet he never even told the guy he had a brain met!"

"Well, I don't know what he told them, but I did. I thought I had to tell him and his wife because, well, he should know, shouldn't he?" Autumn asked, doubting whether she should've said anything. But the faces nodding in affirmation encouraged her to go on.

"Dr. Tomlinson gave me hell for that. He was pissed off that Dr. Lake wanted the family meeting at all. Do you know what he said to me?" Autumn asked rhetorically. "He said, 'it's only one small brain met.' Can you believe that? He now has cancer in his brain and Tomlinson looks at it like he stubbed his toe."

"Ridiculous," Karen, a tough former rower agreed as Chuck reappeared with a fresh Corona for himself and one for Autumn. Autumn steeled herself for the rest of the story by quickly taking a few gulps of beer as Karen continued. "It makes the whole idea of 'informed consent' a joke. We ask patients to make decisions for themselves and then give them only the information that will lead them to the decision that the doctor wants them to make. The oncologists are the worst. It sucks that you have to have onc so early in your internship. It will make your intern depression come on sooner," Karen said sympathetically, referring to the doldrums that seemed to overtake the overworked, overstressed interns sometime between February and March of each year.

"Okay, so I have a good joke," Chuck said. "Autumn,

finish so I can tell it."

"Right, well, I arrange the meeting, and I'm there. Dr. Lake, the nephrologist is there. Dr. Tomlinson is there, and so are Mr. and Mrs. G and their son. Dr. Lake starts off saying that though the dialysis is going well, Mr. G's body overall is in pretty bad shape and that we should think about what would be the best course of action if his pneumonia gets much worse, though we think we can make it better right now. *If* it were to get much worse and Mr. G should have more problems with his breathing, then perhaps it wouldn't do much good to intubate him. Putting a tube down his throat would only cause discomfort, because, well, Dr. Lake now turns to Dr. Tomlinson and says it doesn't seem as if the cancer is curable. This pisses Tomlinson off like you wouldn't believe," Autumn continued, pausing to finish the rest of her beer. "He smiles his scary forced smile and says, 'Dr. Lake, cancer therapy is now much like dialysis in that we can *manage* disease effectively for years even if we can't cure it.'"

"Bullshit," Karen spit out. "Maybe they can manage leukemias and some lymphomas, but not lung cancer metastatic to brain. Maybe one person in a hundred, but most people are in for it, and Tomlinson knows it."

"Right." Autumn nodded. "But what can Lake say to that? So, she smiles in agreement and the conversation degenerates into when to schedule the brain radiation and which experimental chemo protocol to try after Mr. G recovers from the pneumonia."

"But Mr. G doesn't recover from the pneumonia," Chuck finishes. "Two days later, I have to call a damn Code Blue, since he was still a full go and now Mr. G is in the ICU, unresponsive, and he's not likely making it out alive from what I hear. If by some chance he makes it out alive, he'll be a damn vegetable."

Autumn stared at her shoes. She was going to start in the ICU in a month and wondered if Mr. G would still be there.

"Oncology, gotta love it." Vinay, the stocky, usually quite even keeled resident, sighed. "It's all about hope and sometimes that descends into false hope. They just don't know when to let go. It can seem so pointless."

"Ha!" Chuck exploded. "Not 'pointless.' Money, baby! There's big bucks in oncology. Have you seen the offices? Have you seen the Aeron chairs on the Bone Marrow Transplant Unit? Those puppies are close to a thousand a piece. But enough; this is a party," Chuck commanded, holding up his hand. "Here's the joke."

Taking a dramatic swig of his beer, Chuck continued, "There's a priest who's trying to give last rights to a patient in the ICU, but he can't find him. 'I think he went to endoscopy to get a gastric feeding tube,' the nurse tells the priest. So, the priest goes down to endoscopy, but the patient isn't there either. 'Try dialysis,' the nurse at endoscopy says. So, the priest goes down to the dialysis unit. 'Oh,' the nurse says at dialysis. 'I'm so sorry, the patient coded mid-way through his dialysis run and died. I think he's down in the morgue.' The priest goes down to the morgue and still can't find the patient. He goes up to the pathologist. 'Please, can you tell me where the patient is,' the priest asks, concerned. 'I heard he had died.' 'Yes, he did,' the pathologist says. 'But you just missed him. The oncologist just came and took him for his chemo.'"

A wide grin spread over Chuck's face as polite laughter

emerged from the group.

"Ugh," groaned a deep baritone from behind Chuck. "That doesn't seem at all funny to me. Maybe one day I'll get it." Chuck just shrugged, still pleased with himself.

"Hopefully not, Jay." Vinay smiled.

"Hey," Jay said, turning in Autumn's direction, extending his hand, "I'm Jay—I'm a friend of Rob's. I don't think we've met."

"Oh sorry," Vinay said. "Jay, this is Autumn—one of the new interns. Autumn, this is Jay—one of the old medical students."

Jay laughed and smiled at Autumn, flashing a prominent dimple on his right cheek. He had dark hair and light eyes—undeniably her favorite combination. "Pretty much, that's about right. I'm M.D.-Ph.D., in the fourth, and hopefully final, year of my Ph.D. When I'm done with the Ph.D. part, I get to go back and finish up the last two years of my M.D. If I do my residency here, I might be here forever."

Autumn felt her heart skip a beat and the skin around her abdomen tingle when Jay smiled at her. His black hair, just a bit on the long side, was gelled to fall casually on his forehead, and his light green eyes seemed to pierce through her.

"So, when I finally get to residency, am I going to lose all capacity to talk about anything else besides medicine?" Jay asked playfully.

"That's a distinct possibility. Two months in and I think it may have already happened to me," Autumn said, raising her meticulously plucked eyebrows slightly. She was suddenly glad she had decided to take a little extra time getting ready for this party.

"Well it all depends on how much you've had to drink," Rob countered. "Alcohol helps to treat nasty hospital-acquired thoughts."

"In that case, I better get another drink," Autumn said, waving her empty bottle.

"I'll go with you. Despite their imbibing, it's actually impossible for these guys to talk about anything but the hospital. Trust me. You're new, there may still be hope for you," Jay offered, displaying his charming smile once again.

Autumn's mind was racing as she struggled to think of non-medical things she could talk about. It had been a while since she had had an actual conversation with someone who didn't take care of patients on a daily basis. She hadn't really talked with her family or her old friends much since starting internship.

Autumn felt the air around her get incrementally warmer. Jay smelled deliciously spicy and woody, a cologne she had smelled before, but not for months. She took an extra deep breath in and smiled, accepting the drink. No one in the hospital wore fragrances out of consideration for the scent-sensitive patients. Autumn recalled the hairless, emaciated woman on the oncology service begging her not to even use the hand sanitizer mounted on the walls. If Autumn forgot, the woman would immediately start retching when she entered the room. Consequently, everyone working in the hospital wound up smelling like a sour combination of latex and antiseptic soap, especially after an on-call day. Jay smelled so good. *This was how people were supposed to smell*, she thought.

One thought led to another, which led to another, which led to Jay driving her home. Once there, she had realized that while she might not typically be able to control a lot of what happened in her day, she was certainly in control now. And blissfully, for yet another time that night, the gods of parking were on her side and they found a spot right outside of her apartment. As soon as Autumn had closed the apartment door behind them, Jay used his large, strong hands to turn her at the waist, grabbed her arms, and applied the weight of his well-toned body to hers, kissing her gently at first. She responded more forcefully, slipping her tongue lightly into his mouth, as they both started using their hands to explore each others' bodies more thoroughly. Soon his mouth replaced his hands, and he lifted off her shirt and slipped down her pants. Thankful that she had such a small apartment, Autumn maneuvered them to her bedroom.

Autumn unbuttoned and unzipped Jay's pants, slowly sliding her other hand down his stomach, stopping only when she found what she was looking for.

"Autumn, how did you get your hands on Jay's notebook anyway?" Mark pulled Autumn away from her memory halfway down the hall to lunch.

Though she realized she was in the hospital, for a moment she didn't recognize where exactly. Autumn could still smell Jay and shook it off. Yeah. Mark wasn't wrong. She had kinda just met him.

Her eyes focused on the large, open wooden doors of the noon conference room. Her daydream had finally evaporated. She stopped and stared at Mark. The notebook. She must have mentioned it to him in her email.

"The lab assistant, Luba, gave it to me. Actually, I don't

think that I would have thought much about it, but she was so weird about handing it to me. Like it contained some kind of state secret or something," Autumn said. Adding in a whisper, "I think maybe something was going on in the lab and maybe Jay knew about it. Maybe that's why she gave it to me."

Mark shook his head. "Autumn, really?"

Autumn shrugged. "Yeah, maybe it's nothing, but can you help me take a look through it anyway?"

"I will, but I don't think anything nefarious is going on. Doesn't a suicide attempt make the most sense?" Mark sighed. "Maybe Jay was just a pretty intense guy and things got overwhelming. You know, med students have a pretty high suicide rate."

"I know I just met him, but Jay was not suicidal," Autumn said through gritted teeth. "I could go back and talk with Luba. Maybe she is just paranoid, but I think she might know how well Jay's experiment was going. Or not. Maybe she even knows a little more about the PI, Withering. He seemed shady."

Mark snorted, grabbing a plate as they got in line for food. "Yeah, like you'll have time for that. Didn't you just pick up your service? I'll go home with you after we finish up today," Mark offered more gently. "Then we can get some dinner, and I'll have a look at that notebook."

Autumn closed her eyes for just a moment, her mind still with Jay. Hopefully Mark would find something helpful. She breathed in deeply, trying to re-conjure Jay's smell from her memory, but there was only barbecue with antiseptic in the background.

TWENTY

CASSIE

Cassie threw her shoulders back as she began her power-walk to the conference room on the first floor. It was too busy a day for the team to leave the ICU, and a unanimous vote had given her the honor of retrieving the lunch to bring back. The interns agreed that she often stayed back so she should be the one to go, but Cassie half suspected that they wanted to get rid of her in order to enable them to slack off for the fifteen minutes she would be gone. She smiled a little at that thought. "Better to be feared than loved," she remembered from a political philosophy course in college, though she couldn't quite recall who had said it. Love was certainly a more difficult emotion to attain. That she saw every day.

Staring at the blank white hallway walls, she wondered how Marsha and Larry were ever married to each other. They seemed so different. Marsha looked like she walked out of a page of *Martha Stewart's Living*, and Larry looked like he just finished working on his car. Sometimes people were just too different to work out.

She shook her head, her thoughts turning to herself and her ex. They were very different from one another, too. It would never have worked out. He was a quiet man, a deep thinker, and not terribly ambitious in his career, content with teaching high school history. Though he had been so incredibly supportive over all of the years of her training, there were a lot of things she never told him about her work. How could she? How could she explain the little things she missed—that they all missed? Things like the small speck on the chest X-ray or the slight abnormality on the EKG. Other people usually caught the oversights, the radiologist or her attending physician. But sometimes an error happened and there was no one there to remedy it. Like Jay Abrams. He was in a coma. Cassie couldn't shake the feeling that she could have saved him earlier if she'd done something differently. Her mind kept looping back to this singular thought. As the tedious elevator made its way to the first floor, she again pondered the possibilities, replaying that night. What if she had thought about digitoxin poisoning when he first coded? What if she had given him digibind? There was no one at home she could talk to, and she couldn't share her feelings with anyone at the hospital. There was nothing they could say that she didn't already know. And she didn't want their false reassurances. Most days she was surrounded by people. But really, she was alone and had been since she'd started her journey toward becoming a doctor.

"Cassie," she heard her name called from the food line as she walked into the noon conference room, breaking her out of the endless Abrams thought loop.

"Hey, Autumn, how are you?" She called out, grabbing one of the large metal trays that were supplied in case the residents needed to bring lunch back for their teams. The faces of the residents she had cut in front of softened when they saw her grab the tray. Those who had to hurry back to the ICU were granted priority in the lunch line.

Autumn shrugged as Cassie marched in front of her, too. "Okay, I guess. Getting back into the routine of things, you know. This is Mark, he's one of my co-interns," Autumn said, casting a look back at Mark.

"Good to meet you, Mark. I'm Cassie," she introduced herself, reaching her right arm around Autumn while balancing the still empty tray on her left forearm.

"Hey," Mark smiled shyly, shaking her hand briefly.

"Mark is going to help me try to decipher Jay's notebook later today. He was a chemistry whiz in college."

Mark only sniffed in reply. "I think it's barbecue day, and the good stuff is going to go fast."

Humble. Shy. Cassie was starting to warm to him.

The room hummed with loud pre-lunch chatter broken by the jarring pager beeps going off every few seconds. Right before noon conference was one of the rare occasions that the residents and interns got to socialize and blow off steam, and they had about five more minutes before the renal fellow would show up to teach them about kidney failure while they inhaled their lunches. It seemed they all intended to maximize their socializing time except for poor Vinay, who had probably arrived a few seconds before everyone else, because he'd been cornered by the drug rep for Zeno-Graphium Pharmaceuticals. It would be rude not to talk to the man who supplied their food several days a week, and so Vinay, not yet able to get in line for his lunch, had to suffer through hearing about the merits of Zeno-Graphium's newest medication. Just a few yards away, Cassie shot him a sympathetic smile, half listening to what Autumn was saying.

"And it's obvious that he didn't approve of the work Jay was doing," Autumn said matter-of-factly.

The sound of Jay Abrams's name brought Cassie back to the conversation. "Who didn't approve of what Jay was doing?"

"Dr. Withering. I think he's hiding something and it has to do with Jay."

"Autumn, calm down. When you hear hooves, think horses, not zebras. Lots of young guys try substances they aren't supposed to. Maybe he was bored or depressed." Cassie would have loved to lay blame on someone else, but she had to be sensible.

"He didn't seem depressed to me. He seemed happy that he was done. Or almost done."

"Well, if he wasn't depressed, then he wouldn't have intentionally hurt himself. But it didn't have to be intentional. Maybe it was just an accident," Cassie reasoned as she piled her tray high with pulled pork or pulled beef or pulled whatever it was. She would have to remember to get enough rolls, which Cassie noted were in a basket after the plastic utensils. She'd have to remember those, too.

"Maybe," Autumn said, but the lines creasing her forehead said she thought otherwise. "I don't know, Cassie. Something's not right here," she insisted.

Cassie thought about Jay's dire condition and his family

who she still hadn't had the end of life talk with. Not in any meaningful way.

"No," Cassie agreed. "Nothing is quite right, but I'm not sure we're going to figure it out here." She was mostly trying to figure out how to keep the dressing on the coleslaw from mingling with the other things on her tray and if it was worth it to even add the slimy stuff.

Autumn shook her head. "But maybe if I could explain the inconsistencies in the notebook, I would be able to make some sense of things. It just doesn't make sense to me that he would hurt himself." Autumn tapped Mark's shoulder. "Mark, why would someone write on the backs of some of the pages in a lab notebook but not others?"

"Maybe they meant to write on all the pages, but they got stuck together with barbecue sauce?" he said, smiling and turning his attention back to the quickly disappearing ribs.

Autumn tapped him again. Harder. "Be serious."

"I don't know. Maybe the brilliant Jay Abrams had become forgetful or not very neat or maybe he ran out of notebooks." He shrugged and raised his eyebrows, his gaze quickly going back to his food, where his attention would obviously stay until he was fed.

"Maybe he was recording something he thought was important," Autumn hissed between clenched teeth.

Mark just shrugged and turned to grab a plate, his hand awkwardly grazing the approaching pharmaceutical rep instead. Keeping his head down, he mumbled an apology.

"No worries," the pharmaceutical rep, who had released Vinay, replied over-enthusiastically. He greeted Mark with a broad smile and nodded to Cassie and Autumn. "Have you heard about Zerochol yet, the most effective cholesterol-lowering medication on the market?"

"Sure, and I bet I'll need it after this meal," Mark joked.

"Chris Delano. I'm one of the senior representatives for Zeno-Graphium," Chris said, extending his hand from the arm of a very neatly tailored navy suit.

"Mark Callahan, I'm one of the lowly interns."

"Autumn Johnson," Autumn said with full hands, nodding to Chris.

"Cassidy Ellison," Cassie said and turned her attention back to the food.

Chris looked back at Mark. "But you won't be forever." Chris winked. "I'd love to give you some materials I have with me on Zerochol and answer any questions you might have."

"Sure. I'm happy to take whatever you've got," Mark said, reddening just a little as the unbearably handsome man flirted with him.

Chris widened his grin and handed him a pamphlet with his business card stapled to the front, along with a bunch of clear, yellow plastic pens with the bold, blue "Zerochol" insignia printed prominently at the top. Mark quickly pocketed the branded pens. They were considered serious contraband by the hospital higher-ups—an obvious sign of pharmaceutical company influence.

"This really is the most effective cholesterol-lowering drug on the market," Chris continued. "In fact, one of your esteemed professors, Dr. William Withering, will be speaking at a dinner Zeno-Graphium is sponsoring in a few days. He'll talk about the importance of cholesterol lowering in your patients and how Zerochol is the best way to go about it. You should come and bring your friends along," Chris added while handing Mark a flyer, never breaking his thousand-watt smile.

"We'll be there if we can get done with our paperwork, orders, notes, and figuring out who does or doesn't have a death wish," Mark tried to joke again. This time it fell flat.

Cassie released all the air from her lungs and glowered at Mark. Her high opinion of him evaporated. Was he about to divulge confidential patient information?

Chris's perpetual smile disappeared for a moment as his eyebrows raised. "Really?"

"Oh, you know how it is. Everything is the intern's job," Mark retreated as Cassie continued to glower at him.

"Absolutely. Well, you won't be an intern forever and hope to see you at the dinner on Thursday." Chris smiled quickly, showing off his movie-star white teeth, and then walked to the back of the line to chat up another group.

Cassie grabbed two handfuls of rolls, dropped them into her tray, and then reached for a handful of plastic utensils before turning to Mark.

"That was almost a HIPAA violation," Cassie admonished him, her warm feelings toward him evaporating.

Mark's face turned a shade not dissimilar to the barbecue sauce. "I wasn't going to say anything specific," he argued.

"He was cute," Autumn teased Mark, trying to change the subject.

Cassie couldn't believe these two. "He's a pharma rep," she said between gritted teeth. "They do not want to help you. They want to use you."

"Well, he's still cute," Autumn challenged, glancing at the flyer in Mark's hand. "And his dinner is at one of the best seafood places in Boston. We'd never be able to afford to eat there on our own. Plus, Withering will be there. Maybe we can talk to him about Jay."

"You two should go just for the experience, but don't be surprised if the food doesn't taste as good as you expected. Bullshit in the air has a way of doing that," Cassie added, noting the look of shock on Autumn's face. No, she wasn't always the prim and proper resident the interns thought she was.

Cassie doubted that Mark and Autumn would discover anything in Abrams's notebook. But she could appreciate that they were trying and tried to let her anger simmer down to a low boil. She lowered her voice as the renal fellow started her talk at the podium.

"I'm on call tonight in the ICU, but let me know if you find anything in the notebook." And with that, she hurried out of the room, the smell of the food she was carrying growing more unappealing with every step.

TWENTY-ONE

CHRIS

Chris Delano smiled at his reflection as he straightened his tie in the bathroom just outside the ICU. Not a hair out of place, just how Zeno-Graphium liked their reps to look. True, Zeno-Graphium was not the biggest outfit out there, but they were certainly good enough for his needs. He would be collecting a nice big bonus from the company very soon and was sure to get a promotion after all of the long hours he had been putting in.

"I could have been a doctor," he told himself, brushing the non-existent lint off of his shoulders. He had a photographic memory. He could recall every scene from every moment of his life. He could recall every page of every textbook he had ever read. His grades had been good enough, and he knew he was just as smart, if not smarter, than these residents. But he had a better plan. Insurance companies hassling you, patients calling you at all hours of the night, and then the lawyers lining up to take everything away from you at the slightest slipup. No. He had made the right choice after college. His chemistry friends were piling on the debt, going for masters' degrees that they would do what with? Teach? Or the pre-meds who spent their entire junior year preparing for the MCAT and then piling on even more debt interviewing at medical schools senior year. If they wound up getting in, that meant four more years of tuition and then at least a three year residency where they would make about ten dollars an hour.

He would wind up making a lot more money than they did for years, maybe forever if things went according to plan. And anyway, doctors were just marionettes, weren't they? He was certainly skilled at pulling their strings. Chris needlessly patted down his perfectly gelled hair and smiled in the mirror again. That mousy little doctor –Cassidy Ellison she said her name was—was going to be almost too easy. He had walked her back from the conference room to the ICU, gentleman that he was. She had needed help carrying those trays back, hadn't she? Shaky hands. A slight look of nausea on her face. Being a good salesman was all about picking up on subtle cues.

"And where are you off to with all my food?" he had winked at her.

"The ICU. Team's too busy to come down," she had replied, a little coldly he had thought.

"Well, if I remember correctly, that's quite a ways from here. Let me help you," Chris had offered. Not waiting for a response, he lifted the top tray of food, on which the rolls were teetering, threatening to tumble to the ground.

Cassie just shrugged.

"You look a little stressed out," he offered kindly.

"Yeah," Cassie answered, her tone a bit softer. "Some weeks are more stressful than others."

Chris tried to look solemn. "I can imagine. Must be hard being in the ICU, patients close to death. Maybe seeing yourself in them?"

"Um, no, not exactly." Cassie paused for just a second too long. "I don't think I've got a lot in common with my patients. They have a lot going wrong with them. I don't."

"No." Chris shook his head. "Doesn't seem like it. So, do you think they're all going to make it?" He tried to smile reassuringly.

Cassie snorted. "Not unless there's a miracle. But we all like to believe in those, don't we?"

Chris nodded, the hint of a smile playing on his lips. "Well, if there is ever anything I can get for you, Doctor?" He paused. Of course, he remembered her name, but feigning ignorance could be useful.

"Ellison." Cassie finally returned his smile outside the doors of the ICU. "Cassidy Ellison."

"Dr. Ellison," he repeated. "Let me know if you ever need any samples. I've got them all."

He watched her eyes widen ever so slightly in a way he was all too familiar with as she quickly cast her gaze to the electronic door pad and pressed it. His hometown had once been known for coal mining, now it was known as one of the addiction capitals of the U.S. Addicts had a few things in common no matter where they lived. The hungry look they gave at the hint of a fix was one of them. And at that moment, Cassidy Ellison confirmed for him that he had something she wanted—and it wasn't his good looks. The doors hissed open. "Sure," she said, motioning to take the second tray back from him.

"Oh no," he said, "Let me carry this in for you."

Cassie just shrugged again as Chris followed her into the ICU. He quickly scanned the glass doors, but most of the curtains on the inside of the glass were pulled shut.

Chris followed Cassie to the rear of the ICU. "You can just put the food on this table," Cassie said as she placed her own tray down. "Thanks."

"My pleasure," he said, quickly fishing a business card out of his shirt pocket and handing it to her. "Remember, if there is ever anything I can get you . . ." He flashed his pearl-like teeth. "For your patients," he added as an afterthought.

"Thanks," she muttered and slipped the card into her white coat pocket. "Let me walk you out."

She escorted him quickly back out through the ICU doors just as a well-dressed, middle-aged man charged in.

"Excuse me," the man muttered, nodding at Cassie and staring for a second too long at Chris.

"Sir," Chris paused and smiled, "excuse me."

Wing-tipped shoes, slicked back hair, sharp eyes. Chris recognized the man immediately. He was an executive with a chemical company that was working on a deal with Zeno-Graphium for basic ingredients. His name was Pierce Morris. He was Jay Abrams's stepfather—Chris needed to know the backgrounds of all the people involved in his endeavors, and Jay Abrams was working in Withering's lab. So, of course, Chris had Googled him. Facebook provided the rest, including telling him that Jay was in the hospital. Being detail oriented was the key to success. And Chris had planned on being successful for a long time.

TWENTY-TWO

AUTUMN

"I think we should call the police," Autumn heard Mark say to her back as she examined McAdams's chart outside of his room. McAdams's temperature had been steadily rising all day and was now 100.6.

"Huh?" Autumn turned around, her mind still preoccupied with what organism could have infected McAdams's body. He was already on levofloxacin for his pneumonia, the other antibiotics he had gotten in the ICU having been pared down. Maybe he needed one or two of those back.

Autumn focused her eyes sharply on Mark. His brow was furrowed and a few beads of sweat glistened on his upper lip.

"I said I think we should call the police."

"For what?" Autumn was still silently reciting the gram-positive and gram- negative organisms that might be circulating in McAdams's body.

"For Jay. I changed my mind. I do think something is going on here." More beads of sweat glistened as Mark licked his lips.

"Why?" Autumn stopped her mental recitation.

"I got a very disturbing page just after lunch. Check it out," he said, handing her his pager.

Autumn pushed the message button and looked at Mark quizzically.

"Mrs. S needs an order for Tylenol. She has a headache," she read.

"Scroll back one." Mark sighed, looking nervously into the hallway.

"back off ja," she read. "What the heck does that mean? Did they mean to write 'jackass,' but hit the enter button on the keyboard before they were done?" Autumn sighed. "It's a prank page. People send them all the time."

"No, Autumn. I don't think so. J. A., for Jay Abrams."

"But it's lower case, no periods. Not initials. Just ask telecom to trace it to whichever computer signature signed the page and then send them a better one back."

Mark huffed as his face reddened.

"I did call telecom. It wasn't sent from a computer. It was sent from a phone. That's why nothing is capitalized and there's no way to trace it since no one had to sign into a computer to send it."

"We can page from a telephone? I thought we had to use the computers."

Mark glared at Autumn. "Well, it's a brave new world, I guess, and the person who sent me this knows how to send a text message to a pager from a phone."

Autumn's face fell as she examined the page again. By this

time, Mark's face had turned an irritated shade of crimson.

"We need to call the police. This is serious, Autumn."

She *had* felt someone following her from the parking lot. Luba *had* given her Jay's notebook. And Jay. He had said he was almost done when Withering implied that he wasn't. There was certainly enough weirdness going on. Yes. It was probably best to call the cops. They might think she was crazy, but at least someone who knew how to look into things like this would get involved.

Autumn started to nod her head to agree with Mark, when a loud "Hey, Doc!" came from McAdams's room. Autumn turned around to his open door. She thought he had been asleep when she was looking at his vital signs sheet, but now he was sitting up in bed, a bit breathless from the effort that soft shout had taken. Autumn made eye contact with her patient.

"Can you come in here for a sec and bring yah friend?" he asked.

Autumn and Mark stared at each other, confused by the request, but they both took the few steps past the doorway of his room.

"Mr. McAdams, this is Dr. Mark Callahan, another one of the hospital's interns."

"Pleased to meet you. I'm Detective McAdams. Ah, at least I used to be." McAdams waved a weakened arm over his bed-bound body by way of explanation. "I heard you talking about calling the police? Are you in some kind of trouble?"

"No, sir," Mark said, shaking McAdams's atrophied hand. "But a friend of hers is."

McAdams looked at Autumn differently than he had

before. It was a probing stare, like he was trying to look through her.

Autumn paused and closed her eyes, unable to tolerate McAdams's stare. What could she say? Well, Mark wanted to call the police and here it was, the police coming to them. Sort of. She figured that he, at least, wouldn't think she was crazy. She decided to launch into an explanation. She didn't have as much regard for HIPAA as Cassie, at least not when it got in the way. What did her mom say—you had to break some eggs to make an omelet—or something like that.

"A friend of mine is in the ICU. You came out of the ICU to open up a bed for him a few days ago. Everyone assumed he had intentionally or maybe unintentionally taken the stuff that put in him the ICU, but now I'm not so sure that someone didn't try to poison him or something," Autumn added, grinding the ball of her left foot firmly into the linoleum. Maybe she had said too much.

"So," Detective McAdams hung onto the word without breaking his stare. "Why haven't the police been called already?"

"I don't know," Autumn demurred. "Maybe they have been. But no one suspects anything nefarious was going on. He's just an M.D.-Ph.D. student. He works and studies and that's it and all we know is there was some disagreement over how well his experiments were going and some sloppiness in his lab notebook."

"And this page," Mark added, holding up his beeper for the detective to read the message.

"Hmmm." McAdams continued staring, waiting for more.

"He was doing stem cell research. It seems like there was something controversial about it," Autumn added.

"Do you know if he had received any threats of any kind?" McAdams probed.

Mark rolled his eyes at Autumn. "I don't think so," he mumbled.

"Well, the principal investigator he worked for would know if he was threatened." Autumn glared at Mark. "And I think he does know more about Jay than he is letting on. Either he doesn't care about Jay, which is probably the more likely scenario, or he knows something was going on that he doesn't want to talk about."

"Principal investigator?" McAdams raised an eyebrow.

"The guy in charge of the experiment," Mark explained.

"What's this guy's name? I can get someone to at least check this guy out for you," Detective McAdams offered. "If there's anything to it, we can get BPD involved and sort this all out."

"William Withering. He's a doctor here."

"Okay, give me a couple of hours to make a few calls. Things take me a little bit longer these days," he said matter-of-factly.

"And, Detective, one more thing," Autumn pressed her luck. "We think Jay might have been poisoned with a medicinal plant. It's called foxglove."

"Foxglove, hmmm." McAdams closed his eyes, either deep in thought or drifting off to sleep. Autumn couldn't decide which one and rested her hand on McAdams's arm. He was warm. And not in a good way.

"Thanks, Detective, we really appreciate your help. But I've got to get some blood cultures and a urine sample from you. They'll take you for a chest X-ray, too. You're starting to develop a fever again," Autumn informed him, releasing his arm.

McAdams opened his eyes and smiled. "You do what you gotta do to get me outta here, and I'll do whatever I can for you."

Mark kept shooting Autumn exasperated glances, but he waited until they had finished drawing the blood cultures and were far down the hall from McAdams's room before he said anything.

"I don't think that's the same as calling the police," he said behind gritted teeth.

"No. It's better," Autumn insisted. "Because he's taking us seriously and he'll give us something concrete to take to the cops. Otherwise, I don't really think anything would come of calling them."

Mark's face softened and she noticed the sweat had dried from his upper lip.

"Maybe you're right." Mark shrugged. "I'll go finish up my work and you do the same. I'll meet you back outside the great Detective McAdams's room in two hours and we'll see how far he got from his hospital bed."

"Deal."

Autumn felt her spirits lift. She would save McAdams and he would help her figure out what had happened to Jay. Things were finally working out.

TWENTY-THREE

CASSIE

Jay had come out of his coma. At least that's what the neurologist responsible for reading the EEG had reported to Cassie. But when he used the word "coma," it was with the most medical of definitions in mind—it didn't mean Jay was awake. According to his report, the EEG had shown "high voltage bursts of spikes with low volts in between." This meant he had severe anoxic brain injury. His brain had been oxygen deprived for too long while his heart wasn't pumping. His brainwave pattern confirmed that he could never wake-up. His brain had been pretty much destroyed.

Pierce and Marsha Morris and Larry Abrams were waiting in Jay's room for the report. Cassie was waiting in the charting room for Dr. Goldberg to arrive to have another family meeting. She didn't want to have to break the news about the EEG to the family without the attending physician present. She didn't want to bear the brunt of Larry's anger. Christine, the nurse-in-charge who was caring for Jay the last few days, was also supposed to be there. Chiwete, Autumn's replacement intern, would not be present for the meeting. He was busy taking care of other patients in the ICU and since Jay wasn't much physical or intellectual work anymore, Chiwete was instructed not to get involved with the family.

Cassie was known to be a competent, some days even an excellent resident, particularly when it came to performing procedures. She was cool in stressful situations, but in truth, nothing caused her more angst than dealing with an irate family member. More time in a bronchoscopy suite as a pulmonologist or in the catheterization lab as a cardiologist meant less time having to emotionally struggle with patients. Both of those specialties had appealed to her before she settled on gastroenterology. Her father was a successful cardiothoracic surgeon in New York and though he was disappointed his daughter was going into internal medicine instead of surgery, when she was thinking about a fellowship, he cautioned her to "pick something where you have a procedure you can do." Not only did procedures pay more than talking to patients, they also got you out of having to do a lot of unpleasant things for which there was no remuneration, financial or emotional.

The sound of the door to the charting room opening pulled Cassie away from her thoughts. She spun around and saw that Dr. Goldberg had arrived.

"How did the EEG look?" he asked, taking a seat next to her.

"Not good. No real evidence of thought. No response to external stimuli. Lots of non-specific spikes with low voltages in between."

"Did the neurologist call it anoxic brain pattern?"

"Yes," Cassie answered and cast her eyes downward.

She felt Dr. Goldberg's hand on her shoulder. "Are you worried that you should have stopped the code earlier and let him go?"

Cassie stared back at him, startled that she could have betrayed her thoughts so easily. "No. I don't think I should have let him die. I wish I would have seen then and there what you saw on the EKG the next day. Maybe I could have suspected digoxin or digitoxin poisoning earlier, given him the Digibind antidote, and stopped this whole thing from happening."

"I don't think so," Goldberg said reassuringly. "That," he began, but Cassie cut him off.

"Well, Anu, the cardiology fellow thought so."

"Did he now? Well, Anu is one hell of a Monday morning quarterback, isn't he? I'll have a talk with him."

Cassie bit her lip, worried she had gotten a friend in trouble. Dr. Goldberg cursed even less than she did.

"Anu didn't mean anything by it. I think he felt bad he didn't make the diagnosis that night either." Cassie's voice faltered. "And Abrams's digitoxin level just came back from the outside lab at eighty-seven, pretty darn high, clinching the diagnosis," she added softly.

"Dr. Ellison," Goldberg said firmly, "no one could have made that diagnosis the night he came in coding. I wouldn't have made that diagnosis. I wouldn't have even started to think about the QT interval as abnormal if you hadn't mentioned the digoxin theory to begin with. There's not a lot of time to think in a code. You are just going through the algorithm."

"The diagnosis missed is the diagnosis never considered," Cassie mumbled absently.

"In the calm light of day, things look a lot different than when you are in the heat of the moment. We were able to figure out what happened the next day because of you. You are a doctor, not a crystal ball reader. All you can do is your best. And you've done a great job." Goldberg gave Cassie's shoulder a quick, friendly squeeze and removed his hand, signaling that this conversation was over.

Cassie felt her eyes start to get heavy, but she refused to cry in the hospital. Instead, she got up from her seat.

"I'm ready to go talk to the family. And thanks for the encouragement," she said, smiling weakly.

As they approached Room 7, Cassie tapped Christine on the shoulder. "You ready?" she asked.

"Sure," Christine said, jotting down a few more vital signs.

With Dr. Goldberg leading the way, the three of them slid open the glass door to Room 7. Larry had positioned himself squarely at the head of Jay's bed, sitting where the ventilator had been, stroking Jay's hair every so often. Marsha was on the other side, holding her son's hand. Pierce had taken to pacing. He was speaking a lot less recently. The configuration of seats had changed somewhat but the acrimony between Jay's parents still hung thickly in the air. The family had been let back into the hospital under strict instructions that there be absolutely no physical contact or voice raising.

"Shall we go in the family conference room?" Dr. Goldberg said solemnly and everyone followed him down the hall.

They had all been there before. The plain white room

with seven gray-upholstered, wooden chairs arranged in a squared off circle with burnt-orange matted carpeting covering the floor. Dusty magazines and a box of tissues sat on single end table in the back corner. It was a bare room, built to serve no other function than breaking bad news. Larry sat by himself against the wall opposite the door, Pierce and Marsha held hands sitting against an adjacent wall, and along the remaining blank wall sat the three medical professionals. They all stared at one another as if they were about to negotiate a cease-fire. Or perhaps restart the war.

"Well, what did the EEG show?" Larry demanded as they all settled into their chairs.

Dr. Goldberg looked to Cassie and raised his eyebrows to signal her to start.

Cassie swallowed hard. "The neurologist thinks that he has suffered a great amount of brain damage. He isn't responding to the outside world."

"He's in a coma?" Marsha asked.

"No. Not a coma. The time he spends asleep and awake is normal according to the EEG. When he's awake, he just doesn't seem to be thinking, hearing, or seeing. It may actually be worse than a coma. His brain just isn't working anymore."

"So, he's brain dead?" Marsha asked, her upper lip quivering.

"No. Not quite. At least not officially. The parts of his brain that control breathing and other basic functions are working."

"What are you saying?" Larry directed his question at Dr. Goldberg. "This doesn't make any sense. Why would some parts of his brain be working and others not working? Why does he look like he is in a coma, but you say he's not in a coma?"

Goldberg nodded patiently and responded dryly, "The part of his brain that's working is the most hearty. It takes a lot to knock it out. It is also the most primitive, the brain stem, it's called. It performs the lower functions of the brain, like breathing, but none of the higher functions, like thinking."

"Can he get better?" Pierce asked. He was calm, almost abnormally so.

"We hate to say never," Dr. Goldberg started, "but honestly, his condition is as about as bad as it can get without being officially brain dead."

"So, there's a chance," Larry offered.

"That's not what the doctor said, Larry," Pierce answered condescendingly.

"I'm warning you to stay the hell out of this," Larry boomed at Pierce.

Marsha squeezed her husband's hand and shot a warning glance at Larry. "Concretely, doctors, tell us what his chances are."

Cassie swallowed hard and remembered that the question the patient's family was asking wasn't necessarily the question they wanted answered. "He will never be the way he was," Cassie tried to explain.

Her words hung in the thick, tense air of the room. For several seconds, no one spoke.

"I'm sorry," Christine said, breaking the silence with merely a whisper. "This must be so hard for all of you."

Marsha started crying. Larry flew out of his seat.

"I want a second opinion. Another neurologist," Larry demanded.

"That's understandable," Dr. Goldberg offered calmly. "We can ask for another one to weigh in or if you have someone you'd like with privileges here, just let us know and we'll call him or her."

"I will get back to you," Larry said quickly, moving toward the door. "You will not write off my son so quickly," he growled and stormed out of the room.

"They've both previously lost a child," Pierce explained, his arm around his sobbing wife. "This is very hard for them."

"As it would be for anyone," Christine said softly, with a hint of disdain.

"Why don't we give you two some time alone," Dr. Goldberg offered and walked out, motioning for Cassie and Christine to follow.

The two doctors and nurse walked silently back to the ICU. Christine smiled gently and took her leave of Cassie and Dr. Goldberg to check in on Jay. Dr. Goldberg stopped by a few of the sicker patients' rooms before leaving the ICU for the night. Cassie would be on call with Chiwete tonight, for which she was thankful. He was extremely competent and gung-ho. Probably the best of this lot of interns. More likely than not, he would let her get a few hours of sleep and handle all but some of the worst crises without her.

Keeping her energy level up for the nearly thirty hours she would be in the hospital for an on-call ICU shift had never been a problem before. Miraculously, the adrenaline flowed freely enough to keep her going and keep her sharp through the day and night and even into the next morning. But now, she felt deflated and she still had at least twenty hours to go. Her brain, usually buzzing with a to-do list for her patients, with differential diagnoses to consider, with teaching ideas for the interns, was blank and heavy. It was as if the electrical activity her cerebral cortex normally produced was short-circuiting, producing only sludge where ideas for patient care should have been. And the sludge was toxic, causing her to tremble on the inside, to doubt everything she did. She said a silent prayer for a quiet night since was almost completely out of her Xanax and hadn't been able to wind down in days.

TWENTY-FOUR

AUTUMN

Mark had visibly calmed down by the time he and Autumn met up again outside of Detective McAdams's room. His cheeks were no longer flushed and his mouth betrayed the hint of a smile.

"Autumn, you were right. A bunch of other interns got prank pages this afternoon. This is all your fault. You've gotten me all worked up about Jay, and I'm seeing ghosts around every corner."

Autumn shrugged. "Who got texts?"

"Alphonso and Iman," Mark sighed. "They were paged to empty patient rooms. I ran into them arguing with the nurses on the tenth floor, who insisted they hadn't paged. Probably a third-year resident has a little too much time on his hands."

"Doesn't sound like the text you got."

"No, it doesn't." Mark's face fell. "Thanks a lot. Let's see what the detective has come up with."

It had only been three hours since they had left him, but McAdams looked much worse. His eyes seemed as if they had sunken back into his head and beads of sweat covered his forehead and upper lip. Autumn grabbed the vitals chart from the door. His temperature was now 101.

"Hey, doctors," he tried cheerfully. "I have some information fah you."

"How are you feeling? You're really developing a fever now," Autumn said, her face stern.

"I'm just not used to all this activity. It's good for me though. It'll help me get my strength back," he said, brushing her off. "I talked with some of my boys at the precinct. Your professah doesn't have a record. But one of the guys was in his neighborhood and drove by his house."

McAdams paused and tried to cough but was too weak to do anything except make a soft grunting sound. The ALS had begun to attack his diaphragm and coughing was one less thing he could do. Autumn and Mark both waited for him to catch his breath and finish.

"He does seem to have a lot of plants in his backyard. But my guy couldn't legally get onto the property without a warrant, you understand."

"We could. I mean probably not legally, but we could just go have a look," Autumn offered. The hint of a smile now completely gone, Mark's mouth dropped open in response.

"I don't know if that's really smaht. But based on what you told me, I don't think a judge would give us a warrant to search the place."

Autumn looked at Mark, her eyes pleading. He sighed.

"It's early. I bet Withering is still in his lab. Even if he is home, we can just have a quick look around the yard. But would we get into trouble if he did see us? It is trespassing, right?" Mark asked to the space between Autumn and McAdams.

Autumn answered before McAdams had a chance. "C'mon! We're practically done for the day. Let's go. Where does he live, Detective?"

"Not too fah. In Wellesley. 525 Woostah Street. Probably take you twenty-five minutes or so to drive ovah. But you didn't heah any of this from me. And you bettah just have a quick look and that's it. Don't hang around, okay?"

"Okay, and thanks so much," Autumn said. "Before we go, though, I'm going to make sure you get another antibiotic. You look like you could be getting sick again."

"I thought I was sick already." McAdams smiled.

Autumn smiled back. Of course he was sick. Everyone in the hospital was sick. When she said "sick" she was actually worried he might die in the next few days. But not if she could help it.

While Mark wrote down the address that Detective McAdams had memorized, Autumn went to a computer to order an antibiotic. She didn't know what he had exactly but hoped that vancomycin might kill it. The most likely possibilities were a now-resistant pneumonia to the levofloxacin he had been on for the last few days or an infection from the central line she had just cut out. The blood cultures would probably be back in the morning, but Autumn didn't want to wait. Her senior residents had told her early on that internship was a lesson in figuring out "sick" from "not sick." In other words, who might die in short order and who was not making an active attempt to do so. It seemed to her that despite his deceptively strong constitution, Detective McAdams was falling into the former category. She added yet another antibiotic, metronidazole, just in case he was choking down bacteria since he didn't seem to be able to generate much of a cough lately either. She sent her supervising resident a page to let him know about McAdams's fever and the two new antibiotics she had just added to his regimen. Pretty standard stuff, so she didn't expect him to have any difference of opinion on it. She also texted that she would be leaving the hospital after signing out to the on-call team.

Just as Autumn finished asking the nurse to order up the antibiotics from the pharmacy STAT, Mark ran up to her. "Let's go."

William Withering lived on a quiet, private, well-maintained residential street in Wellesley, one of the tonier Boston suburbs. The size of the house was awe-inducing. It was a large, pale yellow, two-story home with high pillars out front and an expansive backyard. Land was at a premium in and around Boston and he certainly had a lot of it.

"This place must be worth at least two million dollars," Autumn said, her jaw opening wide.

"Maybe, but it needs a good paint job."

And on closer inspection, Autumn saw that Mark was right. The paint was peeling off in several areas and small bits of concrete were chipped in conspicuous places, including the bottoms and tops of several of the grand pillars.

"How does an academic researcher afford a place like this?" Autumn wondered aloud, starting to explore the lawn connecting to the back of the house.

"He's lived in Boston a while, you know," Mark offered. "I bet fifteen years ago, this place wasn't worth nearly as much."

Autumn snorted as she looked around. Detective McAdams's cop friend was right. Withering's backyard was a veritable forest rather than a tidy English garden. Oaks and maples peppered the yard with all manner of flowering plants coming up in between. While most had lost their flowers by this time of year, several pink and white rhododendrons were still clinging to white lattice walls on either end of the sizable garden.

"What exactly are we looking for?" Mark asked, turning to look behind them, visibly nervous.

"The foxglove plant. A plant with purplish flowers."

"But what if it flowers in the summer, which it probably does, like most things around here? What does it look like without flowers on it?"

"Damn. You're right." Autumn's gaze jumped from one plant to the next, hoping something would pop out at her. "I don't really know. I think I read that the plant itself is like three to four feet high. We could look for that."

"Look around, Autumn. That could be nearly any of these."

Mark had pulled out his phone to search for a picture.

"No," Autumn suddenly insisted. "If Jay was poisoned by the flower of the plant, then it has to be flowering now, right?"

"Not if it was picked and dried three months ago," Mark offered skeptically, his eyes focused on his phone.

"True. But let's say that it wasn't. Let's say that it was fresh.

Otherwise, we would have to assume that this was being planned for months ahead of time, which maybe it was, but it'll be simpler if it wasn't." She thought about the detective shows on T.V. They never got as overly complicated as this. The same was true for the medical shows. T.V. didn't do complicated. Real life didn't do simple.

Mark looked up from his phone and flashed a picture of bright green triangular leaves at Autumn. He scrolled past and showed another with purple bulbs cascading down. "For it to flower this time of year, he would need a greenhouse, which he doesn't seem to possess."

"What about inside? That's a pretty big house, you know," Autumn said, walking toward the house.

"What the heck are you doing, Autumn?" Mark hissed.

"I'm just going to peek in some of the windows, that's all."

Mark groaned but followed her anyway.

They started from the left side of the backyard and began looking into all of the windows on the ground floor. Besides a lot of photos and plaques, Autumn didn't see anything of interest. There were a few plants but nothing that looked unlike a typical potted houseplant. And no greenhouse.

When they got to the far right of the house, they came upon a screened door entrance to the backyard mud room. Autumn tried the screen door. It didn't have a lock on it. She turned the loose doorknob—it opened instantly.

"What are you doing?!" Mark hissed more loudly.

"Shhh! I'm just going to take a quick look inside and then close the door."

Suddenly, from inside the house, there was the pounding of footsteps and before they could react, the interior door flew open.

"What are you two doing at my house?" Withering demanded, looking from Autumn to Mark and back to Autumn again, a baseball bat clutched in his hands. He glowered at Autumn, a look of recognition replacing his startled glare. "You came to my office the other day. About Jay."

"We were in the neighborhood," Autumn tried weakly.

"In twenty years, I have never seen anything like this." Withering was nearly shouting. "Were you trying to break into my house?"

"No, Dr. Withering," Mark started gently. "We had this crazy idea that we should look around your backyard for a foxglove plant."

Autumn raised her eyebrows at Mark. He just shrugged.

"Why would I have a foxglove plant?" Withering asked sincerely, slowly lowering the baseball bat.

"You wouldn't," Mark said. "We think that Jay Abrams may have ingested the foxglove plant, and we're trying to figure out where he got it. Since he worked in your lab, we thought maybe you had some."

"Well, I don't have foxglove. I'm a rhododendron fan. I like growing lilies in the summer. Anything else that grows in my garden grows wild. I've never seen foxglove growing here. And for that matter, I've never invited Mr. Abrams over."

"You didn't approve of the work he was doing," Autumn tried. She figured she was in trouble anyway. Withering didn't respond. *A deer in headlights*, Autumn thought, looking at him hard. He either really had no idea what they were talking about or he was an excellent liar.

Autumn was in a mood to presume the worst.

"He was doing stem cell research for *you*," Autumn pressed. "And as far as I know, it was going quite well," she added, putting her hands on her hips. "Perhaps you saw him as competition?"

"Oh, for goodness sakes," Withering said coolly, resting the bat like a cane by his side. "Research is a tough game. It takes years and years to be able to get grants and make a name for yourself. Your friend was barely able to write an abstract, so not much competition there. I'm not the villain here. I'm a doctor, too, you know, and I help people. That's what physician-researchers do. We're the unsung heroes of medicine. *Anyone* can treat a patient once we figure out what the treatment should be."

Autumn snorted. "By the looks of this place, you make a nice bit of coin doing it. Unsung heroes don't live in two million dollar houses in Wellesley."

"I make okay money, but nowhere near what I could make in private practice, my dear. And this house has been in my wife's family for some time," he said, shifting his weight from one foot to the other and breaking eye contact. Autumn snorted again. He was obviously lying.

"Furthermore, I don't need to explain myself to you. You broke into my house!" The coolness gone from his voice, Withering was nearly shouting again.

"What about Jay? Don't you think you should have cared a little bit about your student?" Autumn shouted back.

Mark squeezed her shoulder hard this time to let her know it was time to go. She ignored him and kept shouting. "Jay has anoxic brain injury and will never walk, talk, eat, or think again."

Withering let out a heavy sigh.

"My dear, I had nothing to do with what happened to your friend. I can't concern myself with what everyone in my lab is doing on their own time—I have my own job to do and it keeps me quite busy. All I know is Jay was a mediocre student. But I wasn't going to hold him back and I don't know anything about what happened to him. I do know that my wife will be home shortly, and I'd rather she didn't have to deal with finding you both here," Withering added, motioning for them both to get off his porch. Autumn felt hot tears gathering in her eyes.

Mark muttered, "C'mon, Autumn." He stared at Withering as he held the screen door open for her.

"She's been through a lot this week, you know," Mark said by way of explanation.

Withering looked down at his house slippers for a moment. "I'm sorry for your friend. I hope things work out for you all." And with that, he slammed his door shut.

Autumn and Mark said nothing to each other as they walked off of Withering's property. When they got to the car, Mark looked over at Autumn, who was staring straight ahead.

"You know," Mark started, a note of frustration in his voice, "you embarrassed us in front of an attending. Worse, you could have gotten us arrested."

The hot tears rolled down her flushed cheeks. She sat in silence, sniffling.

Mark softened his tone. "Autumn, do you really think Withering did something to Jay or are you just looking for someone to blame right now?"

"I don't know," she said, the act of speaking triggering

heavier tears to start falling. She had never seen anyone die before she started internship in July and now it seemed that everyone was dying. Mr. G, Jay, sort of, and maybe soon, Detective McAdams.

Mark reached over and put his arm around her. "It's okay. It's going to be okay." He paused a moment, then asked, "Do you mind if I tell you what I think?"

She shook her head.

"I think Withering is a little bit in his own world, but I don't think he would intentionally kill anyone. He takes his job seriously. He's not a fanatic, Autumn, and believe me, I've known a few fanatics in my day. Remember the red-jacketed preachers on the Plaza at the University of Florida?" He winked at her.

Autumn smiled through her sobs. She remembered. The Plaza of the Americas. Designed by Frederick Law Olmsted, Jr., the son of the man who had designed the Boston park system she drove along on her way home from the hospital. And like the Boston parks, the Plaza was open to anyone who wanted to be there. The "plaza preachers" would yell "fornicators" at all the girls in short skirts and tell anyone holding hands that they were going to straight to hell. But they reserved their most biting insults for the openly gay students. Mark would have been happy to ignore them. But Autumn wasn't. Not her style. She would march right up to them and call them out on their bullshit. She figured she was still doing that, sniffled, and smiled over at Mark.

"Does Dr. Withering seem fanatical when you really think about things?" Mark asked.

"No," Autumn admitted. "Withering is in his own world

NOT QUITE DEAD

and a dick, really, but probably wouldn't do anything to hurt anyone."

"So, let's cross Withering poisoning Jay off our differential diagnosis and see what else we've got," Mark said, starting the car.

"Let's keep him on the list, but just lower down for now," Autumn insisted, staring out the window. Surely, anyone could have tried to hurt Jay, but hadn't she heard somewhere that most victims of violent crime knew their assailants? If Jay hadn't hurt himself, then it was most likely that he knew the person who had harmed him. But she had only known Jay for a few weeks. She definitely didn't know everyone he hung out with. She decided to confine her suspects to the medical center. That was at least manageable. The police could handle the rest of the world. Maybe there was something in the lab notebook that would give her some direction if she could figure it out. Maybe she should ask Detective McAdams what to do next.

ALS hadn't affected his brain at all—just his body. That was the curse of ALS. At least the dementia patients she took care of weren't quite aware of their decline. It was a merciful, if cruel, compromise. But McAdams had a front row seat to his body's betrayal. No matter how weak his body got, he would still possess the sharp mind of a detective. Autumn focused on the trees whipping past, their formerly ordinary green leaves morphing into bright hues of yellow and orange before they met their wintry demise, and hoped the antibiotics she had prescribed had started to improve McAdams's condition. As much as his condition could be improved anyway.

TWENTY-FIVE

AUTUMN

After a brief stop to pick up a pizza at the thin crust place in Brookline, they were on the Jamaicaway, speeding around the perimeter of Olmsted Park, heading to Autumn's apartment with the smell of fresh baked dough filling the car. Mark had agreed that now was as good a time as any for him to go over Jay's lab notebook with her.

"That guy is awfully close, isn't he?" Mark asked, darting sideways glances at his rearview mirror. The dusk on the way to pick up the pizza had darkened to night and the SUV behind them was sporting tinted windows and a halfway tinted windshield. Mark tried to speed up, but the black SUV kept close.

"Damn those headlights," he said as the height of the SUV forced him to turn his rearview mirror up to deflect the glare. Mark finally saw an opening and pulled into the right lane. "Okay, so pass me then," he said to the windshield, throwing up his left hand.

Instead the SUV pulled behind him in the right lane and seemed to creep even closer than before.

"What does that guy think he's doing?" Autumn asked. "Why doesn't he just use the left lane?"

"I don't know." Mark swallowed hard. "Autumn, get his plate number from the front so we can report him. I can't look at those lights through the rearview."

Autumn turned around in her seat. "There isn't one."

"What do you mean? It's the law. There has to be one."

"Well, there isn't," Autumn said, her words becoming higher pitched as she spoke.

Her eyes widened as she watched the SUV.

"What does the driver look like?" Mark asked.

"I don't know. All I can see is that he's wearing glasses and a hat, maybe a beard. Everything is so dark."

"Shit," Mark said. "He's still on my ass."

They were near the Jamaica Pond. Centre Street was a quick cut to the left. Autumn pointed. "Get on Centre Street. There's a fire station there. We can get help."

Mark skidded across the lanes and took the left turn as two cars furiously honked, the oncoming traffic just barely missing them. The SUV was gone.

"What the hell kind of driving was that?" Autumn yelled.

"I dunno. I was trying to get rid of him. We're nearly to Centre Street now, aren't we?"

"Yeah. But I said go to the fire station. We could have gotten rid of him there and not gotten ourselves killed by oncoming traffic."

"You aren't dead," Mark replied dryly, readjusting the rearview mirror. "You're welcome. I didn't get us killed and that guy is still on the Jamaicaway."

Mark drove past the fire station and on to Autumn's apartment with slightly shaky hands and a hearty respect for the speed limit, his gaze drifting back to the rearview mirror every few seconds.

"Now do you want to call the cops?" Mark challenged.

Autumn breathed in deeply. She considered the text Mark had gotten: "back off ja." She thought about the fact that they—well, mostly she—had tried to break into a professor's house. And then there was a bad driver behind them, maybe following them. And Mark had probably broken a traffic law or two trying to avoid the SUV. What would they tell the cops? Just that, she supposed. And it didn't make any sense. Except the parts where they were breaking the law. Her stomach growled.

"No. Now I want to go home. I want to eat. And I want to figure out what is in the notebook. Then, tomorrow, when we understand what's going on, let's call the cops."

Mark sighed heavily and shook his head, his rust-colored bangs falling into his face.

Autumn's eyes again filled with tears.

"Please, Mark. I'm hungry; I'm tired. Our nerves are frazzled. We encountered a bad driver after nearly breaking into a professor's house. Is that what we would tell the cops? If we want them to take us seriously, let's have some actual information to bring to them."

Mark looked over at Autumn and then back at the road. They drove in silence the rest of the way to Autumn's apartment.

Autumn resigned herself to the fact that her apartment was in a little more disarray than usual due to her more than full-time job as a mediocre intern and now part-time job as a crappy detective. She quickly washed the few white plates and plastic-handled forks that were in the sink so that they would have something to eat with.

"So, really, what do you think was up with that SUV?" Mark asked, breaking the silence and lifting the top from the pizza box. "You don't really think it was just a bad driver."

"Well, if it wasn't a bad driver, it must have been a friend of Withering's who knew we were on to something or someone else checking out his house, right? Maybe someone followed us from there."

"But who?" Mark asked. "Who would know that we're on to something? And by the way, Autumn, we're not on to anything."

Autumn shrugged as the plate she was lowering slipped from her hand and clattered onto the dish rack. "You're right. I know that. He could have gone right past us when you changed lanes, but he didn't."

Mark frowned and grabbed a slightly grubby-looking dishtowel to dry. He stared at the towel a second before throwing it back on the counter. "That's why we're calling the cops tomorrow. The *real* cops. Give me the notebook and let me see if I can figure out what Jay was keeping records on."

Autumn quickly grabbed Jay's lab notebook off of her desk and placed it on the table next to Mark while he put a slice of the pepperoni pizza on each of their still dripping plates. Mark eyed the notebook, then his pizza. He took a big bite and chewed loudly.

"How much was the pizza?" Mark asked.

"Don't worry about it. After today, I think I owe you

pizza for the rest of the year," Autumn said, picking a piece of pepperoni off her slice and popping it into her mouth.

"Well, you know me, I won't ever turn down free food. Speaking of which, do you want to come with me to that drug company dinner this week?"

"Maybe." Autumn shrugged. "That creep Withering is speaking there though."

"He'll only talk for like a half hour or something. The rest of the time, we'll be eating steak and lobster on Zeno-Graphium's tab and flirting with, what was his name?"

"The drug rep?" Autumn asked.

Mark nodded, his mouth full.

Autumn thought for a moment and brightened. "Chris. Okay, I'll go. But I'm just warning you, I think he's straight."

Mark smiled and winked at Autumn. "He's too good-looking to be straight. You know that."

Autumn shrugged. She didn't actually want to flirt with anyone, but the idea of something besides cheap take-out food was appealing. Mark grabbed a thin paper napkin from the stack on the table and wiped the pizza grease from his hands. He quickly inspected them, then reached for the notebook.

"You said Jay was trying to grow stem cells to produce insulin?"

Autumn looked over at the notebook. "Yeah. Is that what you're seeing?"

"Everything's abbreviated, but it makes sense. 'S.H.H.,'" he read each letter out loud. "Looks like he was trying to get hedgehog proteins to stimulate insulin production in his cell lines."

"Hedgehog proteins? That sounds like something I

learned about once."

"Sonic the Hedgehog, to be exact," Mark said raising his eyebrows.

"Oh, maybe that's why it sounds so familiar. Isn't that an old school video game? Be serious."

"I couldn't be more serious." Mark instantly transformed himself from shy kid to future professor before Autumn's eyes. She hadn't seen this side of him in a while. He continued with his lecture.

"Twenty-five years ago or so, some Norwegian guy was working with fruit flies in a dark, dank, windowless lab. He discovered an obscure protein. The scientific community let him name it whatever he wanted. No one cared. A few years later, oops, they realized he had discovered one of the most essential signaling proteins in the human body. So, one of the most important proteins in human cell development, hormone production, cancer—almost anything you can think of—was named after a small blue Sega video game character popular in the nineties. By the time they realized its importance, everyone had gotten on the protein-naming bandwagon. Now there's an Indian Hedgehog, a Desert Hedgehog, you name it."

"Interesting," Autumn said, but she couldn't bring herself to care about this particular scientific footnote right now. "Does anything seem out of whack in the notebook?" she asked, pulling up a chair next to him and trying to get him to focus on Jay's notes.

"Let's see," Mark said, continuing to flip through the pages. "Standard cellular growth media, mRNA isolation, cDNA hybridization, Western blots, and an insulin level assay. All in order."

"Can you tell if it was working?"

"Well, it looks like Jay could get cells to grow, but the better they grew, the less he could get them to produce insulin."

"That's what Withering told me. So, he was telling the truth. There was nothing he wanted in that notebook, and Luba is just some nutty lab assistant?"

"Maybe. Maybe not. That's what's on the front side. Remember, about twenty pages have writing on the back side."

"And?" she asked leaning in.

"And they're from something else. They don't follow the sequence of the experiment Jay was doing. There are groupings of numbers, lot numbers or measurements, I don't know. But what I do know is that none of these notations have anything to do with growing cells or producing insulin. They don't follow the pattern of the rest of his notations."

"Maybe he decided to work on something else since the stem cell experiment wasn't going very well."

"Maybe, but he would have used another notebook for it. No one would do this. A first year college student would know better than to mix two experiments in one lab book."

"I bet Luba would know if Jay was working on something else. I'll ask her tomorrow," Autumn offered, remembering that she had meant to talk with her earlier that day anyway.

"You're on call tomorrow, and for that matter, so am I," Mark pointed out.

"Damn. I forgot. What time is it?"

"8:30."

"Ugh, we left my car in the hospital parking lot."

"I'll come get you in the morning, but I better get going. We both have to get some sleep. Before we left, I heard the admissions from today were already overflowing the emergency room. Tomorrow will be busy."

"Okay. Thanks for all your help today, Mark, and sorry for almost getting you into trouble," she said, walking him to the door and giving him a hug.

"No problem. Someone's got to provide me with some excitement in my life," he said, hugging her back.

After Mark left, Autumn threw the box of leftover pizza into the refrigerator and brushed her teeth. She gave a sideways glance at the dental floss, decided it had been a week too long since she had flossed, and opened it. She pulled on the white string and it unspooled a mere two inches before it ran out. Autumn threw the sad little piece of floss into the trash, grabbed the lab notebook and brought it to her room. Pushing the giant white down comforter aside on her unmade bed, she climbed in, propping herself up on two pillows. Not knowing quite where to begin, she held the notebook in front of her and flipped though the pages with her thumb. The photograph of Jay's brother that she had placed into the notebook fell out of the front and landed softly on her chest. She carefully put the notebook on her nightstand and picked up the picture of the wiry adolescent with thick glasses.

The picture showed a kid with a determined grin, Autumn decided. If any diabetic kid could have done it, he would have found a way. *If he would have lived*, she thought, running a finger softly over the face in the picture.

It felt uneven. Bumpy. A bumpy picture?

She ran her finger over the picture again. The left side of the picture was smooth, but the right side was slightly and unevenly raised.

Like letters. Someone had written on this photo. On purpose? By accident?

Autumn leaped out of bed and hurried to her desk. She grabbed a blank piece of paper and a pencil. Placing the paper over the photo, she carefully rubbed the pencil over the bumps. It looked like Jay's handwriting.

"Problem with," was on the far right corner. "OB mice," appeared about an inch below. That was all she could make out. Most of it was just some randomly placed squiggles and lines, too light to make up a coherent word. She tried to convince herself of a capital W and a lower case f in the space between the "problem with" and "OB mice" phrases, but wasn't sure. It didn't seem intentional. It was as if Jay didn't realize he was leaning on the photograph when he was writing. But what was he writing about? He didn't work with mice.

Autumn convinced herself that the letters "OB" were truncated from a longer word. But what? SOB? Contrary to its meaning in popular discourse, SOB meant short of breath in the hospital. Why would mice be short of breath? Better to start at the beginning of the alphabet and see what she could come up with.

BOB mice? No. JOB mice? That didn't make much sense either. MOB mice? Autumn giggled to herself at the thought of mice with fedoras and little machine guns. ROB mice? Maybe the mice had been stolen?

None of it really made much sense. In medical parlance,

OB stood for obstetrical. Maybe these mice were pregnant?

Autumn's lids were growing heavier. Weeks of sleep deprivation made it near impossible to think clearly when all her mind wanted was rest. She forced herself to picture Withering's lab again. It was a typical lab. There was nothing out of the ordinary. She tried to picture the mice that she saw. Withering's mice were fat, extremely fat. Some were even unable to walk. Obese. They were obese!

Could OB stand for obese mice? Jay was doing work in type 1 diabetes. In type 1 diabetes there was autoimmune destruction of the pancreas, which produced insulin. In short order, there was no insulin being produced and without insulin patients couldn't store glucose, instead peeing it all out. As a result, they lost weight and were thin. If Jay had any mice, they should have had type 1 diabetes and would have been thin, not fat, Autumn reasoned.

But she clearly remembered the obese mice. There were other experiments going on in the lab. Maybe these notes weren't on Jay's work.

Bleary-eyed but determined, Autumn turned her computer on and loaded her search engine. She typed in "obese mice." Hundreds of hits appeared instantly on her computer screen. In 1994 a breed of mouse had been found that was genetically predisposed to obesity. They ate and ate and ate. She read on. Apparently, it had something to do with being deficient in a hormone called leptin. Some of the mice even developed type 2 diabetes. But it turned out that hardly any human beings turned out to be leptin deficient. The mouse model didn't work in people. It was a scientific non-starter.

She pushed back from the computer screen and rubbed

her temples. It didn't make any sense. Jay wouldn't have been working with both type 1 and type 2 diabetes—they were two very different diseases even though they shared a similar name. He must have come across something in one of Withering's other experiments dealing with the OB mice.

Autumn read on. There were some researchers who had decided that, in people anyway, it wasn't leptin deficiency that was the problem, but leptin resistance that created the imbalance in obesity, not unlike the insulin resistance that was the problem in type 2 diabetes. There was currently a race to develop a leptin-sensitizing drug, but so far nothing had panned out, at least not according to her Google search.

Autumn looked at the time on her computer screen. It was nearly midnight and Mark would be coming by in five-and-a-half hours to take her to work. She needed to get to sleep, though her brain was buzzing with the thought that the obese lab mice were the key to everything. She powered down the computer and headed back to bed. She lay buried beneath her comforter, staring at the ceiling. All she could think about was how she was going to find the time tomorrow to head over to Jay's lab and talk to Luba. Being the full-time lab assistant, she was bound to know something about all of the experiments in the lab. Autumn was sure Luba would be able to tell her what was going on.

TWENTY-SIX

CASSIE

Cassie rolled to her side on the narrow, springy cot and yawned, not bothering to cover her mouth. She looked down at her watch. It was 2 a.m., and she hadn't heard from Chiwete since she had gone to her on-call room two hours earlier. Mercifully, and inexplicably, they hadn't gotten any new admissions since Cassie's arrival in the ICU at 7 a.m. the day before. She rolled out of bed and absently walked the fifty steps to the ICU.

She found Chiwete huddled over a stack of textbooks in the back charting room. "Why don't you go ahead and get a little sleep? I'll handle things for the next few hours," she offered.

"Thanks, but I can't really sleep on call. I'm too wired. I just had some coffee anyway." He pointed to an empty Styrofoam cup and turned back to his reading.

He reminded Cassie of herself when she had been an intern—intense. She was worried he would burn out (like she was?). No one could keep up a pace of being on call every third or fourth night forever. Maybe in her third year, she was finally hitting a wall. She certainly didn't have the energy she used to but felt guilty for getting the two hours of sleep on call that she already had. She had to push on. *Push, Cassie. Push,* she told herself as if trying to deliver a baby.

Out loud, she said, "Why don't you just put your feet up for a few minutes then, while I check on the patients?"

"Okay," Chiwete agreed reluctantly, lifting his feet to a nearby chair without breaking his stare on the page. "Thanks."

Cassie looked briefly at each of the giant paper grids lying on the nurses' drafting tables. Chiwete had done a great job of titrating all the blood-pressure-augmenting medications and ventilator settings, so that it looked like everyone would survive the night. She got to Room 7 just as Sue, a senior nurse doing a rare overnight shift, slipped out of the room.

"Hey, how's he doing?" Cassie pointed toward the room.

Sue shrugged. "The patient's the same. The father's looking worse though."

"Mr. Morris?"

Sue gave her a quizzical look.

"Mr. Abrams?" Cassie corrected.

"Of course, Mr. Abrams. For the past two days, nonstop, it's been Mr. Abrams. Why do you think he looks so disheveled during the day?"

"I guess I didn't think about it. I thought the mother was staying with the patient overnight," Cassie offered meekly.

"She was, up until two days ago. I think she just had

enough or maybe her husband had enough." Sue frowned. "Either way, the father's pretty much been sitting a 24-hour vigil for his son."

"Has he been all right?"

Sue raised her eyebrows, confused.

"You know, stable?"

"The patient?"

"No, the father."

Sue rolled her eyes. "Yes, he's been 'stable.' Isn't that a silly question?"

"Not really. During every family meeting, he's totally thrown a fit. He constantly seems like he's going to break."

"Well, maybe he's upset, and he has a right to be. He's not detached like the other one."

"Detached?" Now it was Cassie's turn to shoot a quizzical look. Sue had said the word like it was a bad thing. Being calm, cool, and collected—was that the same as detached? That was what was expected of everyone in the hospital. Detachment. Decorum. How could they function if everyone was having emotional outbursts all the time?

Sue sighed. "You see the family for all of five minutes a day and make an assessment. It's either Christine or I who are in there for hours. Believe me, the father is a good guy who is constantly being put down by the new husband. Looks can be deceiving, just remember that."

Cassie stiffened, embarrassed that Sue didn't think she knew what was going on. Maybe she didn't. She pictured Larry Abrams, always so physically close to his son in a way that Pierce never was when they gathered together in Jay's room. Pierce would stand, Pierce would pace, or Pierce wouldn't be there at all. Maybe that's what she preferred about him.

"I'll go in and talk to him," Cassie announced and turned just as Sue shrugged her shoulders, clearly unimpressed.

Gently sliding the glass door open, Cassie walked into the room. Larry Abrams had one of his son's hands cupped between both of his. He startled and dropped the hand as Cassie walked in. Cassie gave a quick nod to Mr. Abrams and then moved her gaze to the monitor above Jay's bed. Heart rate, blood pressure, respiratory rate, and oxygenation were all normal. Couldn't have been better. Cassie allowed herself a moment of pride before recalling that her patient was in a vegetative state in spite of his perfect vital signs. She cast her glance down from the monitor. Larry Abrams's hair was matted and greasy, his face darkened by several days' growth of facial hair. When she finally made eye contact, his were red-rimmed and puffy.

"Sorry, I must have drifted off for a sec," Larry whispered.

"No, please don't apologize. I'm sorry for disturbing you," Cassie whispered back.

"You're not. Do you have any new information?"

There was so much hope in Larry Abrams's voice.

She shook her head, taking a fortifying breath while doing so. "No, sorry. I just was going by, checking in on everyone. Are you doing okay?"

Larry smiled weakly. "I'm not the patient. I only care if my son is going to be okay."

"He's stable," Cassie offered and immediately regretted it. The well-worn doctor tropes consistently misfired on Larry Abrams.

"But that's not necessarily a good thing," Larry challenged.

"No, it's not," she agreed, pulling up a chair to sit beside him. Cassie's shoulders slumped downward. She rested her elbows on her lap and placed her face in her hands.

"He's an amazing boy." Larry looked down at his weather-worn sneakers. "Man, I mean."

"I've been hearing," Cassie replied, smiling gently.

"You know, he graduated first in his class in high school. He got nearly a full scholarship to Harvard and then the M.D.-Ph.D. scholarship that pays for everything. He never had to ask me for a thing. He's so proud. He likes to take care of things for himself. Real independent. His brother Nathan needed lots of help, but not Jay."

Cassie looked down at her shoes, shiny black clogs that reflected the harsh ICU lights back up at her. She almost never thought about who her patients had been before they arrived in the hospital, weak and broken. Jay would never be who he was before. And that was, at least in part, her fault. She looked back up at Larry, nodding for him to go on.

"Nathan got diabetes when he was five years old. Jay helped out a lot when Nathan was younger, even checking his own blood sugars to make Nathan feel okay about it. But when Jay became a teenager, well, you know how teenagers are. He wasn't around as much for his brother. He never let himself live that down after Nate died."

Cassie swallowed hard. Maybe her penance would be to learn about who her patient had been, who his family had been. Maybe this was more important than sleep. "What exactly happened to Nate?"

Larry looked at Cassie, his eyes wide and sad. "He stopped taking his insulin one day, but didn't let anyone know. By the time we realized how sick he was, it was too late. Jay thought it was that Nate wanted to do the things he was doing. He didn't want to be diabetic anymore." Larry sucked in a deep breath. "Nate was just a kid. His mother and I should have been double-checking his sugars. But he had been adjusting his own insulin based on his blood sugar readings for eighteen months all by himself and was doing great. He was only twelve years old."

"I'm sorry," Cassie said, reaching over to lay her hand on his. She quickly added in her practiced words, "That must have been very hard for all of you," immediately regretting it.

Larry flinched, but he continued. "Marsha and I blamed each other. It destroyed us."

One of the alarms began to beep rhythmically from a nearby room. Cassie turned to it, trying to decide if it was an IV alarm, a ventilator alarm, or something else, but one of the nurses quickly quieted it, so she turned back to Larry.

"It sounds like Nathan really inspired Jay's work," Cassie offered gently. The words flowed naturally this time.

Larry nodded, blinking to force back the tears. "He was doing good work."

"He was," Cassie agreed.

Larry shook his head. "How'd I ever get a boy like Jay?"

"Good genes?" she offered sincerely.

"More like good luck." Larry shook his head and released his hand from Cassie's, clasping his son's again.

Cassie pointed to the pale blue pleather-covered chair Larry was sitting in. "You know, that chair can recline, if you'd like to get some sleep."

Larry smiled at her. Possibly for the first time. "I know. I will in a little while. Thanks for talking with me."

Cassie returned the smile. "No problem. Thank you for talking with me."

Cassie wasn't sure if talking with Larry Abrams had made her feel better or worse. She knew more about Jay and more about his father. And his brother. Tragedy and loss. Too much of it. The acid in her stomach was churning, giving her a sour taste on the back of her tongue. She swallowed it down. She had more patients to round on.

Thirty minutes later, finished with her patient rounds, Cassie made her way to the charting room in the back of the ICU. Chiwete had moved on to the thickest, dog-eared, blue ICU textbook with his feet still up on the chair. The book was read so rarely that the cover had a thin layer of dust on it, making it more of a gray-blue color.

"How can you read at three in the morning?" Cassie asked him.

"I don't have time to study otherwise," he answered matter-of-factly, placing the book onto the desk with a small sigh. "There are only twenty-four hours in a day."

"And you're up for most of them it seems." Cassie smiled supportively.

"I want to do a good job."

"Well, you've been doing a great job so far." Cassie collapsed into the chair next to him. "What do you want to do with your life anyway?"

"You mean after residency?" Chiwete clarified as Cassie nodded. "I'm going to specialize in infectious disease and hopefully work internationally."

"Huh. What inspired you to do that?"

"I grew up in Nigeria. The real problem everywhere else except for the West is infectious diseases, malaria, tuberculosis, HIV. Those kill more people than what we worry about here: heart disease and cancer. But the world is a small place. Those diseases can touch us all and if we don't do anything about it, they will be just as prevalent in America, too."

Cassie nodded and paused for a second to consider that sobering fact. "Do you want to work in Nigeria?"

"Maybe. Or maybe I'll go explore somewhere else. You know, Nigerians are sort of like citizens of the world. I've been thinking about Russia lately. They don't like to admit it, but their TB and HIV problems are exploding right now."

"Hmmm, until right now, I thought you wanted to do critical care."

Chiwete had a mock-frightened look on his face. "Why?"

"Well, you're really good at it. And you might be the first person to have picked up that ICU text in years." Cassie waved at the dusty tome.

Chiwete's smile revealed his upper teeth at the compliment. "Who knows where I'll wind up and what they'll expect me to be an expert in. I may need to do it all one day. But ICU in the U.S. most definitely isn't for me."

"Me neither," Cassie agreed wholeheartedly. She had three years of gastroenterology fellowship to look forward to after she finished residency, and she was hoping to line up a place where there would be lots of research time. She admitted she could use a year or two away from death.

Chiwete leaned back into his chair, the intense look back on his face. "It's funny. In most of the countries in the world, death after a long suffering is welcomed. I went to college in Europe and over there, it's seen as an inevitable part of life. Here, in the U.S., it's an option we ask people if they'd like to exercise."

Cassie just stared at him. It was as though he had read her mind. How could anyone accept death in the U.S.? Death was bad and bad things weren't supposed to happen. Ever. She nodded for him to continue.

"We try to make everything out to be a choice in America. Choice is good, but not everything in health care can be a choice. Death isn't a choice. It's a fact."

Everything can't be a choice. Chiwete's words rang true to Cassie and not just in the ICU. She remembered her rotations in medical school. In pediatrics, parents wanted to be able to choose when or even if to vaccinate their children, public health be damned. In obstetrics, women wanted their birth plans adhered to no matter what. Even as their babies lay dying within them, they needed to be convinced to go to the operating room when it deviated from their choices. But life and death were more out of their control than most Americans felt comfortable admitting.

"Do you think Jay Abrams as good as dead?" Cassie asked softly, sounding more like the intern than the resident now.

Chiwete gave her a wan smile. "Doctors are too afraid to answer that question too?" He shrugged and reached for the textbook.

Cassie nodded in agreement and left Chiwete to his reading. Settled back in her call room, Cassie dug into her overnight bag. One Xanax left. She would need it to sleep when she got home tomorrow. And then what? She pulled out her wallet. In the front pocket was a business card. Cassie fingered the edges. Bright green and deep purple writing drew her attention to the Zeno-Graphium logo prominent in the upper left corner—a G and a Z intertwined in the shape of an Erlenmeyer flask. Cassie ran her finger over the raised writing in the middle of the card and read the name: Christopher Delano. The senior pharmaceutical representative who had offered to get her anything she needed.

TWENTY-SEVEN

AUTUMN

The words leaped out of the computer screen:

Gram-positive cocci in clusters
2/2 bottles positive
Speciation testing to be completed in 24 hours

A chill ran down Autumn's spine as she grabbed Detective McAdams's vitals sheet. She had been right to administer the antibiotics. According to the blood cultures she had drawn, he had bacteria in his blood and since it had taken less than twenty-four hours to grow out, it was likely a high-grade bacteremia. Thankfully, his temperature had come down and his pulse and blood pressure remained stable overnight.

Her pager went off.

Call me re: McAdams bacteremia. Vinay. Ext 3962.

She peeked into McAdams's room before placing the vitals book back in the basket attached to his door. He seemed to be sleeping soundly. Autumn felt a small sense of pride as she dialed Vinay's extension. He had just taken over as her supervising resident and was undoubtedly calling to compliment her on adding the antibiotics yesterday.

"Dr. Krishnamurthy here," she heard on the other end of the line.

"Hey, it's Autumn. You're here early. I thought residents didn't get in till seven or so."

"I like to come in early and review everyone's labs. Anyway, did you see the positive blood cultures on McAdams yet?"

"I did. I thought he looked bad yesterday, so I added on vancomycin and metronidazole, just in case. He's already on levofloxacin for his pneumonia."

"Good. What do you think you are treating?"

"Well, considering that he had a central line in for five days and the site looked a little red, I would suspect a line infection and knowing the high rate of resistance in the hospital, I would say MRSA until proven otherwise."

"Sounds reasonable," Vinay agreed. "So, keep the vancomycin on board, but do you think he needs the metronidazole for anything?"

Autumn took in a deep breath. Adding on additional therapies was pretty basic. Remembering to take away the unnecessary ones was a higher-level skill. "Well, I think he's aspirating, but since we know it's a gram-positive organism, I guess he doesn't need the metronidazole for now. I'll get rid of it. I'm gonna finish pre-rounding, unless there's anything else."

Autumn knew she sounded curt, but she had a lot to do this morning and Vinay definitely wasn't excited enough about her foresight, merely criticizing the use of the additional antibiotic she hadn't thought to discontinue yet.

Vinay sighed audibly. "Okay, Autumn. I'll see you on rounds."

Autumn hung up the phone, a little more loudly than she had intended to. She would have gotten rid of the metronidazole even if Vinay hadn't told her to. It gave people horrible nausea and if her patient didn't need it, of course she would have discontinued it. She did think to add the antibiotics on early, didn't she? If not for her good judgment, McAdams would have landed right back in the ICU. With Jay. She shook off the thought quickly and marched back to her patient's room.

She knocked softly on McAdams's door and walked in to examine him. He had slept through the knocking, so she shook his shoulder gently. Then she shook it harder. He stirred.

"Good morning, Detective," she sang, still proud of herself for giving him the right therapy based solely on her developing intuition. Maybe she really could do this.

"Good mahning," he replied in a low voice, then, realizing who it was, added, "How'd it go last night?"

Autumn paused for a moment, recalling the events that had been pushed briefly away by the few hours of sleep she'd gotten. "Not great. Withering caught us outside his house. Actually, he caught me trying to get inside his house," she confessed.

"What!" McAdams tried to muster an angry tone but could really only produce a mildly annoyed whisper.

"That was dumb, I know. Sorry. We didn't find what we were looking for. I may have the wrong guy. I still think something is going on in the lab. William Withering's lab," she added to be clear.

"Hmmm," the detective replied, still in the fetal position and drifting back off to sleep.

"Sorry for rambling. You're not feeling very well today, are you?"

He smiled slightly and shook his head.

"You have an infection in your blood, but we're treating it." Autumn briefly considered not sharing the remainder of the details from the previous night. McAdams was sick. What was he going to do about the SUV that had followed her? The chill ran down her spine again. She closed her eyes and sucked in a breath through her teeth. Who else could she tell?

"And we may have been followed by an SUV. I think the driver was just trying to scare us. I think maybe he followed us from Withering's house."

McAdams turned back to Autumn, his eyes now wide open. He shook his head.

"Doc, yah need to stop what you ah doing. You ah going to get hurt. This isn't yah job."

Autumn nodded.

McAdams continued to stare at her. Hard.

"Write this down." He wagged his finger weakly at her. "Detective Defranco. The numbah at his precinct is six, one, seven …" McAdams panted for breath and paused. "Three, fah, three, fah-tee five hundred. Tell him the story. Tell him I told you to call." McAdams finally broke his stare, closed his eyes, and used what was left of his energy to roll onto his side.

"I will," Autumn promised, slipping her pen into the chest pocket of her white-coat and the paper she had written all of her patients' vital signs on and now the detective's information into her side pocket. "How about I take a quick listen to your heart and lungs and let you get some rest?"

"Okay, Doc," he answered in a whisper.

Autumn produced her stethoscope from another one of her white-coat pockets and listened quickly as she had promised. After hearing nothing abnormal, she pulled the numerous inadequately thin sheets and blankets over the detective. "I'll stop by a little later to check on you," she said, but he was already in a deep sleep.

Autumn made her way to the elevator to examine the rest of her patients on other floors. When the doors finally opened, Autumn quickly stepped to the side as a gurney was being wheeled out.

She let out a small gasp. It was Jay, motionless, the beeping monitors announcing his stability. Cassie, Sue, and Larry Abrams trailed behind the transport tech pushing the stretcher out of the elevator.

"Hey," Autumn finally figured out how to say as they passed by her.

"Oh, hey," Cassie managed back, looking exhausted. Autumn wondered if Cassie was post-call. Her eyes were downcast and she was in the back of the procession instead of leading the way, as Autumn would have expected.

"He's coming out of the ICU?" Autumn asked her stupidly as she walked past.

"He's stable. So stable, in fact, that Dr. Goldberg has

charged the ICU team with still caring for him as an 'outlier' for continuity of care." Cassie shook her head, clearly unhappy with this arrangement.

Autumn frowned on Cassie's behalf. One of the few comforts of the ICU was that there were only ten beds. That meant you could only have ten patients. Except when Dr. Goldberg was attending. He was a hard worker who expected the same from everyone else. If there was a relationship built up by the ICU team and the patient was expected to be discharged from the hospital soon, he insisted the ICU team continue caring for the patient. Even though, by all rights, if the patient was on a regular medical floor, the ICU team could pass off responsibility to a floor team.

"It's okay," Cassie shrugged. "I have to get going." She waved toward the stretcher and its entourage as it disappeared from view.

"I'll see you later," Autumn blurted out after her, cursing under her breath as the elevator doors closed before she could get in.

After writing down her last patient's vital signs, she flipped the page over to reveal Detective Defranco's number. She spent at least ten minutes on hold with the precinct to find out that Detective Defranco was not in. The officer on the other end of the line wanted to know if this was an emergency, was she in any immediate danger? Autumn glanced around at the doctors, nurses, medical assistant, medical students, all illuminated by the unceasing fluorescent lights. She felt pretty safe right now, she admitted to the officer. He let her know the detective would call her back when he was able.

At noon, Autumn got the results from the lab. McAdams was confirmed to have MRSA. Methicillin-Resistant Staphylococcus Aureus, one of the most feared bacteria in the hospital due to its aggressiveness and the dearth of antibiotics able to treat it. Though it was called "methicillin-resistant," the name of a toxic antibiotic no longer used, that usually meant the bacteria was resistant to almost all antibiotics. When the MRSA came in the blood-infection variety, vancomycin was still the best option. Even though some patients developed a skin reaction to it, if it was given slowly enough, that usually didn't happen. There were other antibiotics they could use, but the hospital tried to avoid them because they were either incredibly expensive or potentially toxic to the patient. Hopefully the vanco would take care of the infection. Since he was on the right antibiotic, she hoped he still would be able to leave the hospital in a few days. McAdams would be the rare ICU patient who was discharged in his usual state of health (or illness in his case). If McAdams was the exemplar of an ICU success story, Jay was just the opposite.

Autumn still had one more lead to track down for Jay. She had told Detective McAdams that she would contact his friend, and she had. She had told him that she would let the professionals handle this, and she would do that, too. She wouldn't do anything that took her away from the medical center. But she still wanted to talk to Luba about the notations Jay had made about the OB mice. And technically, Luba was on the medical center's campus. There were people everywhere. It was safe.

Autumn approached Vinay as he was heading down the hall to noon conference and its accompanying lunch. Since he had been efficient on rounds and quite amenable to her ideas, she had decided she would push her luck.

"Hey, Vinay, can I ask you for a favor?" she called after him.

"Sure," he said, still charging down the hall. Lunch waited for no resident.

"Will you hold my pager for, like, thirty minutes? I need to run an errand down the street."

"Autumn, you're admitting. Can't you run the errand on another day?"

"Not really. Look, I haven't gotten any admissions yet and all my patients are stable. I'll owe you, okay?"

"McAdams is stable?"

"Yes. He's got MRSA. It just came back from the lab. He's on vanco and his temp and other vitals are normalizing. I'll make it quick. How about twenty minutes?"

"Okay," Vinay said, shaking his head to indicate his disapproval. "I sincerely hope you are doing something important," he mumbled as she handed him her pager.

Her good mood evaporated. She was plenty sick of not having a minute to herself. Other people got to leave their workplaces for lunch, at least sometimes, she reasoned. What was the big deal? She was leaving the hospital for twenty minutes out of the twenty-four hours she was going to be there. Well, maybe a little more than twenty minutes. Her stride became a little more buoyant as she charged toward the revolving glass door and glorious sunshine welcoming her to the outside world.

It was a crisp fall day that portended the coming of winter, and one of the most beautiful days Boston had seen in weeks. But Autumn barely noticed as she quickened her pace toward the grand marble buildings. Moving fast was a great antidote to the cold. If she really pushed herself, she could get there in five minutes. Then back in five, which would give her ten minutes to talk with Luba. That was all she needed if Luba was forthcoming, and Autumn couldn't think of a reason why she wouldn't be. After all, she had given her the notebook. Autumn briefly considered that Luba had absolutely no reason to trust her, but Luba seemed to really care for Jay, and hopefully that would help her overcome any distrust she might have.

Though her legs were scissoring rapidly, her too-full white-coat pockets were causing her to move nearly without an arm swing as she kept her elbows tucked in closely to her sides for fear of losing the contents of her coat. She wasn't getting to the collection of lab buildings as fast as she hoped she would and she figured she looked rather silly. But not as silly, she decided, as the well-groomed man with the "Stop Stem Cell Research" sign marching up and down the sidewalk. She didn't have the time to argue with him but somehow felt compelled to. Her annoyance from having to ask her resident for a furlough like she was a prisoner bubbled up to the surface as anger. Just as she had in her undergraduate days, when the red-jacketed Plaza Preachers shouted "fornicator" at her because her shorts were short or her shirt was figure-flattering, Autumn couldn't just keep going. The man, with his button down shirt buttoned all the way up wasn't paying any attention to her, but she was in such a foul mood, he may just as well have been shouting directly at her.

"Idiot," she called out as she raced past him. It wasn't

quite a nuanced argument, but it was the only thing she figured she had time for at the moment.

"Save the innocent," he called back.

Autumn felt like calling back "that's what I'm trying to do," but she thought of it too late. She began to breathe more heavily and threw her shoulders back. That *was* what she was trying to do. Jay had ingested something, and it wasn't like he was a little kid who would take candy from a stranger. Someone he knew must have given him the foxglove and told him it was okay or maybe secretly slipped it to him. Luba would know who that might have been. She probably spent more time with him than anyone else. Luba was her last hope for any leads.

Not having really exercised since internship started, Autumn found herself breathless upon entering the building, her hair spilling out of its ponytail and sticking to the sweat beading up on the sides of her face. The burly guard eyed her suspiciously.

"Yes?" he asked, staring her down.

"I'm here to see Withering, Dr. Withering, lab 410," she panted, holding up her hospital ID, hanging from a chain around her neck.

"Sign in," he pointed to the book.

She half printed, half scrawled her name quickly and headed for the elevator bay. She looked down at her watch. Seven minutes left. She hoped that Withering would be out to lunch otherwise she didn't know how she would be able to get any information from Luba. The last time she was there, Luba had quieted down when Withering had appeared, and given the encounter at his house, if he were there now, he probably wouldn't let Autumn set foot in the lab.

She strode quickly but carefully down the corridor to lab 410. She knew enough not to run in a lab building. You never knew who would be carrying what in breakable test tubes.

Most of the doors to the labs were closed, including those of rooms 410 and 412. Autumn knocked softly on both of them, with no response. She knocked harder. Still nothing. She tried to turn the handle of room 412, but it didn't move at all. Locked. She then tried the handle on room 410, assuming it would be locked, too. Everyone gone out to lunch. And yet, it turned! The lights were all off except for dim fluorescent bulbs above the mice cages casting very large shadows from the slow moving, obese mice. She had absolutely remembered that correctly, and she congratulated herself.

"Hello?" she called out.

She flipped on the light switch by the door. The large overhead fluorescent lights crackled on. At the far end of the lab was the large mahogany desk belonging to Dr. Withering—a gold nameplate announcing that fact. Nearer to the door was a small, badly chipped light wood desk with two drawers toward one side. A few papers were scattered on top of it and in the far right corner was a faded black and white picture of an older wrinkled woman and several very skinny blonde children in front of a building with several Russian-looking onion domes. Luba's desk, Autumn reasoned. She had about three minutes to either go searching for Luba or just look through the desks. Autumn decided to use her time to pick over her small, chipped desk in search of something useful.

The pages on top turned out to be bills. They weren't even lab-related bills, only her gas, electric, and cell phone.

On paper. Well, Autumn figured, not everyone did online bill pay. Some people actually had free time. Autumn opened the creaky side drawer of the desk, cringing as it screeched. It was filled with hanging folders, labeled with Cyrillic letters. Of course.

"Shit," she cursed under her breath.

She closed the top drawer and opened the bottom one. At the front of the drawer were two brown-colored glass bottles, labeled in Russian with a smiling woman's face on the front. Autumn opened one of the bottles. They didn't look like any medication she could readily identify. There was also a cardboard box of sugar substitute. Autumn opened that. It was filled with small yellow packets that looked very similar to the ones Autumn had resolved to start using once she went on her diet. Tomorrow.

Behind the box, there were two sets of keys on plastic fluorescent pink and green key chains. Autumn picked them up and held them side-by-side. There were five identical keys on each of the rings. Would Luba miss one set? Autumn hoped not, slipped the pink ring into her bulging white coat pocket, and returned the green one, hoping the keys opened the lab so she could come back when she had more time. She reached for her wallet in the back pocket of her scrubs and took out one of the business cards she gave to her clinic patients. It had her pager number on it.

"Luba," she wrote on the back. "I borrowed a set of keys. Call me if you need them back. Thanks, Autumn (remember me? Jay's friend)."

She put the card on top of the box of sugar substitute packets and closed the drawer. It was already 12:25 p.m.

She was supposed to have been back at the hospital by now. There would be no chance of talking to Luba today.

Unless she called her. The cell phone bill! She reached for the bill on top of the desk, quickly scribbled down Luba's number and address onto another one of her business cards, and slipped it back into her wallet.

Autumn raced back to the noon conference room. She was ten minutes later than she told Vinay she would be and guessed he was not going to let it slide. The speaker was well underway. There was a rheumatologist giving a talk on scleroderma. It looked interesting and she felt a slight pang of regret for having missed it. But as her fingers traced the outline of the pink key ring, the regret evaporated. It had been a productive, if brief, thirty minutes. Okay, maybe it had been closer to forty. She spotted Vinay leaning against the wall in the back of the room and continued her speed walk over to him.

"Hey," she whispered to Vinay, breathless.

Vinay, not breaking his gaze away from the lecturer, unclipped her beeper from his scrubs and placed it firmly in Autumn's palm. "Here," he whispered angrily. "You have two new admissions in the ER and two of your patients need more potassium and one needs an order for hemorrhoid cream. The nurse made it sound like a national state of emergency, so you better get on it or she'll be on your ass all day. Like a hemorrhoid." He turned to Autumn with raised eyebrows.

"Okay." Autumn shrugged, no longer in a mood to fight. "Thanks for holding the pager."

"You're welcome," Vinay snarled and turned his

attention back to the speaker.

Her stomach was starting to growl as she walked out of the noon conference room. *I did just do some exercise,* she reasoned and ducked back in for a slice of pepperoni, its cheese starting to congeal unpleasantly. Her admissions and the hemorrhoid cream would have to wait another five minutes, she thought, biting down hard into the cold pizza.

TWENTY-EIGHT

CASSIE

"Extremely unlikely to recover any meaningful function and rather impossible that he would make a full recovery," Dr. Maryam Ebadi reported to Cassie at the nurses' station in the ICU.

"Did you speak to the family about this?" Cassie asked, hopeful that she had.

"Of course, why wouldn't I have?"

Cassie shrugged. "Sometimes consulting specialists are reluctant to give bad news and prefer that the primary team does it." *The resident was usually stuck having to do it*, Cassie added silently.

"Right, well, being a neurologist, I have quite a bit of experience in breaking bad news of this sort."

"How did they take it?"

"Not well, but I imagine they were expecting as much, weren't they?"

Cassie nodded in agreement, wondering if Larry Abrams

had given Dr. Ebadi as hard a time as he had given her. She thanked Dr. Ebadi, hoping that this second opinion was the last the family needed to move ahead with discharging Jay Abrams.

Cassie looked around the ICU, and it seemed as if everything was under control. Brooke was watching as Mei was putting in an arterial line into a patient's wrist to monitor his blood pressure. Though she seemed to have just started, she was almost done and it seemed like Brooke was loath to find anything to criticize.

"I'm going to head out," Cassie called to Brooke from outside the room.

"Okay," Brooke said, breaking her singular focus and possible opportunity to find fault with Mei. "Can you check on Abrams on the medical floor on your way out?"

"I was just going to do that. The neurologist just gave them some bad news, and I need to see what, if anything, they've decided about him."

"I bet they're going to want to PEG him," Brooke said, referring to a tube inserted into the stomach through the skin, opening to the outside world, and used to feed patients who had lost the ability to eat. "You should hurry up and call GI to put it in tomorrow, otherwise we're going to be babysitting him forever. No nursing home will take him with a temporary nasal feeding tube. He needs some permanent hardware."

"What would you want?" Cassie asked softly.

"For myself? If I were a vegetable?" Brooke looked as if she had just tasted sour milk.

Cassie nodded.

"Let me go, for Chrissakes. Who would want to go on

like that? Ugh." She shuddered.

"Then why do you want to shove a PEG into Abrams?" Cassie asked mimicking Brooke's shudder.

"I don't. I want to get him the heck off our service and have one less patient to worry about and only a PEG tube can accomplish that. Unless the family is ready to send him off to hospice," Brooke added coolly.

"Maybe I'll go see if they do want hospice," Cassie said, surprising herself. She wasn't sure she had ever recommended hospice to a patient or a patient's family. Better to call a palliative care consult and let them handle that sort of thing.

"Good luck." Brooke snorted.

"You don't think they will?"

"Look around, Cass. Half the patients·in the ICU right now should be in a hospice, but their families can't do it. They think the next brilliant doctor will find a cure for dying or that God will perform a miracle. How many miracles have you seen so far?"

"Not many."

"None?" Brooke asked, raising her eyebrows.

"None," Cassie admitted.

"If the families could see what we see every day, they wouldn't want a PEG tube for their loved one. Ask the residents and nurses here what they would want for themselves. It's not a PEG tube."

"Maybe we need to do a better job of explaining things, then."

Brooke shrugged. "Good luck," she repeated and turned back to Mei.

"Done," Mei announced, pointing to the monitor

showing a beautiful wave-like arterial line tracing.

"Good job," Brooke offered flatly. "But you got blood everywhere. You better clean it up before the nurses throw a fit."

Cassie tried to shoot a supportive half smile to Mei before she turned away, not sure if she saw it. Brooke was a tough resident to work under, at times tougher than Cassie was. But she was right about Abrams. When Cassie really thought about it, she wouldn't want a PEG put inside her if she couldn't think or feel anymore. But what if it were her parents? What if she had to make the decision to let them die? Could she do it? What did they want for themselves? She didn't know. They had never talked about it. They were Catholic. Pope John Paul had had a PEG tube before he died, she reminded herself. But the Pope died at the Vatican, his home, not a hospital. He had drawn the line somewhere. At the end, there were probably no IV antibiotics and probably no ventilator he had to be attached to. How did he know when to stop? Why hadn't he left better directions for the rest of us?

Cassie got off the elevator on the tenth floor where they had moved Jay Abrams earlier that morning. The door to his room was closed. Cassie wondered what was going on inside. Unlike the sliding glass doors in the ICU, which she had become accustomed to in the last month, the rooms on the regular medical floors had heavy metal doors. She heard raised male voices inside. They hadn't heard her knocking or possibly had chosen to ignore it. The beauty of the opaque door. She decided to go ahead and open it anyway.

Larry and Pierce were standing at the far end of the room, their noses inches away from each other. Marsha was sitting next to Jay's bed, sobbing, her head buried in a tissue.

"What do you have against my son?" Larry roared.

"Nothing, Larry. I understood Jay. Maybe I just understood him better than you did."

"Do, Pierce. He's not past tense yet."

"Fine. Frankly, it doesn't matter to me what you want to *do*."

Pierce shook his head as he passed Cassie on his way out of the room, mumbling something about going for coffee. Cassie took a deep breath in and exhaled slowly.

"Should I come back?" she asked, hoping they would say "yes."

"No, please stay," Larry said, collecting himself. "We just got some news from the neurologist that we need to discuss with you."

"Is that what you were arguing about?" Cassie asked, already knowing the answer.

"I want to take my son home with me and care for him there. Pierce wants to put him in an institution. He doesn't think I can handle it, which is not true, but also not his concern," Larry explained.

Marsha wiped at her nose with a well-used tissue and looked up at Cassie and her ex-husband. "If you take him, he'll be far away from me. Pierce has already found a very good place near the city. They would take excellent care of Jay."

Larry opened his mouth to answer his ex-wife when Cassie quickly intervened.

"How would you be able to care for him at home?" Cassie asked Larry, trying to sound concerned rather than confrontational.

Larry shook his head. "I don't know yet. But I don't want my son institutionalized. He wouldn't have wanted that. It sends chills down my spine just to think about it, let alone me having to see him in a place like that."

Marsha started crying again. The tissue disintegrating as she dabbed at her eyes.

"Doctor," Larry started, "the neurologist said to ask you about a permanent feeding tube for Jay since he won't be able to eat or drink anything and can't leave the hospital with the temporary tube you have going down his nose. She said you could arrange that while he's already here in the hospital."

Cassie took another deep breath in, recalling her conversation with Brooke. "We certainly could. But I have to ask if that is something you think Jay would have wanted?"

Larry intensified his gaze at Cassie. "What is the alternative?"

"Not to put one in," she said simply.

Marsha looked up again, staring at Cassie, gripping the small white pieces of tissue between her hands as if in prayer.

"I thought you said, and the neurologist said, that the tube in his nose couldn't stay in much longer. He could get a sinus infection or it could come out and there wouldn't be any doctors around to put it back in when he leaves."

"That's true. And if that happened, you could allow nature to take its course." Cassie swallowed hard, not sure where her words were coming from. She wanted to start crying, too, after seeing the horror on Marsha's face her last statement provoked.

"Let him starve?" Marsha shook as she whispered, her

eyes getting wide.

"What the hell are you talking about?" Larry raised his voice in a way that was becoming very familiar to Cassie and not nearly as threatening as it used to feel. His original attack on Pierce notwithstanding, the kindness in Larry's tired eyes led her to think that when it came to everyone except his ex-wife's husband, the guy was all bluster.

"We can call in the palliative care specialists, but I don't think he would feel discomfort if it came to that."

Marsha and Larry seemed stunned into silence by what she had just said and stared at her blankly. Cassie somehow found the words to keep going.

"Why don't I have someone from hospice come and talk with you? This is their area of expertise, and I feel like I'm getting you both all worked up because I'm not able to explain these things very well. At the very least, they might be able to offer you some help to take him home," Cassie tried, meeting Larry's gaze.

That seemed to diffuse the thick tension in the room. The temperature on Cassie's face felt as if it had dropped a full degree as Larry sat down next to Marsha. Cassie was relieved to have the two sets of eyes off of her as they looked at each other instead.

"Help?" Marsha asked.

"Home health aides, nurses. They work with the hospice to allow people to be cared for at home."

Larry looked up at Cassie. His eyes stared into the middle distance and the corners of his mouth turned downward connecting with deep lines that Cassie swore hadn't been on his face when she had first met him.

"All right. Let them come and talk with us," Larry said

and Marsha nodded her assent. "If they can give me help to take him home, I'll listen."

Thinking more of herself, Cassie asked, "Would it be at all helpful if the hospital chaplain came to sit with you?"

Marsha and Larry looked at each other again. "It's been a while for me," Marsha said. "I imagine for you, too, Larry?"

Larry nodded.

"A rabbi, though," Marsha corrected. "Sure, why not?"

"Okay, I'll put a call in to the on-call rabbi right away," Cassie said finally and hurried out. "I'm sorry," she added as she tried to close the door quietly behind her.

Mustering those two words as the door was closing was the best Cassie could do by way of an apology. She was sorry for what the Abrams family had to go through, but she was sorrier still that she had kept Jay Abrams's code going for as long as she had. "A vegetable," Brooke had called him, and she was right. Cassie had taken a bright, young medical student and turned him into a vegetable. After she called the social worker, hospice, and the rabbi for the Abrams family, she felt her ears perk up with every beep from the monitors at the nurses' station. They were so loud. She could usually ignore them, but now each beep rattled her nerves. She felt beads of sweat pop up on her forehead. She needed to leave. Her heart was beating too fast and her jaw began to throb again. She ran her finger across her gum line and winced when a bolt of electricity shot through her jaw to the back of her head. A bad tooth? When had she last been to the dentist? She couldn't recall. She needed to relax. Get a good night's sleep. Making her way to the hospital lobby, she dug her wallet out of her bag and found the Zeno-Graphium card the rep had given her.

She read the card: Christopher Delano. He seemed nice enough. For a pharma rep. She would tell him she needed the medication for an indigent patient who couldn't afford her meds. Surely, it was within Zeno-Graphium's largesse to help a poor patient out, Cassie snorted to herself, dialing his number.

TWENTY-NINE

CASSIE

Cassie's feet felt leaden as her heart continued to race. Chris had graciously offered to walk with Cassie to his car to retrieve the samples. Cassie wished she didn't have to keep talking to him. Every time she opened her mouth she was overcome with a wave of nausea. Every time she closed it, her jaw ached.

"You guys have a really tough job," she heard Chris saying. He was going on and on about how hard residents work and the hours they put in. She wasn't really listening. Just staring straight ahead, breathing deeply through her nose. This was illegal. Sure, taking the initial Xanax her patient had given her was wrong, but it wasn't like she had stolen it. But now a drug rep was giving her meds for a fictitious patient. Would she have to give him the patient's fake identity, too? She wasn't sure she could do that. What if he checked it out? Tried to call this poor woman? Who didn't exist.

Maybe she would call her Barbara. Barbara Smith.

"So, how's that young guy in the ICU doing?"

"Huh?" Cassie was concentrating on coming up with Barbara Smith's demographic information, her heart pounding in her head.

"I saw him after dropping off the lunch trays. Through those glass doors you have in the ICU. He looked about twenty-five or so. Looked like that guy was in pretty bad shape."

Cassie wondered how Chris had noticed any patients that day. He had been there less than a minute. She just wanted to get her hands on the meds and be done with Chris. But she had to answer. It would be rude not to.

"Oh, him. Yeah. Not so good."

Chris grunted. "What was it? Accident? Suicide attempt?"

Cassie shrugged. "You know, I can't really talk about patients. HIPAA privacy laws and all that."

Privacy laws! Cassie felt her heart rate immediately slow. Chris couldn't ask her who the meds were for. She could invoke patient privacy laws. She wouldn't have to make up a story after all.

Chris flashed her a bright smile. "Oh, yeah, I don't want you to break privacy laws. It's just when they're young like that, you know, we think about ourselves being in that position."

Cassie nodded, maybe a little too vigorously. Did this pharma rep actually get it? Maybe he had spent enough time with doctors to understand them. He seemed so caring, so professional. Not the usual sort of greasy pharmaceutical rep. But he needed a haircut, Cassie decided. She figured most women her age liked Chris's look. Maybe most men, too. He was very good-looking in a generic sort of way. Cassie had always gone for nerdier guys, clean-cut guys who were responsible and safe. Chris was the kind of guy that she had consciously avoided, disarmingly handsome, dangerous, the ones who knew just how good-looking they were.

They slowed their pace entering the darkened parking garage as Chris looked for the right row to his car.

"I don't think what he had was transmissible." Cassie smiled at Chris for the first time. "Anyway, my intern is playing detective and I'm sure will have it all sorted out soon enough."

"Hmmm." Chris's eyes seemed to brighten as the corners of his mouth turned up slightly. "I hope so. Well, here we are." He pointed his key chain at a dark blue Mercedes SUV and disarmed the alarm. "Can't be too safe carrying around medications. You know how people are these days." He smiled a model-perfect smile at her.

She replied with a thin, weak grin as her stomach did a quick summersault and the right side of her jaw begged for relief. This wasn't her. She was supposed to be the perfect doctor, the perfect daughter. She was supposed to be better than this. *It's just to get through these next few weeks*, Cassie promised herself, one hand resting on her stomach, the other one extended to receive her pills.

THIRTY

AUTUMN

Seven new patients, twelve doses of potassium, and a manual disimpaction later, Autumn finished her on-call day. She had signed out her pager to the night float intern at 10 p.m. and had managed to get five hours of sleep. By 7:30 a.m. the next day, which was really just a continuation of her same endless day, she had finished pre-rounding on her ten patients, including Detective McAdams, who was doing dramatically better. Internship was by no means easy, but at least it was becoming increasingly manageable. She had thirty minutes before morning rounds started and she decided to use them to visit Jay.

She was feeling incredibly competent and level headed for the first time in weeks, months perhaps. She strode confidently to Jay's room—this was *her* hospital. She had decided that Jay had been her boyfriend for a short time, and ultimately, he was a good person, a little wrapped up in his own head, but so was she. And even though she still had no idea what had happened to him, she felt like she was on the right track. She might figure it out and even if she didn't, her detective work was helping her to come to terms with what had happened.

Autumn stood outside of Jay's room and pondered the prospect of spending the next three years without a serious relationship. She just didn't know how she could combine medical training with anything else. She sighed and knocked on the door to Jay's room.

"Come in," came Marsha's now-familiar voice.

It was early, but the overhead fluorescent lights were all on. Marsha and Larry sat next to each other with a hand each on Jay. Pierce wasn't in the room.

"Sorry I wasn't able to come by yesterday," Autumn offered as a greeting. "I've been trying to figure out what happened. To Jay."

Marsha tried to smile, but Autumn wished she hadn't. It was a pained expression.

"I've been looking everywhere I can think of for the plant that may have hurt Jay, but I haven't had much luck," Autumn admitted.

"Thanks," Marsha said. "Really, thanks. I know you are a busy person. But, you know, it's not important anymore. We can't look back. We have to look forward."

Autumn tried to mask her disappointment in Marsha's lack of interest in trying to figure out what happened to her son. Didn't she want to know?

"That's true." Autumn nodded. "Moving forward is good, but I think I may have a new lead. I'm happy to keep looking into things." Autumn made a mental note to call Luba that morning when she was done visiting with Jay's family. She still had her phone number in her pocket but hadn't found the time to do it while on call the night before.

"I appreciate your help. Really, I do," Marsha insisted. "But, however Jay got hurt, he's here with us now, and we have some tough decisions to focus on." She paused, stared at Autumn, and then added, "Whether or not to put a permanent feeding tube into him."

Larry furrowed his brow and glared at his ex-wife. "Jay didn't just get hurt, Marsha. Someone must have done this to him. Something happened and I'd like to know what that was."

Marsha didn't say anything. She seemed to be ignoring Larry, who turned to Autumn, hopeful, and asked, "What do you mean you may have a new lead?"

Autumn swallowed hard. She didn't want to upset Marsha, whose rounded shoulders and sunken eyes, surrounded by dark circles, made her appear ten years older than the woman she had met a few days prior. But she couldn't stop herself.

"Well, I wonder if someone could have tried to poison Jay. I'm going to talk with a woman in his lab who seems to suspect something later today."

Autumn turned to Marsha and asked, "Do you think there is any possibility Jay could have tried to hurt himself?" She was immediately sorry she had done so.

"Yes!" Marsha burst into tears.

"No!" Larry insisted and stood up from his chair, glowering at Marsha. "I don't. I don't care what Pierce says."

"What does Pierce say?" Autumn asked, confused. She hadn't wanted to disturb the momentary familial peace, but she was too invested to stop now.

"Pierce said Jay called him for some advice on his experiment. He was very upset or something. Pierce didn't make much of it, but he's now convinced that Jay was suicidal when he spoke to him and he's sorry for not doing anything at the time." Larry shrugged. "What the hell does he know about my son anyway?"

"Why would he have called Pierce for advice?" Autumn asked.

Marsha picked her head up and slowed her sobs down. "Pierce had been involved in laboratory science for a long time. He was very good. The company he's VP for does some work in Jay's area."

"Who cares?" Larry snorted.

"Jay cared, Larry. Why can't you accept that? He loved you, but he and Pierce had a relationship, too."

"Where is Pierce?" Autumn wanted to speak with him herself. She wondered what he and Jay had talked about.

"Working," Marsha said simply. "He spent as much time with us as he could, but he had to get back to Maryland for a couple of days. He'll be back this weekend."

"Can't wait," Larry muttered.

Autumn walked nearer to Jay, ignoring Marsha and Larry. She rubbed his arm over the sheet that was covering it. His arm felt different. He had already lost some muscle mass. A lot, actually.

She swallowed hard. He needed more nutrition than he was getting.

"Do you think you'll put in a feeding tube?" Autumn asked. She hadn't spoken with the ICU team, but even as a first-year trainee, she knew that's what came next.

Larry sat down again and both he and Marsha shook their heads.

"We don't know," Larry spoke first. "Hospice met with us and will help us either way, but we don't know if we want to put him through poking a hole in his stomach. The hospice woman asked us to think about our 'ultimate goals' for him and we haven't figured out what those are yet."

"What would you want, Autumn?" Marsha pressed, tears still streaming down her cheeks, creating rivulets in her makeup.

"For myself?"

Marsha nodded.

"I've actually thought about it," Autumn admitted. "Maybe I'm a little morbid or maybe I'm just a worrier. I think a lot of doctors worry about getting a fatal or horribly debilitating disease. At least, I do." She shrugged and took a deep breath, thinking about her stacks of alcohol wipes and newfound fear of bodily fluids. Disease and death were just around every corner and that was mostly all she thought about anymore. So, yes, she had pictured herself lying in the ICU, dying a horrible death. But worse, she had pictured herself not dying, merely going on and on, forever attached to a bed and ventilator.

"If I couldn't think or feel, I wouldn't want to be kept alive artificially," she said emphatically, no longer thinking of Jay but picturing herself. "I would want my family to let me go."

Marsha closed her eyes. Larry kept staring at her. "Have you told that to your family?" he asked.

Autumn shook her head. She hadn't. How do you bring something like that up? Her mother would just tell her not to be morbid. Her mother hated "doctor talk," as she called it.

"You should. You should tell them," Larry said and then turned his gaze back to his son.

Autumn nodded and turned to leave, making her apologies for having to return to her work. She only had a few minutes before she was scheduled to meet Vinay and the wind had been sucked out of her sails. She no longer felt like the world's greatest intern. Her confidence high had been very short lived. Jay's family had more important things to worry about and she was busy playing Nancy Drew. Walking out of the room, she decided she needed to call Luba now, clear things up, and be done with this whole mess.

Autumn reached into her wallet and pulled out the scrap of paper with Luba's cell phone number on it and dialed from one of the phones at the nurses' station. It rang several times before the voicemail picked up. It was almost 8 a.m. and Luba should have been awake. In fact, she should have been in the lab by now. Maybe she was there and just too busy to pick up. Autumn would have to remember to call back at the end of the day, get Luba to explain why she had given her the notebook, and put an end to the Jay Abrams mystery. She committed herself to finding out what happened by the end of the day or she would drop the whole thing and let them all move on.

She had a few more minutes, so she decided to try the number for Detective McAdams's friend again. Miraculously, the officer who answered the phone informed her that he was at his desk and transferred her call.

"Defranco."

"Yes, hi, Detective? My name is Autumn Johnson. Doctor Autumn Johnson. I'm an intern at Boston Memorial Hospital. I'm taking care of Detective McAdams. He gave me your number."

"McAdams!" Defranco nearly shouted. "How is my old partner?"

"Ummm, he's doing okay, everything considered."

"I keep meaning to visit," Defranco still boomed, forcing Autumn to move the phone a few millimeters from her ear. "But, argh, work gets in the way. What can I do for you or for him?"

"Well, you see," Autumn stammered and proceeded to tell Defranco about Jay, Luba, the notebook, and about how she and Mark had gone to Withering's house, conscious to leave out the part about trying to get into the house. Finally, she told him about the car chase, where she might have exaggerated a bit.

Defranco sighed. "You've been a busy doctor. Did you say you had a phone number and address for the lab assistant?"

Autumn wasn't quite sure what she had said, but she looked down at her watch. 8:02 a.m. She was late for morning rounds. She quickly gave Detective Defranco Luba's phone number. He promised to contact Luba that morning, adding that he would be back in touch with Autumn soon so that she could file an official report. In turn, Autumn promised to take good care of Detective McAdams and then hung up, her spirits starting to lift again.

"Do you still want to go to the drug company dinner tonight?" Mark paged Autumn several hours later while she was finishing up her notes. She had forgotten all about the Zeno-Graphium dinner. It was four o'clock and though her eyelids were starting to get a little heavy, a free steak and lobster dinner sounded much better than mac n' cheese from a box. She grabbed her phone and called Mark back.

"So?" he asked.

"Sure," Autumn said flatly. "It's at six, right?"

"I think so. We can take the 'T' directly from the hospital, so we don't have to worry about parking downtown."

"I can be done with my patients soon, but can I go over in scrubs?"

"Ooh, very chic," Mark teased. "Don't you keep something halfway decent in your locker for when you have clinic?"

"Oh yeah. I do. I can change into my clinic clothes. Good thinking."

"I know. You gotta look good for Chris, remember?"

"Oh, I thought he was all yours," Autumn sang, sitting up just a little straighter.

"I want to give you a fair chance." Mark laughed and hung up.

The less than twenty percent battery notification flashed on Autumn's phone. She absently set it to low power mode, figuring it would make it through the night. She didn't necessarily need it, but she was hoping to hear back from Detective Defranco.

Autumn finished writing her patient notes at five and went to the residents' lounge for her clothes. Brown linen slacks and a silk tank top. Not bad from a fashion perspective, but she was going to freeze walking to and from the "T" in her thin tank. She hadn't thought to bring a jacket that morning. Autumn changed into the slacks and top and slipped her white coat on over it in the hopes that it would provide a little warmth. She threw her stethoscope, reflex hammer, tuning fork, and stack of papers from her white-coat pockets into her locker, significantly lightening her load. She would either stuff the white coat and what remained in its pockets into her giant tote after they got to the restaurant or coat check it. She imagined turning her white lab coat in to the coat check person and giggled a little. Lab coats were a little ridiculous out of the hospital. They were also a little ridiculous inside the hospital— probably just carried germs around. They were meant for a lab after all. *Lab! Luba!* She still hadn't heard from her.

She pulled out her cell phone and dialed Luba's number. It went straight to voicemail. The less than ten percent power warning flashed on the screen. She didn't want to turn it off in case Detective Defranco had had better luck contacting Luba than she had. She flipped through the phone's screens and closed as many open apps as she could.

Maybe her inability to connect with Luba was a sign for her to forget about playing detective. She was becoming obsessed when she needed to focus on her patients and maybe just get a good meal. She threw her cell phone into her bag and headed out of the hospital. She would just try to have fun tonight. The professionals had been contacted; she was officially dropping the Jay Abrams case.

THIRTY-ONE

CASSIE

Her jaw hurt, but so did everything else, so she tried to ignore it. Cassie looked down at her takeout burrito and watched as her hot tears fell onto the foil wrapping, each drop making a soft tap as it landed. Like a heartbeat. Like a heartbeat she could keep going if she chose to. Drop. Drop. Drop. She reached for a napkin. Or stop if she chose to. She wiped hard at her eyes and clumsily at her nose and threw the napkin and the burrito into the trash. She didn't want to eat. Abrams would never eat again except through a feeding tube. She figured she deserved to skip a meal as penance. Anyway, her jaw really did hurt, and she didn't want to chew either.

She took off her scrubs and looked at her small, thin body in the mirror, her ribs having become visible under the skin. It was a good body. A body where everything worked. How lucky had she been? Health, good parents, good schools, no loans. And all she had to do to repay life's largesse was to work hard and succeed. Her father was a surgeon and he saved lives. And what did she do? Destroy them? She stared at the mirror again and saw Jay Abrams's body instead. He was becoming so thin. Maybe she was, too. She traced the outlines of her ribs. Just like his, expanding and contracting with every breath. She pictured her arms covered in the same bruises that now covered Jay's—a result of the multiple blood draws he had had. She imagined various red spots portending pressure ulcers in the bed-bound that formed from disuse. She thought about his brain, which would never work again. Because of her mistakes.

A searing pain shot through her jaw. Cassie wandered into her bathroom, peed, washed her hands, and reached for the bottle of Advil sitting on her bathroom counter, carelessly tossed there during her last period. When had that been? Weeks ago probably. Maybe it had been a few months. She couldn't really remember. She poured three Advil into her palm and swallowed them dry. She grabbed an old T-shirt from her closet, slipped it on, and crawled under her comforter. She just needed to sleep. But every time she closed her eyes, she saw Jay Abrams's face, slightly swollen and immovable. Her jaw was still throbbing. She just wanted to sleep.

Cassie angrily threw off her covers and grabbed her purse off of the front table in the hallway. She pulled out the small rectangular box labeled Zenon, the benzodiazepine that Chris's company was marketing for sleep. Underneath, in smaller letters she read, "Tranzenolapam 5 milligrams." This was a new medication. She had never prescribed it. But she didn't feel like looking up the dosing, figuring a sample pack generally contained a starting dose of a medicine. She tore open the cardboard and slipped the foil blister pack into her hand, counting twelve light green tablets. Chris had given her three cardboard boxes. Plenty. She popped a green tablet out of its pack and attempted to swallow it, coughing as it hit the back of her dry throat. She ran into the kitchen and grabbed a dirty glass out of the sink, filling it with lukewarm water from the tap. She swallowed the water down hard. Cassie closed her eyes for a moment and waited, a few lingering coughs sneaking up from the back of her throat. She wandered back to her bed, dropped the blister pack onto the dresser, took another small sip of water, lay down, and pulled the covers to her chin. Her head began to feel heavy, a mixture of the benzodiazepine starting to kick in and her jaw throbbing.

Cassie lay awake, staring at the ceiling. She looked at her clock: 6:15 p.m. She stared back at the ceiling. She saw the whole Abrams family. Pierce, Larry, and Marsha. She even pictured the kid brother, whose image she had never actually seen. In her mind's eye, the brother looked like Jay. But his image faded, became bluer, more dead. She kept staring at his dead body, but it didn't change. It stayed dead. Only it wasn't his brother at all. It was Jay. *You can't save him*, she told herself. *You didn't.* She looked at her clock again: 6:35 p.m. Fuck! Why wasn't she asleep yet?

Cassie reached for the Zenon blister pack on her dresser and popped out another pill. She thought for a moment and then popped out one more. The one pill hadn't done a damn thing. She may as well take three. She needed to stop thinking. She needed to sleep. She put both small green tablets into her mouth and swallowed them down hard with a gulp of warm tap water from the glass. She stared back up at the ceiling and waited for Jay's bruised, thin body to go away. Finally, it did.

THIRTY-TWO

DEFRANCO

Detective Anthony Defranco pulled his white Dodge sedan into the driveway of the small Brighton house. He hoped Lyubov Myshkina would be in. It had been a long day, and her phone kept going straight to voicemail. His plan was to ask this woman to confirm what the doctor had told him and maybe get enough information to get a warrant to search the lab she had talked to him about. Quick in and out, and he could go home. Better yet, maybe Ms. Myshkina would tell him nothing was going on. He loved his old partner, Joe McAdams, but he wasn't sure that Joe should be trying to play cop from his hospital bed.

Defranco rang the front door bell twice. Nothing. He pounded on the door and saw a curtain covering the front window move slightly to the left. A wrinkled woman's face appeared. He moved his navy blazer aside to show the gold badge on his hip and pointed to it. A few seconds later, the door opened.

"Hello," he began gently. "I'm Detective Defranco with the Boston Police. Are you Lyubov Myshkina?"

The woman screwed up her tissue-paper face. "What?" she asked in a heavily accented yell, pointing to her ear. "Hearing aid no in."

Defranco knew not only to raise his voice, but to deepen it if he expected the elderly woman to hear him. "Lyubov Myshkina?" he growled as non-threateningly as he could.

"Ah, yes. Luba. She live in apartment. Upstairs. I rent to her," the woman said pointing up.

Defranco needed her permission to enter. "Can I come in? I need to talk with her about an important matter." He reached for his wallet identification, opened it, and held it up for the older woman to inspect.

The woman squinted her eyelids over the whitish film covering her blue eyes. She stared at his I.D. for what seemed like an eternity. What she was hoping to discover there, he had no idea. He breathed in deeply, thinking of his own grandmother, and admonished himself to slow down.

Finally, she motioned for him to come in. Her home was neat, smelled slightly of mildew, and had furnishings he hadn't seen since he was a kid in the 1970s. Yellow and orange floral was the pattern of choice.

"Luba live upstairs." She pointed at the staircase. "But I no think she here."

Defranco raised his eyebrows.

"I no see her for two days. She usually say 'hi' to me every day when she come home."

Defranco felt the thick hairs on his arms stand at attention. He nodded to the older woman and walked slowly up the stairs, keeping his hand inside his blazer in case he needed his sidearm. He pounded on the door.

"Boston Police," he shouted, pounded again, and shouted again. There was no answer. And he had no warrant to enter. He trudged back down the stairs.

"No answer," he said to the landlady, as though she hadn't been watching the whole thing. "Can you let me in?"

The older woman sighed deeply, shuffled to the kitchen, and returned with a set of keys. "Come," she ordered.

Defranco let her lead him up the stairs. He returned to the image of his grandmother and reminded himself to have patience as she took each step painfully slowly, her knees audibly crunching with each step. His right hand was resting on the butt of his gun, his thumb ready to release it from its holster.

When they got to the landing, the woman took her time finding the right key, turned it, and opened the door. Then the old lady screamed.

That was all the permission he needed. He drew his weapon with his right hand, simultaneously using his left arm both to shield and to gently move the woman aside. On the floor of the small upstairs efficiency apartment, there was a strawberry blond woman who also happened to be very blue. Defranco's arms prickled. His day was about to get much longer.

THIRTY-THREE

AUTUMN

She noticed him from across the room. His hair was held in perfect position by unknown forces since there didn't seem to be a trace of sticky gel in his locks. His medium-gray suit was perfectly tailored to his athletic frame, and he even dressed it up with a small white flower on his lapel. He flashed his Hollywood-white smile at Mark and Autumn as they made their way towards him.

"Glad you two could make it," Chris said, shaking both of their hands in quick succession. "You both look great," he added, looking from Mark to Autumn.

Mark flushed, and Autumn started to feel a bit warmer, too. "Thanks," they both mumbled absently as Chris left them to continue working the room, filled with much more senior doctors.

"He was talking to you," Autumn whispered, nudging Mark with her elbow.

"I don't think so." Mark shrugged. "His eyes were

resting on you when he said it."

"The big, dark circles under my eyes are a huge turn on, I'm sure. Let's grab a couple of drinks—open bar, courtesy of Zeno-Graphium," she added, winking at Mark.

Mark ordered a rum and coke, and Autumn had an Amstel light. She was tired already and if she drank anything more than a beer, Mark would have to carry her back. They shuffled to the edge of the bar to make room for others getting drinks. Since no one was sitting down yet, a hoard of people had gathered around the bar making the air thick and loud.

"Ouch," came a man's cry from behind Autumn.

She spun around, realizing that she had just stepped on the foot of a broad-shouldered, dark-haired man of about thirty. "Oh, sorry," she choked out after forcing down a mouthful of beer. Mark patted her on the back as he turned around, too.

"That's okay. I'll survive." He smiled at her and then Mark. "I wanted to come over and meet you two anyway. I think we're the only people under thirty here. I'm Bradley, Brad Koslowsky," he said, offering his hand to Autumn and then to Mark. Brad was stocky with strong facial features and a firm handshake. "What brings you two here?"

"A much needed break from the hospital," Mark said quickly.

"Hear, hear," Brad agreed enthusiastically, raising his beer and meeting Mark's gaze. "Are you both residents?"

"Interns," Mark said, beating Autumn to the answer.

"Me, too," Brad said, his eyes fixed on Mark. "At the Massachusetts Medical Center."

"We're at Boston Memorial," Mark said as Autumn's

gaze drifted around the room, resting on the podium in the front of the room. Chris was making a bit of noise adjusting the microphone. He hit it twice with his hand and gently cleared his throat.

"I hate to interrupt your conversations, but if everyone could find a seat, dinner is about to be served. Shortly after that, we will hear from our speaker Dr. William Withering. Thank you."

"Let's find a table," Autumn interrupted Mark and Brad.

"Do y'all mind if I grab a table with you? My colleagues from Mass Medical were too tired to show," Brad asked, brushing his dark hair off of his forehead.

"Not at all," Mark said too quickly. "Where are you from anyway, using 'y'all'?"

"Atlanta. And where are y'all from?" Brad asked, overemphasizing the "y'all." Autumn headed toward a table in the back in case her post-call fatigue kicked in and she wanted to duck out early. Mark and Brad followed a bit behind her.

"I'm from Melbourne, Florida, and Autumn here is from Miami. We went to college together at the University of Florida."

"No kidding. So, we're sworn enemies, then," Brad said, using a tone of voice indicating that they were most definitely not enemies. "I'm a Georgia Bulldog."

Autumn knew Mark didn't much care for football and thought she would spare him from Brad's tiresome conversation by taking the seat next to him, leaving Mark the vacant seat on her other side. When Mark took that seat and shot her an ugly look, she was confused for a moment, but only a moment. She had clearly misread the situation.

"So, you're from Miami?" Brad asked Autumn. His gaze, however, drifted toward Mark.

"Yup, I'm a Southern girl," she said with a slight shiver, remembering the freezing cold walk from the "T" station as the sun had started to go down, and trying to think about how to direct the conversation back to her friend.

"Miami's not really the South, though, is it?" Brad said looking to Mark for support. "You know what they say about Florida, don't you? The farther south you go, the more north you are."

Autumn just smiled at her silverware and waited for Mark to respond.

"You ain't seen nothin' yet," Mark said in a slight Southern drawl Autumn hadn't heard since their freshman year.

"Wait till winter comes!" Brad chuckled.

To her surprise, Mark laughed, too. Autumn smiled weakly and scanned the expressions of the five other people sitting at the round table. Three white-haired men and two unnaturally blond women, all in their fifties, buried in their own conversations.

The waiters entered the dimly-lit room in pairs, one carrying a massive tray containing high stacks of covered plates, while the other carried a folding stand to prop the tray onto beside each table.

"Steak, lobster, or vegetarian?" one of the waiters asked, while the other hurried back to the stand to fulfill the request.

Autumn, thinking briefly of Jay, asked the waiter to come back to her as she was seriously pondering the vegetarian option, while Mark and Brad ordered the lobster. But when the waiter got back to her, she couldn't resist asking for the lobster. She raised her eyebrows at Mark, who just shrugged at her and went back to his conversation with Brad. Realizing that the lobster would have to entertain her for the evening, Autumn busied herself with getting the meat out of her pre-cracked lobster.

"Again, thank you all so much for coming," Chris said, flashing his toothy smile. "Allow me to introduce our eminent speaker for tonight, Dr. William Withering. I'm sure Dr. Withering needs no introduction, so I will be brief. The esteemed Dr. Withering did his medical residency right here at the Massachusetts Medical Center."

Brad brightened up at the naming of his hospital. Autumn made another unappreciated face at Mark, indicating that she might get ill when Withering took the microphone.

Chris continued, "He went on to do an endocrinology fellowship at the Boston Memorial Hospital and has made his mark in the area of diabetes research. I now give you Dr. Withering."

There was a short burst of requisite applause before everyone went back to their meals. Though Autumn was not excited to hear Withering speak, it at least meant that Brad and Mark would not be talking over her anymore.

"Thank you so much for inviting me here," Withering started, giving Chris a tight-lipped smile. "And thank you to Zeno-Graphium for sponsoring this lovely dinner," to which there were a few scattered applause. "I come to you today to speak about some very exciting research that I have just presented at a national endocrine meeting this month. It is an issue that concerns us all: endocrinologists, general internists, cardiologists, and maybe even a few of us personally in this room," he said with a smile, looking around as people guiltily laid down their forks. "First, a bit on the pathophysiology of type 2 diabetes mellitus."

Autumn went back to attacking her lobster with the little trident that had been supplied for the task. She had gotten most of the meat out of the tail and claws and finally just gave up on the little legs when she realized her eyes were just too tired for the fine job. The beer combined with the rhythm of the utensils clinking and Withering's mono-tonal speech began lulling Autumn to sleep. Her chin began to rest on her left shoulder as her lids became heavy.

"Indeed, my lab has uncovered the first successful leptin-sensitizing drug," Withering announced dramatically, smacking the podium for effect and jolting Autumn awake.

"What did he just say?" Autumn whispered to Mark.

"They found a leptin-sensitizer that got obese mice to lose twenty percent of their body weight in a matter of weeks, and they kept it off," he whispered back quickly, turning his attention back to the podium.

"We have now been approved to move on to trials with human subjects and will begin recruiting for this Zeno-Graphium-sponsored study next month. If you have any obese patients whom you feel would be appropriate for this trial, and I'm sure you all have many, I urge you to refer them to my study coordinator. Ladies and gentlemen, we may finally be working toward a real cure for obesity, diabetes, and cardiovascular disease. One drug to cure them all," he added triumphantly to rousing applause.

The coffee Autumn had begun drinking nearly shot out of her nose as she tried to speak and swallow at the same time. Instead, she went into a coughing jag, causing everyone at the table to look over at her. She waved everyone's stares off, stopped herself from coughing, and nearly yelled at Mark, "Did you hear what he just said?"

"Yeah." Mark shrugged. "Very interesting stuff. Good for him for doing something useful."

"That was the other experiment," Autumn hissed.

Mark just stared at her.

"Jay's other experiment," she added.

"Jay's other experiment? How do you figure that?"

"There was another note, on the back of a picture of Jay's brother about OB mice and a problem," she said, raising her voice. "I think Jay figured out there was a problem with this hot new drug."

"Calm down," Mark pleaded, looking over to Brad, who was now shrugging at him. "We'll check it out, okay?"

"I'm going to talk to him now."

"Who? Withering?"

"Yes," she said, pushing her chair back and storming off toward the podium. Withering was surrounded by a group of well-dressed physicians and Chris was to his immediate right. They were all smiling and chatting pleasantly, many holding their after-dinner cocktails. One man who might have been considered fairly overweight, if not obese, had his hand on Withering's left shoulder supportively. "Good job," he kept repeating. Autumn marched into the circle and stood in front of Withering.

He seemed startled for a moment but quickly regained his composure. "Yes?" he asked pleasantly as she glowered at him.

"I need to talk to you about this experiment," she demanded.

Withering laughed. "My dear, everyone wants to talk to

me about this experiment tonight. I suggest you get in line."

"No. I need to talk to you about this experiment and Jay Abrams."

Withering's mouth turned down as he glowered at Autumn. He shook his head and then stretched his mouth into an uncomfortable grin. "She's a bit overwrought," he explained to the group. "Jay, a friend of hers and one of my protégés, is quite ill. If you all will excuse me for just a moment."

Withering took Autumn by the elbow and escorted her to one of the far corners of the room. "Look, I'm not really sure what you are getting at, but I think you ought to call my secretary and set up a proper meeting for us to discuss whatever it is that is troubling you," he tried to whisper firmly.

"What is troubling me is that Jay told you there was a problem with the OB mice. I found part of a note he must have written you. But you didn't mention any problems in your talk tonight," she said in an angry whisper.

"That's because there weren't any. Your friend Jay was mistaken. Yes, he came to me thinking there was a problem, but, no, there weren't any, and I explained as much to him."

"Fine, then. What did he *think* the problem was?"

"That's really none of your business, is it? This drug has a patent already. It belongs to me and to Zeno-Graphium. And the university," he added, implying that her own bosses would be none too pleased with her interference.

"If there isn't really a problem, why not just tell me what Jay thought?" Autumn insisted.

"If that will get you off my back, I will. But not here with people I consider my competitors around. As I said, make an appointment with my secretary."

"For early next week?" Autumn insisted.

"Yes. I will tell her to fit you in."

"Fine," Autumn agreed. She wasn't going to get anywhere with Withering while he was surrounded by people he was trying to impress. She had her answer, or one of them anyway. Withering was a fraud. And Jay knew it. And now she knew it, too. Was Withering capable of hurting Jay to protect himself? She would call Detective Defranco in the morning. She still had to fill out her report. This would all be in it and she presumed the detective would not have to make an appointment with Withering's secretary. Autumn balled her fists as she strode back to the table. She thought of Jay lying in his hospital bed. He shouldn't have been there. He should have been a Ph.D. just sent back to finish his medical school rotations in the hospital. She would have helped him get through that. Hot, angry tears began to pool in her eyes. Instead of helping him on his ward rotations, she would help him finish what he had started.

"What was that all about?" Brad asked as Autumn returned to the table, which now just contained Brad and Mark.

"Personal." She shrugged at Brad, grabbing a napkin she assumed was hers off the table and absently running it across her nose. "I'm going to get him to explain everything," she said with satisfaction to Mark.

"Oh yeah," Mark remarked off handedly, not picking up on Autumn's sour mood. "I wouldn't bet on it."

Autumn glared at him angrily, his words a punch to

her gut.

"Hey, do you want to come out to the bar down the street with me and Brad?" Mark asked, still oblivious.

"Not really," she said dismissively. "But you both have a good time. I'll just grab the 'T' back."

"You sure you're okay?" Mark asked. "It's dark out."

Autumn glanced down at her watch. "It's only 8:30," she said with as much good cheer as she could muster, realizing Mark was about to go on the first date of his intern year. Her anger started to dissipate. She couldn't be mad at him. He'd helped her get this far, and she owed him. "I'll be fine. You kids have fun."

She grabbed her tote from under the table, slipped on her white coat, and steeled herself for what she hoped would be a very quick walk to the "T" station.

THIRTY-FOUR

AUTUMN

The combination of stress, sleep deprivation, alcohol, caffeine, and information overload was making her dizzy. Autumn pulled the edges of her white coat together to protect her from the howling wind as she walked to the "T" station. She regretted not having a real coat with her now that the sun had set.

Autumn's thoughts swirled busily in her head. Maybe Withering was telling the truth. Maybe there was nothing wrong with his experiment and Jay had ingested the foxglove for reasons only he could know. How well had she gotten to know him anyway? Not well, but there should have been some hint that she could have picked up on. What clues had she missed? He had sounded depressed to his stepfather, hadn't he? She shook her head. Jay said he was nearly done. He was busy and upbeat. Lots to do and little time to do it in.

What if Jay had actually found something? Withering

spoke as if he had uncovered some miracle drug. It must be worth millions. Perhaps even billions. Still, people exaggerated the implications of their research all the time. As Autumn remembered from the lab work she did during medical school, it was incredibly boring stuff. The thing that kept people toiling away was the notion that eventually they were going to come up with something great. You needed a lot of patience and a lot more ego. Autumn smiled to herself thinking that Withering certainly had a fair helping of the latter.

She raced down the stairs to the dark and dingy "T" station, quickly inserting her CharlieCard to get through the turnstile. The Boylston stop was, by far, the oldest-looking of all the "T" stops in Boston, most of which had been renovated with new lighting and tiling on the walls. Usually she wondered why this station was kept in all its dilapidated glory, but tonight she was happy just to be out of the wind.

She felt her phone buzzing from inside her tote and dug deep into its recesses to grab it just as it stopped. Two missed calls. The first had been from Detective Defranco, thirty-two minutes earlier and now she had just missed a call from Mark. She smiled. He was probably calling to check that she had made it back okay.

"Autumn, call me right now!" a text came through from Mark.

"Okay, okay," she mouthed to the phone as she pushed his contact. The low battery warning flashed briefly just as his number came up and the phone started to automatically power down.

"Shit," Autumn cursed out loud as she threw the dead

phone into her bag. She made a mental note to call Mark as soon as she got home. She needed to start being a better friend to him, she thought as she took in the sparse crowd around her.

There was the usual mix of about half a dozen students and professionals heading home after a long day in the city. Two loud women to her left with expensively dyed and blown out hair were discussing their conquests from an evening spent shopping.

In the distance, Autumn heard the squealing wheels of a train slowing down. She had a one in four chance of it being the "D" line she needed to get back to her car in the hospital parking lot. She leaned over and peered down the tracks. "Yes," she whispered triumphantly, the front of the approaching train announced itself as "D—Riverside," and she positioned herself to be one of the first on board. Her tired legs were aching for a seat, and she wanted to be sure to get one.

Autumn boarded and breathed a sigh of relief. The train was so empty that no one had to be bothered to sit next to anyone else.

Autumn rested her elbows on her bag, propping up her head on her palms, and watched the dark walls race by. A pill to cure obesity. Could it really be possible? Sure, there were pills now. There were the ones that blocked the GI tract from absorbing fats or the kidneys from absorbing carbs and kept its users on the toilet all day. Then there were the ones that acted like amphetamines and kept getting yanked off the shelves as soon as some horrible, fatal side effect was discovered. Why did it take so long to figure out the side effects anyway? It seemed that lots of people had to use the drug outside of a clinical trial before enough of the side effect was seen to attribute it to the drug. Lab animals could be strikingly similar to people though, and the drugs would be tested on thousands of them first. What if someone could know that a blockbuster drug would cause problems before it was used by tens of thousands of people? She wondered again if Jay had discovered a side effect of Withering's wonder drug. Jay had told her that Withering didn't like him being around the lab mice. Why should Withering care one way or the other if Jay had taken an interest in the lab mice? Unless something was wrong with them.

The train quietly approached the above-ground hospital stop. Autumn rubbed her temples as she deboarded. It didn't make any sense. Withering would report it himself if something was wrong. What motivation could he have for hiding the side effects? He was a doctor. A professor. He took an oath. Plus no one went into research to make money. Only . . . what if he could with this drug? Maybe he didn't go into research for fame and fortune, but what if it came for him?

She remembered that plenty of her medical school classmates had started medical school as altruists and had graduated as something else entirely. Others entered residency proclaiming they would go into primary care and then went on to pursue lucrative fellowships. Money was a powerful lure.

She walked quickly down the dark street, a set of keys jingling with every step. Then she remembered—Luba's extra set of keys were still in her white coat pocket!

She could go to the lab now. Just for a minute to look at

the mice. By tomorrow, Withering could get rid of them now that he knew she suspected something. Did she have keys to the front door on the key ring? She hoped so, but even if she didn't, people worked late in labs. There was usually a guard there and if he wasn't, maybe the main entrance of the building would be unlocked.

Autumn arrived at the heavy metallic rimmed doors to the large brick building and pulled on the handle. It wouldn't open, and the building itself was dark, except for the dimmed lobby lights. Everyone was gone. She hoped. She dug in her left coat pocket for the key ring. A total of five keys were on it. She reached for the largest one. Etched onto the surface was the phrase "DO NOT COPY." She inserted the key, turned it, and heard a click. She pulled on the handle again. The door opened and quickly closed behind her. She was in the entranceway but in front of another set of glass doors. She tried the same key. It worked again, and she opened this door to the lobby. The front desk stood empty—there was no security guard.

She walked quickly to the elevator for fear that the guard had merely gone out for a smoke or to the bathroom and would be back any minute. The elevator doors opened normally, but when she pushed the button for the fourth floor, it refused to light up. She pushed it uselessly half a dozen times before noticing the keyhole next to the emergency button. She looked at her key ring again, chose the smallest one, and inserted it into the hole. It turned and the light for the fourth floor glowed as the elevator doors shut.

A few seconds later, they opened up to a darkened hallway. Autumn strode over to lab 410 and inserted one of the three remaining keys into the lock. It didn't turn. She tried a second key. It still didn't turn. She tried the third key. Nothing.

"Shit!" she said out loud. One of them had to work. She stared at the key ring again and held up the three keys she had just tried. "Shit," she said again, realizing she had used the first one twice. She inserted the third key; the lock and knob turned simultaneously. She pushed the door open, feeling blindly along the wall for the light switch. Her fingertips found two switches on the wall and flipped them both on. The fluorescent lights crackled to life as she stepped farther into the room.

The mice were housed on the black-top against the far wall. About twenty cages lined the counter. Most of them were filled with the familiar obese mice, whom the lights had awakened and who were now scratching at the bottoms of the cages. But there were also two cages with thinner mice and one with decidedly skeletal mice. Autumn pulled that one forward and unlatched the top. These mice were moving as slowly as the obese mice, all the better for her, she thought, as she again remembered back to her lab days, and reached for a mouse by grabbing at the tissue behind its neck.

As she pinched the skin between her left thumb and flexed index finger, the second knuckle of her index finger brushed against a small, irregular, firm nodule just beneath the skin of the mouse's head. She lifted the mouse out of the cage and palpated the mouse's head with the pad of her right index finger to get a better feel. Although it barely created a lump visible to the eye, she could distinctly feel a small tumor.

"It's metastatic renal cell cancer," came a man's voice just as the door to the lab slammed shut.

Autumn gasped and dropped the mouse onto the counter as she spun around. She met Chris's beautiful, glistening eyes. He was still in the finely tailored gray suit, but the flower in his lapel was gone. So was his charming smile.

THIRTY-FIVE

AUTUMN

"So, the game-changing leptin-sensitizing drug causes renal cell cancer? That's what Jay found out," Autumn said weakly, trying to keep her voice from trembling. Looking into Chris's now-cold eyes, she felt her heart leap to her throat.

"In a few mice," Chris growled back in a voice that didn't sound anything like the smooth one she was used to hearing. "Mice aren't people."

"No," Autumn agreed, her head spinning as she struggled to figure out how to get out of the lab. "How did you even get in here?" Autumn looked from left to right, but Chris seemed to be standing at the only exit.

"You mean because my sweet Luba's keys had the words 'do not copy' written on them? Our former presidents' faces speak much louder to certain locksmiths than those words."

Without realizing it, Autumn backed along the counter stacked with the cages. "You poisoned him," she said dumbly, instantly regretting it.

"I bring the residents lunch once a week, but you know that. And sometimes I bring the hard-working folks in the labs lunch. Jay was a healthy guy. He liked salads. But salads can get boring, you know," Chris flashed his bright-white smile at her, but it wasn't attractive anymore. It was maniacal.

"I would add special ingredients, like foxglove petals or bits of poisonous amanita mushrooms. I think he appreciated that, you know," Chris said, smiling again. "He was supposed to quietly die of liver failure or a heart arrhythmia, I didn't care which one, but he got to the ER just in time to wind up brain dead. Well, good enough." He shrugged.

Autumn's back was nearly against the wall in the far corner of the room. Her mouth was dry and her hands sweating, but she did her best to sound calm. She slipped her hands into her white-coat pockets and, as casually as she could, said, "Well, you know, Jay and I weren't that close. I don't have to tell anyone about this. I don't really care, you know." She attempted to shrug carelessly, but it was more like a shudder.

Chris's smile broadened. "Oh, sweetie, I think you do."

Autumn's mind raced. Why was this drug so important to him? He was a drug rep. He sold drugs that had already been brought to market, not drugs that were in development. What could he possibly have to gain?

"Okay," Autumn admitted. "I care. I care that people might die from this drug. Why don't you?"

Chris shrugged. "Dunno. I don't care that much about people. Chalk it up to a rough childhood." He grinned maniacally again.

Autumn balled her fists and jammed her hands farther into her white-coat pockets as Chris came closer. Her right middle finger hit something hard and flat at the bottom. She felt it with her fingertips. It was the handle of the scalpel she'd meant to dispose of after cutting out McAdams's sutures, when the sharps container had been too full. She had forgotten to throw it away! She slid the plastic cover off of the blade with her thumb and her index finger, her hands still in her pockets. It wasn't large, only a one-inch blade, but hopefully it was enough to help her get out of there.

Autumn's voice shook. "You have to care about someone. Your family? They might take this drug one day." She felt her heartbeat pounding in her throat. "And Luba! You just said that you cared for Luba."

Chris's grin faded. "No. Sadly, the busty Russian was useful, but only briefly. I thought I'd just be checking in on the good work they were doing here. But then she let me know about the little glitch you just figured out. She couldn't say anything directly to Withering, of course. She needed to keep her job and her visa. She was hoping I'd help."

Chris's smile returned. "No one would think twice about a Russian immigrant dying of an INH overdose. Big problem, tuberculosis in Russia. God, did she love her vitamins! And conveniently, didn't they just look so much like INH pills?"

He had poisoned Luba, too. Detective Defranco had tried to call her earlier. Did he know? Autumn dropped her gaze slightly to Chris's neck. As casual as he was attempting to appear, the tension in his neck outlined the anatomy of the anterior triangle on its left side. Autumn knew this part of human anatomy very well. Extremely well. She thought about the internal jugular placement of a central line. She had taken a great deal of time to learn how to avoid the nearby carotid artery. She had no intention of avoiding that pulsating artery tonight.

"But you can't poison me," she insisted as he approached, now about five feet from her.

"No, you are right. Too much poisoning would start to look suspicious. But I can strangle you and put your body where no one will ever find it," he said flatly.

He dove at her with outstretched hands, but she kept her gaze fixed on the anterior triangle of his neck. Before he could get his hands around her, she ducked to the right, pulled the blade from her pocket, spilling scraps of paper from her pocket onto the floor, and took her one slice.

Blood splashed from Chris's neck, and she frantically yelled, "That's your carotid," as his hands covered the wound, hot bright red blood flowing through his fingers and onto his perfect gray suit. She ran around him and toward the door of the lab as he stared at her in shock. "Hold pressure, get to a hospital quick, or die," she commanded, swinging open the door and running for the elevator.

THIRTY-SIX

AUTUMN

Cold sweat coated Autumn's skin as she ran, her blood-stained hand still gripping the scalpel. She pushed the elevator call button and listened for sounds of the elevator approaching but heard nothing. She remembered—it was key-activated this time of night.

"Shit!" she cried and ran down the hall away from lab 410. She saw no exit sign, no stairwell. She looked back in the direction of the lab and saw a red exit sign at the end of that hallway. Wrong way. She also saw Chris, who was using his left hand to hold a blood-soaked towel from the lab against his neck, standing in the doorway twenty yards away. His rage-filled eyes met hers, and he strode briskly toward her, his right hand holding a bottle of something he had taken from the lab. She couldn't tell what it was, but she tightened her grip on her scalpel as he approached.

A slow mechanical whine came from behind the closed elevator doors. The elevator had somehow started its ascent. There was no way she would be able to get inside of it before Chris got there. He was losing blood, but not fast enough. She figured that he could live another twenty minutes or so. She would have to fight for her life with a one-inch scalpel blade.

He was now ten yards away. Could she puncture a lung or his heart with the short scalpel blade? She didn't think so. Where could she strike? His eye? He would be ready for it this time and stop her easily.

Five yards away.

"Bitch," he yelled, "I'm taking you with me!" He let the towel fall from his neck and unscrewed the cap of the opaque brown glass bottle in his grip. Blood pulsated out of his neck with every step he took. Autumn stood frozen in place, her mind now blank with fear.

Less than ten feet away and just across from the elevator doors, Chris threw the contents of his bottle at her. At the same time as he aimed, the elevator doors opened, giving him a start and causing the clear liquid to miss Autumn by mere inches, hissing and bubbling as it started to burn a hole in the gray-tiled floor.

"Hands up," boomed a voice from the elevator as two fast approaching figures pointed their guns at the bleeding Chris. He lifted his right arm and dropped the glass bottle onto the floor, shattering it and causing another hole to start bubbling. He instinctively brought his left hand to his neck again. The men seemed agreeable to this.

"Hands up now," one of the men shouted at Autumn. Her eyes caught the flash of a badge on his waist.

"Sorry," she said quickly, dropping the scalpel, lifting her arms up, shaking all over.

One of the cops turned his head and hit a button on his cell phone. "We need an ambulance at the corner of Long Avenue and Bishop, fourth floor."

The taller, bald officer pushed Chris against the wall and patted him down. Apparently satisfied that he wasn't hiding any more bottles of acid or other weapons, he sat Chris down against the wall, his now sticky right hand still holding pressure while the left was tucked behind his head.

The shorter, stockier officer with an almost-grin on his face began patting down Autumn's coat.

"How many freakin' pockets do you have on this thing?"

"Six."

"Are they all filled with crap?" he asked, pulling out a pair of rubber gloves and some of the small books, pens, and scraps of paper that hadn't fallen to the floor when she grabbed the scalpel.

"Yes," Autumn answered flatly, wanting to smile back at the cop, but having enough fear and good sense to suppress it.

"Well, then, would you mind removing it? Slowly."

Autumn took off her coat and dropped it beside her. She put her hands behind her head and shivered as the air conditioning came into contact with her sweat-covered skin. The cop then quickly patted her down.

"What happened here?" he asked her, putting away his gun and taking out a small notebook and pen.

"He attacked me," she said, still trembling, more from shock than cold. "How did you know to come here?"

"We got a tip. But, miss, I hate to break it to you, it looks like you attacked the guy bleeding to death over there." His voice was familiar but booming and made Autumn's trembling worse.

"He was going to kill me," she said, raising her voice. "He already killed two people. I mean almost killed two people. Well, almost killed one person. I don't know what happened to the other one."

"Relax. Keep it together," he instructed as the elevator door opened and two EMS personnel emerged. "Are you okay?" the cop asked her as the man and woman attended to the very pale Chris. Autumn nodded.

"Autumn!" she heard Mark's familiar voice exclaim.

"Mark! Oh my God," Autumn shouted and felt hot tears roll down her cheeks. She was going to be okay.

"Wait there," the cop questioning Autumn commanded Mark, who had just come out of the elevator, Brad following behind him with a decidedly bemused expression. They abruptly stopped. The EMS workers and the tall bald officer loaded Chris onto the stretcher they had brought.

"You okay here?" the officer called out, the fluorescent hallway lights reflecting off of his bare brown scalp.

"You bet," the other cop responded.

"I'm just gonna escort this guy to the hospital. I'll get a couple uniforms assigned to him over there and come back ASAP."

The stocky cop turned back to Autumn. "You ready to start explaining this whole mess?" he asked, pointing to what was indeed a mess. Two acid burns had destroyed several feet of tile, stopped only by the concrete below. The rest of the floor from lab 410 to the elevator, as well as part of the wall that Chris had been resting on, was decorated with pools of blood.

Autumn choked back her tears and started with the night

Jay Abrams had been brought to the ICU. She didn't stop until she got to the Zeno-Graphium-sponsored dinner, her sneaking into the lab, and the confrontation with Chris. She left out the part about breaking into Withering's house because she wasn't sure how many breaking and enterings she could get away with.

"So, you're the young doctor Joe asked us to check out that yard for? The one who called me earlier," the officer said, the suggestion of a smile playing on his lips.

Autumn furrowed her brow. "Detective McAdams?" she asked, remembering that his first name was Joe. "Yeah, I was wrong about that," she admitted shyly.

"But you seem to have been right about something tonight," the cop said, smiling more broadly now. "And you were right about Joe. He said you saved his life. You stopped an infection before it could make him real sick."

Autumn screwed up her face even more. "But he didn't know I was here. How did you know to come here?" she asked again, transferring her gaze to Mark, remembering that he was still standing against the wall.

"I can help fill that part in," Mark said, looking over at the cop to make sure it was okay that he step away from the wall now. Brad seemed content to stay just where he was.

"A few minutes after you left, Dr. Withering came up to me and asked if we had come together. I said 'yes,' and he said that someone who might be dangerous had followed you out. I asked him a few more questions, but he really didn't say much else, just that I needed to make sure you got home okay. Brad and I went into the street, but you were gone already. I tried your phone, but you didn't pick up. I texted you, and you didn't call back. I didn't know what to do, so I called the cops," Mark said, shrugging. "The dispatcher asked where you would be going so they could get some officers over there and I said the Boylston stop and then the hospital parking lot to pick up your car. Brad and I took the 'T' over to the hospital and went straight to the parking lot. These guys were there," Mark said, motioning over to the cop, "but you weren't anywhere, and your car was still parked. Detective Defranco," Mark said, pointing at the cop, "asked where you could have gone since the officers at the 'T' stop couldn't find you there either, and then I thought of the lab. I remember that you had wanted to go there the day we went . . ." Mark stopped abruptly just as Autumn shot him a dirty look. She knew he was about to say Dr. Withering's house.

"Joe said you had a good head on your shoulders and we should take you seriously. That's why I didn't hang up on you when you called me," Detective Defranco added to Autumn. "Seems like he was right. Always was, great instincts," he said shrugging. "It's a shame, you know."

Mark and Autumn nodded in agreement.

"The cops made me wait downstairs," Mark finished. "But when I saw the ambulance pull up, Brad and I jumped on the elevator with the EMS guys. "I was so scared for you. I just can't believe Chris would do something like this."

Autumn snorted. "Why, because he's good looking?"

"No. Because why would a pharmaceutical rep care whether a drug makes it to market or not?"

"I can answer that." Brad beamed from against the wall, seemingly happy to have regained an opportunity to speak. "Lots of them work on commission or stock options or whatever they call it. I bet he had a small fortune at stake in this as much as anyone else. If he had already been assigned to detail on this drug, he could stand to lose a ton, too." Brad folded his arms in front of himself, satisfied with his answer.

"And Withering?" Autumn pressed.

Mark shrugged. "I guess you guys will have to ask him," Mark said to Detective Defranco. "He must have known something was wrong with his miracle drug and he was going to let it go on the market anyway, but he did warn us that you were in trouble. Maybe he never intended for things to go this far."

Now Defranco snorted. Autumn stared at him and his expression immediately darkened.

"I'm sorry," he said. And somehow Autumn knew what would come next. His eyes had softened in the same way she had seen her fellow physicians' eyes soften when they were about to say to a family member or friend that a patient had died.

"Luba?" she questioned. But she already knew the answer.

Defranco sighed. "She was dead in her house. It's a case for the medical examiner now."

Autumn shuddered. Her adrenaline was wearing off and the fear of what could have happened to her just a few minutes ago stuck in her throat. She cleared her throat, but the heaviness in her neck remained.

The elevator opened again, and Detective Defranco's partner walked back out. "Sorry that took so long, Anthony."

"No problem, Roger. I just finished getting this young

lady's statement. Looks like she'll go to any lengths to solve a crime. We can use you on the force," he said and rested his hand on her shoulder.

His hand provided much needed reassurance and actual, physical warmth. The chill began to lift, and Autumn found that she could speak again. "Some days I do think about a career change." Autumn smiled. "But I've had enough police work for quite a while."

Detective Defranco shrugged. "I can understand that. Why don't you all go home and get cleaned up? Don't leave town. We will need more information from you soon. Is paging you the best way to contact you?" he asked Autumn. "Because your cell phone clearly isn't." He frowned to emphasize the point.

She looked down at her sticky, blood-caked pager, nodded, and smiled weakly. At least it wouldn't be a page for hemorrhoid cream.

THIRTY-SEVEN

CASSIE

Cassidy Louise Ellison, who at twenty-eight years old had never missed a day of work in her life, who was never even late to a birthday party, was jarred awake at 9:30 a.m. by her phone ringing. She stumbled into the kitchen to grab her purse but by the time she got there, the caller had hung up. She swiped her finger across the screen and discovered that she had missed a few calls and had two voicemails waiting for her.

The first was from Randall Chin.

"Cassidy, this is Randy Chin. You were due in the ICU an hour ago. This is very unprofessional behavior, and I expect a call back immediately unless you are dead, in which case you can have a little more time to get back to me." Randy chuckled at his joke and then ended his message.

Cassie groaned and hit the next message. It was also from Randy left a moment earlier and just thirty minutes after the first message.

"Okay, Cassie, I'm not messing around anymore. You will either call me back ASAP or magically appear in the hospital in the next five minutes, or I am writing you up."

Crap. She needed an excuse fast. The flu. She had the flu. She called the number for the Chief Resident's office. He answered after one ring.

"Dr. Chin here."

"Randy? Hi. It's Cassie Ellison. I'm so sorry."

"Yes. You are. Now tell me you are on your way to the hospital."

Cassie clenched her jaw down too hard and pain shot through to her temple.

"I have the flu," she said while attempting a weak cough.

"Oh, give me a freaking break," Randy said. "The CDC flu map doesn't even have Massachusetts on it yet. What the hell is wrong with you, Cassie?"

Cassie sighed. Of course Randy would have the current CDC flu map committed to memory. She decided to offer up a watered down version of the truth instead.

"Okay, Randy. It's just that I had a really bad toothache last night and wound up taking some old meds that I had. I guess I took too much and slept through my alarm this morning."

"Hmmm. Better," Randy said blandly. He quickly added, "My office in thirty minutes, Cassie. Don't be late."

Cassie peed, splashed a few handfuls of cold water on her face, brushed her teeth, and threw on a clean pair of scrubs. Food would have to wait; she didn't feel much like eating anyway. Twenty-three minutes later, she was knocking on the office door of the Chief Resident.

"I'm so sorry," she apologized again. Randy both waved

her apology off and motioned for her to sit with a flick of his wrist.

"What's going on?" He locked his gaze with hers, threatening her not to lie to him.

"My tooth," Cassie pointed at her jaw.

"We all get toothaches," Randy said dismissively. "You wait for a day off or if it's really serious, arrange for coverage. Now, honestly, what did you wind up taking last night?"

"Huh?" Cassie asked, starting to tap her foot beneath her seat.

"You took something, right? You said some old pills you had. What were they? And before you answer, remember that I can send you to the ED for a tox screen in a minute."

Cassie stared at Randy. His dark eyes seemed to be looking straight through her. She shuddered before answering, "Benzos."

Randy's lips stretched into a thin line. "Benzos aren't pain killers. They're anti-anxiety. How was that supposed to help your tooth?"

Cassie shrugged. "I just needed to sleep, and I couldn't because of the pain. Ibuprofen didn't work. That's what I had."

"What pain?"

"The pain I already told you about."

Randy's eyes were like laser beams boring into Cassie. She wondered what he saw and tried to stop fidgeting. "Hmmm," he considered. "I think you might need some help."

"I don't need help," Cassie insisted. "When have I ever been late or missed a day prior to today?"

Randy nodded his head in agreement. "Never, Cassie. That's why I'm worried about you. You never stop to take care of yourself. It's clear you've lost weight this year. Something is going on."

Cassie just stared back at him.

"I'll give you the name of a good psychiatrist and a psychologist," Randy said, while scrolling through his phone contacts. "What you do with them is up to you. If you decide to contact them, which I think you should, my other piece of advice is to find the cash to pay for it out of pocket. Don't use insurance and don't leave a paper trail. These guys are good at being discreet. They know a doctor's mental health history can make it hard to get a medical license or malpractice insurance later on."

Cassie raised her eyebrows at him. "I don't have a mental health history."

"I know that. And I'm telling you not to get one. But get help if you need it."

Cassie shrugged again, hoping that would be enough of an answer.

As he handed over the names and numbers of the psychologist and psychiatrist, he asked, "Are you okay to rejoin the ICU? I don't have anyone to cover you today," adding the second part to ensure that only one answer would be acceptable. Just then Randy's phone rang and he said nothing for several seconds.

"What?" he yelled in disbelief into the mouthpiece. "Hold on." Randy looked up at Cassie.

She didn't speak for fear that she would cry. She had never done that in the hospital and she was done with today being a day of firsts for her. Cassie nodded her assent and mumbled a "thank you" as she excused herself from Randy's office. She walked toward the elevators, considering what he had just said. Maybe she would benefit from a psych visit. How would she pay for it? She could ask her father. No. She couldn't. He was so proud of her independence and strength. She couldn't let him down. He would think she couldn't handle residency. And a medical residency, not even a surgical one. She had a few pieces of jewelry her ex had given her. Maybe she could pawn them. That might pay for a few visits. It might be better to get him out of her head completely. No. She couldn't. That would be erasing some of her best memories.

She got on the elevator, giving a curt nod to the well-dressed man and woman already there. She pushed 15 and watched the numbers slowly go up. The man and woman got off at 7. She supposed she could moonlight for the money. Work more for actual doctor-level pay. But when? Her jaw throbbed in response. No. There just wasn't any time.

The elevator stopped at 15, and Cassie got off. She headed toward the pneumatic doors of the ICU. She pressed her I.D. onto the electronic keypad and the doors hissed open. Cassie strode quickly through them, dropping the numbers Randy had given her into the nearby trash bin. She didn't need a psychiatrist. She needed a dentist. Maybe she would be able to get someone to cover for her in the next few days so she could take her tooth taken care of. Then she would be just fine again.

THIRTY-EIGHT

AUTUMN

Autumn awakened to the unwelcome chirping of her pager. She turned her head toward the digital clock as her hand fumbled on the nightstand for the beeping menace. Shit! It was 6:30 a.m. already. Had she forgotten to set her alarm? She couldn't remember. Her mind was a blur. When her hand finally located the small but thoroughly cleaned and disinfected plastic box (she had had the energy to break out her stash of alcohol wipes and take care of that before bed) and silenced it, the display read: "Heard you had a rough night. I will take care of the patients today. Vinay."

Autumn read it again in disbelief. Vinay was giving her the day off! She wondered what he had heard, but she didn't wonder for long as her heavy head met the pillow. It was 11 a.m. before she opened her eyes again. She sat up and for a split second wondered if it had all been a nightmare. Grabbing her pager, she hit the display button showing Vinay's page from earlier in the morning.

It was real. Vinay was taking care of her patients. That meant that he might discharge some of them today, perhaps Detective McAdams if he was doing better. She stretched her way out of bed and decided to get ready in a hurry. She wanted to thank him and say goodbye. She wondered if Jay was going to go today also. Only she still had no idea where he would be going.

It felt weird but decidedly refreshing to walk into the hospital without her white coat on. She wasn't exactly sure where she had left it last night and was fairly certain it was ruined. Today she was off duty in just a sweatshirt and jeans. Detective McAdams's door was closed. She rapped her knuckles lightly on it.

"Come in," she heard a woman's voice call.

Autumn walked in to find Detective McAdams sitting next to a very attractive redheaded woman of about forty. He was smiling brightly.

"Hey, Doc," he called out, "come meet my wife, Darla." He looked over at his wife. "This is the doctor that saved my life."

Darla stood up and put out her hand. "Thank you, Doctor," she said with a firm handshake. "Thank you for giving us some more time together."

Autumn blushed. "I'm off duty," she said, pointing at her outfit. "Call me Autumn, please. And anyway, I came to thank your husband for saving *my* life."

McAdams looked down for a moment and gave a small grin. "I owed you one, Doc," he offered simply.

As she recapped the previous night's events, Autumn soon realized that he already knew everything that had happened. McAdams proceeded to fill in the gaps for her that the adrenaline had wiped from her memory.

"Sounds like you may have a second career in criminal justice," he praised.

"I think I may need a bit of a break from criminal justice for a while," she said and laughed. "How about you getting back in the saddle?"

"Oh, I'll still help out where I can. For right now, I just need to get out of here. Remembah?"

"He's getting a long IV line so he can get the antibiotics at home and then we'll be going," Darla promised him and reassured herself.

McAdams nodded in agreement. "When this infection clears up I'll be getting one of those stomach tubes, so hopefully food won't go down the wrong way anymore and hopefully I'll avoid another bad pneumonia."

"A J-tube?" Autumn asked.

The McAdams couple nodded resolutely in unison.

"Hey, what about Withering? Did you hear if he was arrested for what happened to Jay or not?" Autumn asked, her voice lowered.

"A buddy of mine brought him in for questioning early this morning." He looked up at Autumn. "Confidentially?"

"Of course," she insisted.

"Well, he denied that he evah said anything to that pharmaceutical rep about there being any troubles. He thought he could convince your friend that the few mice with tumahs had nothing to do with the drug. He was planning on just burying the whole thing. Does that sound right?"

"The burying part does." Autumn snorted. "But yeah, it sounds like you got the story as Withering probably told it."

"He did ask Dr. Mark to get help fah you last night, didn't he?"

Autumn shrugged. Too little too late. She hoped that Withering would be going down for what had happened to Jay. To Luba. To the potential victims of that drug.

She gave Joe and Darla long goodbye hugs and strode down the hall. She thought a few people she passed stared a moment too long and thought she heard a bit more whispering than she considered usual. Autumn figured they knew she had been attacked the night before and she just kept her gaze down. Word seemed to spread faster in the hospital than the bacteria did, and she wasn't ready to talk about what happened with anyone she worked with yet.

Autumn slowly approached Jay's room. She hadn't seen him in two days. The door to his room was closed.

Hesitantly, she knocked.

"Yes?" boomed Larry Abrams's voice.

She cracked the door open. "It's me, Autumn."

"Oh, Autumn, come in, come in," replied Marsha, with a strength in her timbre that Autumn had not yet heard from her. Marsha stood up immediately and gave her a hug. Unexpectedly, Larry got up and hugged her, too.

"How's everyone doing?" Autumn asked lamely.

"We're all okay," Marsha smiled, patting Jay's still-lifeless hand. Larry tried to smile as well, but the ends of his mouth refused to turn upwards, merely creating a pained expression.

Larry looked at his son and then turned to Autumn. "I know Jay would want to thank you for everything you've done for him and for us." He rested his hand on his ex-wife's shoulder.

Marsha nodded to her ex-husband and sniffed back her tears.

"We're taking him home," she said. "Well to Larry's home, but I'll camp out in the guest room for a while. We'll both take care of him with the hospice team until it's his time. Pierce has to work and can manage at home by himself for a little while."

"That's really good. I think that's what Jay would have wanted."

"We do, too," Larry said, though he didn't sound totally convinced. "No artificial feeding or anything, but we talked it over with the rabbi and he said that there were two important tenets to consider. Life is the most important thing, but prolonging someone's suffering is the worst thing anyone could do. Right, Marsha?"

"Right," she nodded.

"And if Jay can't use his brains, obviously a gift from his mother, then he's suffering," Larry finished and sat down hard in his chair, looking intently at the floor.

"You guys should have your time with him. I just wanted to say goodbye to Jay."

She went over to the far side of the bed, where there weren't any chairs and whispered softly into Jay's ear, then kissed his cheek as her eyes glazed over. She gave Larry and Marsha hugs as the tears started to stream down her face. Within a few seconds Autumn had managed to cover her face in the tears for Jay that she had been storing up since, well, she wasn't even sure anymore.

After rinsing off her face in a call room bathroom, Autumn decided that she was done with being in the hospital on her day off. Maybe she'd go shopping for clothes that fit her a little better. Maybe she'd go for a walk. She still hadn't been to the Boston Common. As she pushed through the heavy revolving front door, she finally noticed the clear blue Boston sky and, for no reason whatsoever, stretched her arms out as she craned back her neck to look straight up. She felt her lungs fill with air as the wind teased the small hairs at the back of her neck. Alive. She felt alive.

THIRTY-NINE

AUTUMN

A week later, Marsha called to tell Autumn that Jay had passed away. It had been in his own bed with his family around him. No beeps. No alarms. No codes. The funeral would be held the next day. She would be there, Autumn told Marsha. She would find someone to cover for her at the hospital as soon as she finished seeing patients in her outpatient clinic. She looked at her schedule. There was one patient left to see. George Schafer. Eighty-two years old. Complaining of shortness of breath.

George Schafer. Why did that name ring a bell?

She walked into the room and saw a thin, gray-haired man with the classic flat facial expression of Parkinson's Disease. Schafer. Schafer! The sun-downing patient she had made dystonic was in her outpatient clinic, breathing much more quickly than he should have been.

It had started three days ago and was getting worse, he told her. She could see him huffing away, taking a breath every two seconds or so. If he recognized her from the hospital, he didn't mention it.

"Anything else bothering you?" Autumn asked, debating whether or not to tell him that she had given him the wrong medication a few weeks ago.

"A bit of stomach pain," he answered. "Drinking a little milk or having some food makes it better."

"Are your stools darker than usual?"

"Yeah, but my girlfriend said that happens when you take Pepto-Bismol by the gallon, which I've been doing."

Autumn nodded in agreement. *But that also happened when you were bleeding from your gastrointestinal tract*, she thought.

"Why don't you have a seat on the exam table," Autumn commanded. No sense having him get changed. She had a feeling she would be sending him down to the emergency department in a few minutes anyway and Parkinson's patients moved very, very slowly. She helped him onto the examination table.

She grabbed her light and looked at the skin under his lower eyelids. Instead of pink, it was pale. She listened to his heart. The aortic murmur his chart noted he would have, sounded much harsher than any murmur she had ever heard, and she made a note of it. And when she pressed on his abdomen, there was pain just below the sternum, in the epigastric area. She figured that he had an ulcer and it was likely bleeding. She could prove it with a rectal exam and then a quick test of his stool for blood, but she figured she'd leave that to the emergency room residents. She had something else she needed to do before she sent him down to the emergency room.

"Mr. Schafer, you don't by any chance remember me, do you?"

"Not so much," he said flatly. "But I know you took care of me in the hospital."

Autumn raised her eyebrows.

Schafer explained. "My primary care doctor retired a few months ago, and I've been looking for another one, but they are hard to come by these days. So, when I was being discharged from the hospital, the nurse gave me the resident clinic number to call for a follow-up appointment. The nurse wrote down the names of the residents who had taken care of me in the hospital. Yours and Dr. Callahan's. He didn't have an appointment for a few weeks."

"I did take care of you, but only at night." She paused.

Schafer was still staring blankly at her. Because of the Parkinson's, he had completely lost the ability to convey emotion through his expressions. She had no idea what he was thinking. She pressed on.

"One night I gave you a medicine I shouldn't have. It made your muscles contract and kept you in the hospital a few extra days," she confessed. "It could have done more damage than that."

Schafer was still staring at her.

Autumn continued, "I guess what I'm saying is, I'm sorry. And I hope you can still trust me."

He couldn't smile much, because of the Parkinson's, but he nodded. "I don't remember that. But it's okay. I got better and hopefully you learned from your mistake."

She nodded and tried to smile, too, but wasn't able to quite make it either. She looked down, breathed in deeply, looked back up at her patient and launched into more unpleasant news.

"Mr. Schafer, now I think you need to go downstairs to the emergency room. I think you might have a bleeding ulcer."

"Will you take care of me?"

Autumn couldn't believe that the patient she had previously harmed wanted her to take care of him. Yes. She would take care of him. And she would do a better job this time.

"I'd be happy to take care of you. I'll request that you be admitted to my team." And she quickly added, "I promise to take excellent care of you."

He patted her hand and said, "I know you will."

A few minutes later, Mr. Schafer left the clinic in a wheelchair with the nurse and his girlfriend, who had been in the waiting room. Autumn called the emergency department, conveniently just one floor down from the resident clinic, to let them know he was coming. She quickly gave the triage nurse his story. Since his heart wasn't in good shape to begin with, he would be sensitive to the blood loss and Autumn had no way of knowing how bad his levels were, but he might need a transfusion. She asked that he be admitted to her team and hung up the phone. She sat back in her chair, closing her eyes for a moment, and then realized she still needed to find coverage for herself for the next day so she could attend Jay's funeral. To make sure Schafer was taken care of like she had promised him, she'd have to stay late today, off the clock because of the duty hours restriction. She'd record that she left the hospital after clinic like she was supposed to. He trusted her and if a little paperwork lie was what it took to take care of him, that's what she'd do.

Patients over paperwork. Every time. Sick from not sick. Death and how to avoid it. That's what you learned in intern year. All of the other patients in the clinic that day thought they were sick, but now, to Autumn, "sick" meant making an active attempt at dying and only one patient fit that description that afternoon. She had known it the minute she saw Schafer. He was sick. She could help. She was becoming a real doctor. She ran her index finger down the side of her nose, over the small piercing hole that was almost completely closed. Maybe on her next day off she would re-open it.

ACKNOWLEDGEMENTS

This book is the product of many stops and starts and could never have gotten off the ground without encouragement from my own residency program years ago (which, if anything, was a foil for the one I wrote about). In the craziness of life, nothing gets done without the support of my husband, Michael, who was forced to read many versions of this book and whom I can never thank enough for working diligently every day to create space for both of our dreams. Thanks to my sister, Jennifer, who meticulously picked apart early versions the book and who always holds me to the highest standard.

A whole buffet table of appreciation goes out to the ladies of the Wine and Words Book Club. Thanks for making me dust off the manuscript and drag it out into the light of day. Your enthusiasm for the book and suggestions propelled it forward like no one else. I thank fellow authors Martina McAtee and Eva Meckler, who have been generous guides and wise sounding boards throughout this mysterious publishing process. The list of my beta readers is long and I thank everyone who provided words of encouragement, support, and careful criticism along the way.

I could not have put this book together without a fantastic and meticulous editor, Parisa Zolfaghari. Thank you for working through several iterations with me and for being a patient teacher. Thanks also to the amazingly talented cover and layout artist, Molly Phipps. It's like you can see what I am thinking.

Finally, I have to give thanks to my patients, who continue to inspire me to get better and do better every day.

ABOUT THE AUTHOR

DAWN HARRIS SHERLING, M.D. is an internal medicine physician and a writer of both fiction and non-fiction. This is her debut novel. She is a Florida native, and after surviving ten brutal New England winters, returned to her home state. She lives in South Florida with her husband, two children, and their dog.

Made in the USA
Middletown, DE
11 April 2019